Praise for Bonnie Edward

Thigh High

"Beautifully written stories . . . The satisfying finale brings back the mysterious bordello that figured prominently in the author's *Midnight Confessions*."
—*Romantic Times Book Reviews*

"This is without doubt the hottest and the sexiest book that I have ever read."
—Fallen Angel Reviews

"Ms. Edwards puts fire in her characters that can be felt completely. The steam floats off the pages, enticing me . . . hated to see them end."
—Coffee Time Romance

Midnight Confessions

"Erotic, seductive . . . This book is fun, feisty and a frolicking good read. Bonnie Edwards mixes erotic romance with just a hint of mystery . . . Packed full of colorful, interesting characters, gorgeous men and sizzling sex scenes . . ."
—A Romance Review

"Fascinating and intriguing . . . A definite keeper!"
—Just Erotic Romance Reviews

"Edwards establishes interest from the first page with an extremely unique plot. . . . The novel achieves a sensual tone that is tasteful and sexy . . . *Midnight Confessions* is definitely entertaining reading."
—*Romantic Times Book Reviews*

Midnight Confessions II

"Edwards mixes fantasy and reality in this imaginative and romantic ghost story . . . flows with humor, emotion, sex and love . . ."
—*Romantic Times Book Reviews*

"With characters that will entertain and bewitch you, *Midnight Confessions II* is a spicy, delightful read . . ."
—Romance Reviews Today

Breathless

BONNIE EDWARDS

APHRODISIA

KENSINGTON BOOKS

http://www.kensingtonbooks.com

APHRODISIA BOOKS are published by

Kensington Publishing Corp.
119 West 40th Street
New York, NY 10018

All Kensington Titles, Imprints, and Distributed Lines are available at special quantity discounts for bulk purchases for sales promotions, premiums, fund-raising, and educational or institutional use.

Special book excerpts or customized printings can also be created to fit specific needs. For details, write or phone the office of the Kensington special sales manager: Kensington Publishing Corp., 119 West 40th Street, New York, NY 10018, attn: Special Sales Department, Phone: 1-800-221-2647.

Aphrodisia and the A logo Reg. U.S. Pat. & TM Off.

ISBN-13: 978-0-7582-3828-3
ISBN-10: 0-7582-3828-2

First Kensington Trade Paperback Printing: December 2009

10 9 8 7 6 5 4 3 2 1

Printed in the United States of America

For those who dream
For what may be
And to the hard work that means

And for Ted

Always

Contents

Breathless

1

Blue McCann traced the lines of the corset through the glass of the store window. Ivory satin and lace, the exquisite vintage piece looked way out of her league. She admired the delicacy of the hand stitching, as perfectly even and precise today as it had been a hundred years ago. Timeless, the handcrafted corset pulled her toward the window every time she passed by.

Timelessness was alluring to people whose time was up. Today, she'd gone out of her way to stop by just to look. Silly, to dream of having a piece of clothing like this one. Still, the corset pulled at her, made her dream of wearing it. She smiled through her next cough. That's why she came here, in spite of the rain, the unrelenting coughing and pain, the corset reminded her she was a woman: a sexual being. If she wore something like this corset, she could be desired, wanted, maybe even loved.

Loved? She must be delusional. A cough wracked her chest and she turned away, into the wind. Rain lashed her face, so she turned back, chilled more than ever. She had to get home before the wind pushed the rain through her clothes.

The cough went so deep she bent over, hating the hollow feeling in her chest. She leaned on the glass for a moment to catch the little breath she could. Love, the idea was ridiculous, coming from a woman whose very name came from the color of her skin when she was found in a Dumpster. The cop had told the head nurse the newborn girl he'd found had been so blue he'd thought she was a painted doll at first.

On another gust of biting wind and rain, the shop door opened and a woman stepped out. "May I help you? Need to use the facilities? Or maybe a phone?" She stepped around Blue and put her hand on her shoulder. Warmth radiated where the woman touched, even through her thin jacket and thinner sweater.

She'd heard of hands like this—healing, warming. Blue had always hoped she had them.

The woman's body shielded Blue from passersby and the nasty wind. "This corner is a raceway for wind gusts," the woman said. Her warm hands firmly urged Blue toward the entrance to the store, and Blue couldn't resist the softness of the warm air that drew her inside.

Out of the corner of her eye, the corset seemed to shimmy, but a truck went by and rattled the glass. That was all it was. The weight and rumble of the heavy truck had made the glass shiver. She couldn't have seen the corset actually move on its own.

"Thanks." She nodded at the woman. "I was just . . ." she hesitated, knowing she was silly to ask, "wondering how much that corset is? It's beautiful." The heat from the woman's hands infused her back and made her feel stronger. She straightened and squared her shoulders.

"Come inside out of the rain and I'll take a look. I can't remember the price. But with your coloring, it will look fabulous on you." The husky, amused tone made it seem like a done deal, but Blue was broker than broke and living on nothing but dreams and whimsy. And not for long, either.

As Blue stepped to the door, she tried to see the price tag, but a draft twirled the tag like a leaf in autumn. "Whenever I stop here to check the price, the tag's facing the wrong way." She coughed again and the woman helped her to a stool by the cash desk. The woman's healing hands fell away and Blue sank onto the stool, appalled at how weak she felt.

"I don't want to cause you any grief with your boss," she said when she could. She knew how she looked. This kind of store didn't entertain her kind of customer. The broke kind and now that—

"My name's Faye Grantham," the woman's voice cut off Blue's thought, "and I *am* the boss. Welcome to TimeStop."

Blue raised her gaze to see a vision of white and gold loveliness. "Pleased to meet you," she said.

Faye was a '50s movie siren, all blonde curves and a come-hither look that seemed completely natural. "Wow!" Blue breathed. "You're a knockout."

"Thanks, I like the look, although sometimes I go for sixties mod rather than blonde bombshell." She did a twirl and her skirt kicked up, showing a glimpse of crinoline. "TimeStop specializes in vintage Hollywood wardrobe castoffs, but the corset you admired came from the attic in my home, Perdition House."

"Perdition House," Blue repeated, trying to place the name. She came up empty.

Faye tilted her head, letting her gaze slide down Blue's body. "Would you care to try it on?" She waved a hand toward the back where Blue saw a couple of dressing rooms. "I think it will fit. And I'm sure the man in your life would love to see you in it."

As much as she loved the corset, it could never be hers. "I don't have the money for something so beautiful."

"I don't believe that will be a problem. Your name's Blue McCann?"

"Yes, that's right," she said through a cough. "How did you

know?" She'd never been inside the store, she'd have remembered.

Faye took Blue's hand in hers. She clasped it warmly and her eyes held a deep, caring smile that Blue could fall into. "We must have met before because I recognized you right away. Care for a cup of coffee, Blue?" She walked to an old-fashioned coffeepot on a stand at the end of the counter. She tilted the pot and poured a cup without waiting for a response.

"Thanks, but I need to get home," Blue said halfheartedly. The wind had kicked up even wilder. She'd be soaked by the time she got to her place. But when Faye offered her the cup, she took it and settled on the stool as if she had all the time in the world.

"No point rushing out into this kind of weather," Faye said with a shiver.

Blue took a sip of coffee. Perfect. "How did you know to put in half a teaspoon of sugar and two creams?"

"You told me, of course. You've got someone waiting for you?" Faye asked, drawing Blue's attention away from the delicious coffee.

"No, it's not that. I can't afford the corset, so I don't see the sense—"

"We need a part-timer in the store," Faye interrupted in an offhand way. "Maybe you'd be interested?"

"And maybe you don't see that I'm, ah—" Another cough cut her off while she stood, ignoring the pain and weakness that rode her every movement these days. "I'm no charity case," she said. Tomorrow, maybe, but not today.

"This isn't charity, Blue, it's more like a blessing," Faye said, and slipped the corset into Blue's hands. It felt as silky and sexy as it looked. She pursed her lips, wanting badly to give herself permission to try it on.

She clutched it to her chest. "A blessing," she repeated.

Faye smiled and her eyes glowed with warmth and caring.

"I've got a feeling it'll fit as if it were made for you." Her voice sounded hypnotic and soft-toned. Mesmerizing.

She hadn't mentioned how she liked her coffee, she was sure of it. The quiet calm of the store, the warmth of the corset in her arms, and Faye's deep smile soothed her. She needed soothing. Suddenly tired of being brave, trying to be strong, she soaked up the comfort of the store and Faye's kindness.

"This corset has been in a trunk in Perdition for nine decades, just waiting for you. For Blue McCann." Faye's eyes were alight with promise and secret knowledge that gave Blue an odd comfort.

The more Blue thought about it, the more certain she was that she'd never met Faye Grantham before. She had a great memory—strong, clear, precise. She could remember the color of her kindergarten teacher's favorite dress, the feeling of noiseless sobs when she was booted out of foster homes she liked. She remembered being locked in that sweltering car when she was three.

So, no matter what Faye said, Blue was certain she'd never set eyes on her, let alone been introduced. As for the corset? "I doubt it'll fit, but I guess there's no harm in trying it on." Her voice had taken on the same soft warmth as Faye's, and Blue allowed Faye to lead her to a dressing room.

Once in the booth, she kept her eyes trained on the floor while she stripped to her panties. The coziness of the room enveloped her, and she noted the beautiful quality of the heavy velvet drapery that covered the doorway. It blocked light, sound, and drafts of air. Her toes curled into the luxurious rug underfoot.

It had been months since she'd looked in a full-length mirror. She was half the woman she'd been before her lung disease had worsened. Gaunt and rib thin, she had a hard time looking at her wasted body.

Her lungs worked through a wheeze as she avoided her reflection. She held the corset up in front of her and focused on the fine material rather than her body. It felt foolish to try it on, but when would she get a chance like this again? A howl of wind chased along the roof. It was warm in here, and dry, more than enough reason to hang out for a while.

Maybe Faye was bored. That's why she took this time with Blue. The store was empty of real customers.

That was why Faye was being so kind. Blue shrugged and undid the ribbon on the back of the corset with shaky fingers. The material was incredibly silky. She pulled it over her head, making sure to keep her back to the mirror. Her boobs were all but gone, and no matter how tight she pulled on the ribbon, she'd never fill out the demi cups.

The satin felt warm and cocooned her ribs and chest, reminding her of the way Faye's hands had felt. Her cough disappeared. Her wheeze went away. She could breathe! Her pain diminished to a dull ache.

She faced the mirror but covered her eyes with her workworn hands. *Wimp.* She'd dreamed about this corset time and again. She'd wondered at the beauty of the seamstress's hand until the piece of lace and satin had seemed to call out to her.

"Need help with anything, Blue?" Faye asked in a soft, coaxing tone.

Blue blinked and tried to think, but she couldn't tell a stranger how odd everything seemed, or how disjointed and out of place she felt in her own skin.

"No, I'm fine, thanks. I got the back done up on my own." Although she couldn't recall actually doing it. She widened two fingers and peeped out at herself in the mirror.

Her cheeks glowed pink, her thighs were filled out, and shapely curves filled out the corset. And her boobs! They were full and round and perky. She palmed them where the satin gave way to the rounded tips.

She looked healthy again!

Her blood rushed warm all over, and her eyes sparkled in the glare of the overhead pot light. She giggled and preened and spun in a circle as she drank in the sight of the perfection in the mirror. She'd been right about the ivory. It brought out all her golden hues. Her hair looked thick and shiny again, the cut sassy and fun the way it used to be.

The heat from the corset increased; her blood rushed loud in her head as the dressing room mirror went dark. The light overhead faded. She couldn't be sure, but it looked as if her hair was longer than before. She touched it, felt the ends. It wasn't longer; it couldn't be longer. But she finger-combed through long plaits that made no sense. Plaits she couldn't see but felt as clearly as she felt her own skin.

The darkened mirror showed her hair swept up into a Gibson Girl style. She'd seen the style before. Early 1900s. Pretty, feminine, but definitely not her! The image in the mirror flickered as her chest got tight.

Flushed with heat, she tried to find the knot at her back to undo the corset. She had to catch her breath, needed to cool her body.

When she reached back, she felt something more than the ribbons. Something warm, firm. Hands!

She gasped and the warmth she felt changed to something hotter, more sexual. A mouth descended to her shoulder, warm, seeking, giving soft nibbles that stole her breath. But there was no one behind her; no one else stood in the compact fitting room.

Fantasy! That's all it was, she realized as the sensation drifted away. She hadn't felt sexual in months, another sign of her compromised health. She peeked outside.

Faye had left for the front of the store. Blue was alone.

The fitting room glowed softly intimate. Blue let her eyes drift shut as she opened her legs and leaned her back against the wall. Moisture slicked across her slit as her labia plumped; her channel softened in readiness. She palmed her belly where it felt warm and needy, then slid her fingers into her moist recess.

She gasped at the sensation she'd missed for months.

Her fingers coaxed, slid, promised release, filled her while she leaned against the wall, legs splayed. No longer afraid to see herself, she opened her eyes and watched as she played her pussy, rubbing and sliding first one then another finger into her body. She widened her stance, gave her hand more room to slide and slick, while her other hand plucked a nipple. A nipple at the tip of a round, heavy breast—the breasts she used to have.

The sensations changed. The hands that played her were no longer thin and feminine, but manly and strong. Demanding. Heavy and needful, her pussy wept for him—the man, the stranger whose hands and lips performed their magic. She felt him at the nape of her neck, his lips nibbling, his teeth scoring across her skin, dragging her gold chain across her flesh. She reached a hand up and behind her to his head, felt his hair, wavy and masculine, beside her neck.

She cried out and gave in to her urgent need as the light overhead flickered. Hips pumping, she allowed the fantasy to run its course. The light overhead gave off a golden, flickering glow.

She thought she'd seen a pot light with a bright white bulb, but she must have been mistaken.

Her reflection changed to watery and unclear as she rose to the peak of ecstasy, taken there by fantasy and the lure of completion. In the mirror, she saw full breasts, round hips, bright eyes, and a healthy glow. The man of her fantasies dragged her backward into his hips, his erection hard against her buttocks, his hands demanding, seeking, heating her to explosion.

And then he looked at her.

Watched as she undulated against him, his eyes dark chocolate and hot with sexual intensity. He had strong features, dark hair, and a crooked, sexy mouth that teased the flesh of her earlobe while he coaxed her to orgasm.

"Let go," she heard. "Let go for me." His voice was an echo, a specter's throaty murmur.

Called to arousal, she responded with a moan and tried to turn to meet him, feel him, hold him, but her orgasm overtook her and she closed her eyes, swept into sensations so real she lost herself.

She was a sexual being again! A woman who needed and wanted. A woman with a man at her back, kissing her neck, his hands taking her where her need beckoned.

Breathless and in full orgasm, Blue McCann slid to the floor, and the gaslight overhead flickered out.

2

Hours later, back at Perdition House, Faye called out to thin air, "You didn't tell me what would happen when she put on the corset, Belle." She ran her hand through her hair, distraught at the turn of events. "What'll happen to Blue McCann? What have you done to her?"

Belle floated down the staircase from the widow's walk and slid with a guilty glance to her favorite perch on the dresser. Her color went to monochrome beige. Faye had figured out months ago that beige meant her great great aunt, decades dead, was distressed.

"You have no idea what will happen to Blue, do you?" she demanded.

Belle threw a glance to the ceiling. "Not exactly. It depends on her."

"How could you mess with someone's life?" The horror of finding Blue crumpled on the floor of the fitting room flashed through her. Her pulse had been faint, her breathing thready and weak.

Emergency first responders had looked grim when they'd

taken her vitals, and grimmer still when they'd loaded her unconscious body into the back of the ambulance. "How could you do this? You had me encourage her to try on that corset knowing this would happen. I just don't see why you think you had that right." If Blue died because of this, Faye would never forgive herself.

Belle pursed her lips. "It all happened because other lives are at stake, Faye."

"Not *today* they're not. Have you forgotten you're dead? You're all dead! Have been for decades." She swept both arms up and around to indicate the walls of her room, of her house. "This whole house is full of dead people, and you say lives are at stake?"

An angry red appeared in Belle's dressing gown. Oops! "Think of the generations, girl," she snapped. "Lives lost decades ago have a trickle-down effect."

That stopped Faye short. If someone had died prematurely all those decades ago, then of course it would affect today. She forced herself to think. Whom would Belle do this for? Whose life could be so important that Belle would—"Whom did you make a pact with, Belle?" She tilted her head toward the floor and gave her aunt a very pointed glance downward. "Was it you know who?" A cold chill ran through her at the thought of how far Belle might go to survive as a specter.

"I'm not a fool!" her decades-dead great aunt chided. She conjured a nail buffer and used it. "Arrangements were made," she said through a put-upon pout. "But it's anyone's guess how things will turn out. We have to see if this is a good fit. One soul doesn't necessarily fit into another's life."

Faye closed her eyes. When would she learn that her long-departed aunt survived by her own rules and kept her plans to herself. "If I didn't feel so responsible for the souls in this house, I'd sell it out from under you all!" The threat was old and useless, but Faye issued it on a regular basis anyway.

Belle smiled, a mere lift of the lips. A knowing light burned in her gaze. "But you do feel responsible, Faye. Just the way I knew you would."

"I'm going to the hospital to check on Blue." She raised her finger and jabbed it into the chill of the spirit's chest. "And she'd better be alive when I get there."

Belle shrugged. "Why would you assume that decision is mine?" She had the nerve to look huffy.

Faye threw up her hands and headed out into the wildest windstorm the Seattle area had seen in years.

"Miss? Miss!" a woman's voice called to Blue. She groaned. "Are you all right? Bart, she's coming around now. Oh, thank heavens."

Blue considered her condition before answering. She moved her arms and legs, wiggled her toes, took a deep breath and held it, while she took stock. Her lungs held the breath and used the oxygen the way they should. She felt strong again, vital. She sighed, loving the absence of pain. Good drugs. Good, good drugs. She wanted to let them hold her for a moment longer, but the woman kept talking, prodding her awake.

Blue opened her eyes. Grass, weeds, rocks filled the dressing room. And rain! She felt rain on her face.

It was not the dressing room, she saw as she peered past her hands to the muddy ground. Not a hospital room, either. "Crap, where am I?"

"Miss?" The woman's voice sounded shocked. "You've had a bump on the head. That speedster of yours liked to kill you."

Strong arms reached under her and tugged her to her feet. Her head hurt and she held it, felt something thick and sticky. She checked her fingers. "I'm bleeding." Probably concussed too.

"Yes, miss. A bump on the head, like the wife said," a man responded. His voice sounded gravelly and kind, even concerned.

She looked up, then up again to a giant's face. "You're huge," she said, then looked around. She pulled herself to her feet none too steadily, and he clasped her gently by the elbows to help. Rain pelted them, sharp and insistent.

They were next to a ditch filled with a car—an ancient car. The two wire-spoked tires that stuck up in the air were still spinning. She'd had an accident.

"You were thrown clear when that thing slid into the ditch and hit a tree." The woman pointed to a huge fir.

Blue looked up toward the top of the tree, felt woozy, and quickly leveled her face again to save herself from toppling over.

She looked from the giant man to the woman who'd spoken. She was a tiny woman with lively eyes and a warm smile. "Who are you?" she asked.

"I'm Lizzie, and this is my husband, Bart Jameson." She looked worried and waved a hand in front of Blue's face. A blur of movement. "Miss McCreedy, surely you know us?"

Blue shook her head. "Should I?" One minute she'd been in TimeStop, trying on a corset, and the next . . .

She felt her ribs. Yes, the corset was there, under heavy layers of cloth. She looked down and saw that somehow, some way, somebody had dressed her for the weather. She wore a heavy cloak and black boots. A wide-brimmed hat lay in the mud, the fine silk ties trampled.

"Bart, let's get her back to Perdition. Belle will call the doctor."

With nothing more than a sigh, the giant of a man hoisted her gently into a carriage—a carriage!—pulled by a pair of black horses. Wedged between Lizzie and the giant man, Bart, she sat, bouncing and jiggling on the way to wherever they were taking her. Perdition. Another name for hell.

Maybe that's where she was. Or where she was going. Her time had come and obviously she hadn't lived right, or for long enough. She'd lived with a religious family when she was ten. This was what they'd warned her about. If only she'd listened instead of screaming like a brat in church.

But the optimist in her wondered, if she wasn't in hell yet, maybe she could change things. Sleep pulled at her, and concussed or not, Blue closed her eyes, determined to go back to sleep and wake up again in her own apartment, in her own clothes.

In her own body.

When she woke later, it was to the feel of a man's hands on her face. She batted at him. "Go away, leave me sleep."

"Stella, wake up, woman, and stop being difficult."

Patty cheeks again. She peeped one eye open.

"That's a girl, now stay awake!" Concerned chocolate eyes widened as she tried to shove herself to a sitting position. She was in a bed at least. Soft, though, not like a hospital bed. She would recognize one of those.

"Who's Stella?" she asked. Someone had called her Miss Mc-Creedy earlier. She'd never heard the name Stella McCreedy in her life.

The man looked over his shoulder at a woman who came around him to stare down at Blue. "Don't know your own name?" she asked.

"Faye! How did I get here? I remember a carriage and a giant man."

"That was Bart. He and his wife Lizzie were right behind you when that speedster you drive went off the road," Faye said. "You pitched straight over the front of the car and into a tree. It's no wonder you don't know your own name." She frowned. "Or mine. I'm Belle, honey. Belle Grantham. Your . . . friend."

"But you look just like Faye, a woman I met in a store not an hour ago."

"There's no Faye here. Not in Perdition House."

Finally, a name she recalled. Faye said she lived here. Blue was sure of it, but these people were pretty confused, so she kept quiet. She had an excellent memory, always had.

"This is enough for now, Stella," the man broke in. "You need to rest, but I want you to stay awake, just the same." His voice flowed over her. The tone was deep, well-modulated, and intimate. Thrills chased through her chest and down to her belly. *Let go for me.* It was him! The man from the fitting room. The man who'd turned her into a woman again.

She heated through at the memory. Sure, *that* she recalled with crystal clarity!

"I'll try to stay awake, but I'm so sleepy." She wanted to drift again, slide into the deep quiet of unconsciousness, but the man's eyes lured her to wakefulness.

"I'll have one of the girls sit with you," Belle suggested, but it sounded more like an order. "And it's no wonder you're sleepy. You were up all night with Mrs. Barker. You don't remember telling me that?"

"No." Blue looked at the man. A stethoscope hung from his neck. He was a doctor. The one that couple had said would come to the house for her. She wanted him, not someone Belle ordered up.

"Doctor? Do I know you too?" Had she dreamed of him or had he really been with her in the fitting room. Crazy thought.

She tried for a peek at his hands, but they were buried in a deep black leather bag, his medical kit. "Will *you* stay?" she asked.

He gave a curt nod. "If you want me, I'll be here."

"I want you." *Please and thank you.* She shifted her legs under the covers. Thank goodness her body moved the way it should. This talk about her not remembering things frightened her. "I do remember some things," she said, just not the things they expected. The corset! Somehow, this weirdness was connected to the corset she'd tried on.

Belle gave them an assessing glance, her gaze swinging from Blue to the man and back again. "Can she have soup? I'll have Henry bring some up."

Blue's stomach growled, making the man chuckle. "I'd say that's a good sign. Send up a bowl, Belle. I'll see she eats it all."

The moment the door closed, he turned back to her. A strong jaw and intelligent brown-black eyes set his face in the highly attractive range. Yum. "I told you that automobile could be the death of you. You're lucky to come out of this alive." His face flattened with stern anger.

"When did you tell me?" Whatever was happening, it was up to her to figure it out. These people were clueless that she wasn't the woman they saw. She glanced at her hands. Nope, not hers. These hands were larger, stronger looking, and competent. She wasn't sure how she knew about the competency, but she did.

"I told you every time I saw you racing that thing. Women aren't meant to drive automobiles, Stella. Especially not ones that have been modified for speed." His self-righteous tone set her teeth on edge.

"Could you refresh me on the date, please?"

"June twentieth, nineteen thirteen," the man said. "It's Friday." The corset it was, then. That would be about the age of the thing. The date also explained his 'tude about women driving. But if Stella was a speed demon, it would explain the edginess between them. He might not appreciate a forward-thinking woman.

"Am I healthy?" she asked. "I mean aside from the bump on the head. I feel so strong." *Alive!* As if she'd been renewed, given another chance. She looked around the room. Everything looked antique, and the room was overstuffed with furniture, lamps, and bric-a-brac. The heavy drapes and sheers blocked the daylight.

"You're one of the healthiest women I know, Stella." His

smile finally made an appearance. It was crooked, as if one side of his mouth didn't work properly.

It was the most appealing, masculine smile she'd ever seen and cemented her belief that he'd been the man in the mirror. The man who'd kissed her neck, who'd used his hands to bring her to ecstasy. She hoped he would again. She recalled thinking how sexy his mouth looked quirked up that way.

"But you should give up the cigars," he suggested. His mouth dropped back to even.

Oh, crap. Cigars? "No problem." Healthy, huh? Maybe that was why she was so warm under these sheets. A healthy body had healthy needs. The orgasm in the dressing room had only whetted her appetite.

She lifted the covers for a look down her body. Boobs! Heavy ones from the lumps she saw. The corset was gone now, replaced by a white muslin nightie. "No more cigars for me," she said around a smile, as she tucked her blankets around her.

He frowned. "You're mighty agreeable."

Maybe Stella had a mind of her own and didn't fret about speaking it. Cool! Blue had always been too quiet for her own good. The foster system could have that effect on a kid.

"I must look a mess, could you pass me a mirror? And maybe a comb for my hair?"

"You must be better," he said, and went to the bureau top to retrieve a long-handled mirror and brush. He was tall and had a slender build. He'd taken off his jacket and old-fashioned suspenders held up his pants. His shirt was white as snow. The suspenders lifted his waistband so his pants cupped his tight ass. The doctor had a great build. He was trim and fit looking.

When he settled on the bed again, he reached for the top of her head. She felt her hair being released from several pins and let him minister to her as he let masses of reddish hair fall to the pillow and down her chest. From mousy, lifeless brown to luscious red in one fell swoop. She could live with that.

Her nipples peaked under the covers, and she felt heat suffuse her cheeks. She was happy to feel sexual again, but if Stella McCreedy didn't want him, Blue didn't feel right acting on her attraction. She needed to ignore the heat in her belly and the desire in her heart.

His hands on her hair were gentle, the delicate tugs creating waves of relief along her scalp. Was a scalp erogenous? And then she felt it. Definitely erogenous. His fingers massaged her entire head, then combed through the unfamiliar, heavy strands of hair.

She closed her eyes and let out an unwilling sigh at his touch. The man was gifted. First, in the mirror, when he was still a phantom, and now, in flesh and blood. Another sigh rose and escaped, and he stopped massaging and held his fingers still.

She opened her eyes to find his face three inches from hers and still as a statue. If she tilted her head toward him, she could press her lips to his.

And if she did? Would he kiss her back? Could she coax him to slip under the covers and lift her soft muslin nightie and finish her?

"You're very good with your hands," she murmured. "I like that in a man."

His eyes flared hot. He was affected by her. Correction, by Stella. Blue would be wise to remember that.

With her hair unpinned, and the air between them sharp with need, he held out a hand mirror. The last time she'd seen her reflection a whole lot of weird happened, so she was nervous at what she might see. She took the mirror and placed it glass side down on her lap.

"Um, would you mind refreshing my memory on your name? I'd like to know it."

The door opened and a boy of about fourteen entered. He

brought a tray to the bedside. "Here you go, Miz McCreedy. Ma sent it up."

"Thanks, Henry," Blue said, recalling his name from earlier. So, her short-term memory was fully operational. She could move ahead from here if need be. A fresh start. She frowned. If Blue stayed, what would become of Stella?

"Doctor Stephens, Ma wants to know if you'll be down for a bowl or would you like me to bring you some too?"

"The doctor will have some up here, with me, Henry. Is that all right?" She didn't know where this confidence came from, but it seemed to work.

Doctor Stephens stiffened. He nodded to Henry and let the boy leave. "What game are you playing now?" he said as soon as they were alone. "You've never wanted to spend any time with me, alone or otherwise."

"We don't like each other?" That surprised her, because she could swear she saw more than a professional interest in his gaze.

"I wouldn't call it not liking each other. We got off on the wrong foot, and you've never been off your high horse long enough to give me a second chance." He avoided her gaze.

"High horse?"

"Not only have you not forgiven me for my initial impression of your business here in Perdition, but you've got a proprietary attitude toward your patients that can do them harm."

"I have *patients*? What am I? A doctor too?" Startled at the idea, she lifted the mirror to look at her face. Red hair cascaded in waves across the pillow, while green wide-set eyes stared back at her. Her lips were full, and she had a smattering of light freckles across her nose. All in all, not bad. And the pink color in her cheeks radiated health. She smoothed her right one, not sure if she liked being a few years older.

But this body felt like it could chug along for a lot more

years than Blue McCann's, regardless of the extra handful of years Stella had already lived.

"No, not a doctor, Stella, you're a midwife. And a fine one at that." But his tone sounded begrudging. The heat between them cooled at his tone.

A midwife. Stella delivered babies and he didn't much care for her career choice.

Okay, this was officially off-the-charts weird, because Blue McCann was a doula, not a midwife. Doulas had no training in actual deliveries. She had trained to provide emotional support during pregnancy and to help with newborns, a kind of coach for new mothers.

But helping to bring a new life into the world? No, not her. As much as she'd wanted the designation, she hadn't been able to afford the courses.

Stella delivered babies. Blue had wanted with all her heart to have the same career. Then, she'd gotten sick, and it had taken everything she had to hang on financially, emotionally, and physically. Was this a chance to have her heart's desire? What a fantasy!

She glanced in the mirror again, noted the healthy glow, and figured fantasy was better than reality any day.

3

Three days later, Blue was up to speed on everything she needed to know about Stella McCreedy. She felt stronger than she had in years. The only effects from the accident that still remained were some bruises and sore muscles. Her headaches were gone, her vision had cleared, and she'd been catching up on Stella's life since her arrival at Perdition.

Stella had been the mainstay of health care for the women who lived and worked as prostitutes in Perdition House. As a midwife, she had been able to see to their womanly complaints competently. She also provided the house with their supplies of prophylactics. Stella had been quick to see the added birth-control benefit of condom use.

Dr. Colt Stephens had arrived in the area a month ago and had been happy to take the ladies on as patients when they needed help Stella couldn't provide. The morning he'd arrived for a meeting with Belle, he'd taken one look at Stella and made the mistake of assuming she was one of the working girls. Their relationship had been prickly since then. But Colt was definitely ready to move to something warmer between them.

Maybe even blazing.

She had a feeling that Stella had been thawing toward him when she had her accident.

The way Blue saw it, she needed to do three things. First, she needed to figure out why she'd taken up residence in Stella's body. Once she understood the purpose of the switch, she might be able to complete whatever task was required. She was no expert, but things like this didn't happen without some kind of unseen help. To her knowledge, there was also a damn good reason.

Second, if this switch was permanent, she had to learn everything she could about life in 1913, so she could fit in.

Third and most personally, she wanted to get Dr. Stephens into her bed, because she might have only one shot at having a fulfilling relationship before she went back to her own body and it gave out.

It might be selfish, it might be wrong, but under the circumstances, she convinced herself no one would blame a young woman for wanting to live life to the fullest when she had this once-in-a-lifetime opportunity.

The way Colt talked about their more recent conversations, Stella had been attracted to him. Blue wondered if Stella had been afraid of acting on the attraction. These days were very different from Blue's.

As far as life today, she'd read all the newspapers she could get her hands on and had memorized the women's names who'd stopped into her room to say hello. Some of them counted Stella as a true friend and confidante.

Belle seemed to have a particular friendship with Stella and made it clear she saw Stella as an equal. Belle referred to the mansion and grounds as a "retreat for fine gentlemen," and insisted on nothing but the best for her employees and the men who came calling. Some of the names and positions of Belle's client list made Blue's head spin.

Powerful men in high positions, men with secrets and contacts that stretched around the globe, were among Belle's gentleman callers.

Blue didn't much care what the women called the place, she was grateful for the respite and care she'd received. Everyone here was warm, friendly, and kind beyond anything she'd experienced in her life.

Perhaps she should think of it as her *former* life. As each day passed, she felt stronger in Stella's body and more removed from her own sickly one. She'd tried every day to see if Stella lurked somewhere in her subconscious, but there was no sign of the other woman.

Blue had never been much for organized religion, but she had faith that whatever had happened had been for the best.

The clues to why the switch had been made were somewhere in Stella's life. They couldn't be in Blue's own life, because she'd never done anything to get this kind of benevolent attention.

The life of Blue McCann was unremarkable, except for her beginnings, of course. Not every newborn was abandoned in a Dumpster. Since then, the only special thing that had ever happened to her was happening right here and right now.

And his name was Dr. Colt Stephens.

As each day passed, her desire for the doctor increased and the light in his eyes warmed.

Today, she would see exactly how warm the man could get.

He would arrive soon to take her home and she waited, dressed and ready. The pounding in her chest was a good sign, she decided. Her heart was strong, and she had released the fear that she wouldn't be able to enjoy every moment with Colt.

They were adults, attracted to each other, and spent a lot of time in a whorehouse. What more encouragement could they need?

Not every man of this time could appreciate a straight-talking woman, but there were times she caught a smile lurking in his eyes when she said something he thought was outlandish.

Everyone insisted she get more rest. Days of rest. Which suited her just fine, because she was terrified of taking up Stella's midwifery and causing irreparable harm.

Not that she'd be here long. Surely she would return to her own life and time soon.

Which only made her want the doctor more.

She may have to take matters into her own hands, so to speak.

She checked the time and then Stella's reflection. Blue still hesitated to look in mirrors, but the shock of seeing another woman's reflection had faded. Lustrous red hair, wide green eyes, and an hourglass figure were definitely a step up. She'd miss this body if she had to leave it. All the more reason to enjoy it as much as possible while she could.

The good doctor should be here any moment to take her to Stella's apartment. Apparently, she had a place over a general store run by Hope, one of the former girls, and her husband, Jed Devine.

Hope had married the widower, and was busy raising his children and expecting their first. They'd recently moved into a much larger house and Stella had taken their apartment.

A light rap on her door announced Colt's arrival. She opened the bedroom door wide in invitation. She smiled, delighted with him all over again. His face held the male focus of a man intent on a woman and her heart picked up speed.

"Good morning," he said with a tilt of his head. His hair gleamed and he flashed her a grin that set her afire. She motioned him inside and closed the door.

He quirked an eyebrow and let his gaze drift idly down her body. He hadn't seen her out of bed since the accident. She stood straighter, smiled wider, and let him see how much she appreciated his attention. "Surprised I'm ready to go?"

"A little. I thought you might choose to stay another day or so."

She stepped closer and put her hand on his upper arm. "I want to go home. I can't wait, in fact." He was holding something behind his back. "What are you hiding?"

With a flourish he presented her with a bouquet of wild flowers. Daisies, mostly. Her favorite.

"I saw you pick daisies a week ago, so I thought you might care for more." Apparently, she and Stella had the same taste in flowers as they did in men. Good to know.

"How lovely, thank you, doctor." She went to the side table for an ornate crystal vase. "I'd like to call you Colt, if I may." Was that forward by 1913 standards?

"Please do. I've asked you many times to use my given name."

"I guess I spent a lot of time on my 'high horse,' hmm?" she said. She turned and gazed at him, enjoying the sight of a handsome man gazing back. "You should know I'm ready to climb down off that horse, Colt. I'd like to be on equal footing with you."

His eyes flared hot and the sun came out in the room. A surge of female need put a swing in her hips as she sauntered toward the door. "Time to go home at last. A woman needs her privacy."

Until this visit, she'd been sitting up in bed, covered to her chin. Now that she was on her feet again, she let him see the woman she was. She turned and let her expression speak of her need.

He stilled, his body tensed. Even from ten feet away, she could see the battle he fought with himself. She released the doorknob and waited to see what the delectable doctor would do.

She watched as he hovered between desire and control.

With a sigh, she said, "Relax, Colt. I'm not a patient any longer. I've never felt as healthy and strong as I feel right now." *In either life!*

He strode across the room, sucking up all the air, looming large and focused over her. She stepped back and hit the door. Her blood rushed, crazily, along every artery, through each muscle, to every single nerve ending in her body. Alive! Her need made her feel alive, and she reveled in the feeling.

"Colt, kiss me already and put me out of my misery."

His hands clasped her arms, his mouth dropped to hers and hovered a millimeter over her flesh. "Stella, you make me want to roar, to plunder and take. I fear my baser instincts will soon be in control."

Clang! Clang! Her heart slammed against her chest wall in a warning. Overload was imminent, she was sure of it. No, that was her old body, Blue's body.

Stella's body was up for whatever the doctor had in mind.

His lips moved to her ear as he murmured against her. The feel of him there, against her neck, reminded her of the dressing room. It had been Colt Stephens who'd taken her over the edge into orgasm just before she'd blacked out.

Before she'd become Stella McCreedy.

"I've dreamed of this," he murmured. "I've wanted you for weeks, but you wouldn't look at me, wouldn't give me the time of day." His eyes roved her features as his mouth hovered, a pucker away from touching hers. "Now that I have your interest, I'm dumbfounded at the changes in you. Something happened to you, and it changed the way you look at me. And I'm very happy it did."

She placed her palms on his cheeks, held his gaze. "I'm very glad it happened too." She lifted her mouth and let him settle, light as a butterfly, on her lips. Soft and firm, Colt's lips met hers.

Her belly dropped with need; hot, hard, and faster than anything she'd felt before. He was so hesitant, so careful, testing her, coaxing her to respond. If she did what her modern self wanted to do, she would frighten him. She wanted to lift her skirts, wrap her legs around his hips, and invite him inside, here against the door.

But this man came from a different time, had different ideas of men and women and sex. She had to let him lead the way. "Take me home, Colt, and I'll give you anything you want. Just take me home."

He lifted his head, then studied her eyes for a long moment. "Stella, are you sure?" He slid his hands to her rear and cupped her.

She nodded. "The thing you think happened to me. It's true, I've changed. The bump on the head, my accident, all made me think hard about the good things life offers us. About how all those good things can be snatched away at a moment's notice."

She kissed him again and mimicked the way he kneaded her. His butt felt tight and firm under her questing fingers. "Colt, you're one of the good things in life and I won't let you be snatched away. Not yet."

He kissed her so hard then she thought her heart would stop.

They stepped out together into the hallway and walked around the gallery to the head of the wide stairs. As they descended, she heard voices from the hall on the main floor. All the women of Perdition waited below. They were here to see her off amid hugs and best wishes. Blue felt part of a community for the first time in her life and blinked several times as the women clasped her to their bosoms in true affection.

She felt like a thief taking these wishes to heart. They belonged to Stella, not Blue. If she found a way to stay here, she would make it her business to earn the respect and affection of these women for herself.

Outside, the air felt moist and cool. The tang of sea air, salty and fresh, filled her nose. The brothel stood over a cliff that looked onto Shilshole Bay. The lot stretched out all around the building with sculptured gardens to the right of the house and a beautiful expanse of lawn to the left. At the end near the trees sat a lovely gazebo. White with green trim, it looked like the perfect spot for a romantic tryst.

Colt told her about parties and dancing held out there on the lawns. He helped her into his Model T and she watched as he maneuvered the car down the drive. She held on with both hands. "Some day, they'll put seat belts in these things and people won't go flying out onto the road when they hit trees."

He cast her a sidelong glance. "If people kept to a reasonable speed, they wouldn't slide off the roadway."

That much was true no matter what century they were driving in, she thought. There was nothing like holding on for dear life to chase away desire. By the time Colt parked behind the building that housed the general store, Blue's body had been shaken and jostled. The roads were terrible, and every bounce had reminded her that it had been only three days since the accident. Every sore muscle she owned had protested with each jiggle and rough bounce.

As soon as she could, she scrambled out of the rattle trap car before Colt could get around to help her. "I want my feet on solid ground," she said as he reached into the back for his medical bag.

"Oh ho! The speed demon has finally seen sense."

She laughed and even that hurt. Gingerly, she made her way toward the stairs to the second floor, but once she started to move and think about having Colt all to herself, she felt better.

The apartment was much larger than she'd thought it would

be. "This is a lot of space for one person," she said as she walked through the kitchen that overlooked the back entrance.

Colt followed her from the parlor through all the bedrooms. One had a painting easel set up in a corner. Stella was artistic, but Blue couldn't draw a circle. She'd have to find a way around her lack of ability. Closer inspection showed dust gathering on the blank canvas. She smiled and ran her fingertip across the top. "I haven't painted in a long time. I should probably put this away."

"You don't have time for it, I suppose. Since we met last month, you rarely have an evening to yourself, much less a day for painting. Belle told me you used to take your easel and paints out to Lake Washington and spend hours."

She looked over her shoulder at him and drank in the sight of the man she was about to take to her bed. Chocolate brown eyes, dark brown hair, thick lashes, and with a broader chest than her first impression, Colt was everything she could ask for. "Used to?"

"Since I've known you, there hasn't been a day when you haven't been run off your feet. Or any nights off, for that matter."

"I'm not rushing around right now." She lifted her hands to the buttons on her coat and slipped them free.

He stepped closer and set his hands at her waist. His palms burned through her day dress to her flesh. She'd packed the corset, half afraid that if she put it on again, she would return to her own time. He squeezed her gently. "I like feeling your pliant flesh. You're perfect, Stella."

"I don't like corsets," she said. "Besides, styles will change soon and women won't have to wear them anymore." She liked it here too much to chance a return to Blue McCann's nothing existence. With luck, she would soon think of herself as Stella.

Maybe that would guarantee she could stay.

She watched a storm of emotion chase through Colt's eyes. Desire warred with hesitation. "Don't be polite, Colt. Take what you want."

He groaned and pulled her to his chest. His eyes went hungry as desire won. His smile was crooked as always, but his kisses were straight, hot and hard.

She sighed into Colt's mouth as he pressed her lips open and pushed for entrance. His hands moved up from her waist to cup her cheeks. His face filled her view as he set her away from him.

"That's all you want? A kiss?"

He was torn, desire rode him, but the mores of the time held him back. Enough! She would have to take charge.

She tilted her head and smiled. "Colt, I won't break. I'm healthy again."

"So am I. That's the problem, Stella. I'm a healthy man and what I want isn't proper."

"Proper?" This was worse than she thought. She hadn't read anything about what was considered proper behavior for single women, but considering she'd landed square in the middle of a whorehouse and Stella took care of the women there, Colt would surely read her attraction to him.

She tilted her head into his palm, turned her lips, and kissed him there. He sucked in a harsh breath. She extended his index finger and slid her mouth down to the apex, keeping her eyes locked on his. No man could mistake this message, not even a prim doctor. His eyes widened. His belly jerked. His cock rose between them.

"You're hard," she said around his finger. "You want me and I want you. Take me, Colt."

He stepped back, taking his hands away, then frowned. "This bump to the head has affected your judgement. I will not take advantage."

She raised her face to the ceiling, closed her eyes, took a

breath, and took a mental count to three. Without missing a beat, she began undoing buttons. First at her neck, then at her throat, and then down the front of her dress.

Colt stared, his fingers twitching at his sides. "Stella, stop, this is—"

"I know what I want, Dr. Stephens. I'm what? Twenty-five? Old enough to know. Old enough to want. Hell! I've been delivering babies, handing out prophylactics to prostitutes. How sheltered do you think I am?"

By now, she'd undone all her buttons and her dress hung open. His face went deep red; his cock sat just under his waistband, a bulge of promise. His hands clenched into fists. "Dearest Stella, if you persist, I won't be responsible."

4

Blue shucked off the shoulders of her gown. The simple day dress puddled at her feet. Colt's eyes burned through her light cotton chemise until her nipples peaked with need.

"My bedroom's through there," she whispered and pointed. It had to be there, she hadn't seen a room with a bed in it yet and they'd traipsed through the whole apartment.

At long last, he clasped her hand in his and towed her behind him into the room at the front of the apartment. Inside, they found a lace-covered bed, unmade, a simple washstand with water in the bowl, and a single dresser and mirror. A wardrobe stood against the wall on the far side of the bed, still open. Stella had left in a hurry.

She flushed at the sight of the disheveled room. "Sorry, obviously I had to rush out of here."

He grinned, then slipped his finger under her chin. "A hurried departure is part of our lives." He frowned again. "Babies don't wait." His gaze clouded with doubt.

She knew what he was thinking. It was on the tip of her

tongue to say she used birth control; then she remembered. Stella's body was a wide-open baby machine.

"I care for you, Stella, but I'm not sure that's enough for a happy marriage."

"What's marriage got to do with this?"

He stepped away, shock making his face flat. Anger roiled in his gaze. "I wouldn't compromise our friendship unless it meant marriage. What kind of man do you take me for?"

Oh, crap. An honorable man with the moral fabric of 100 years ago. Crap. Again. "You're a good man, Colt Stephens. A man I want with my whole being. But marriage is a huge step, and I can't promise you."

"But if a child results—"

She stopped him with two fingers on his lips. "I have a solution. For everything."

"What is it?" You'd think a doctor would understand there were ways to enjoy sexual fulfillment without the threat of pregnancy, but he was behaving like a man, not a doctor.

"No penetration," she said, and watched his eyes flare heat.

"What else—"

She dropped to her knees and he broke off, quick to see where she would take him. "Stella, you don't have—"

"Colt." She smiled as sweetly as she could. "Ever heard the term *payback?*"

He swallowed, hard. Sweet, sweet man. He freed his cock, and from her position on the floor he was huge—long, strong, and perfectly formed. She salivated and felt moisture gather between her legs.

She ran her thumb from his base to his tip with a firm stroke. "Like a rock," she said. He threw his head back and groaned while he braced his feet wide. She snuggled her knees between his ankles.

His cock slit was dewed, and she tipped the underside of her tongue against the moisture as a tease. Then in a move designed to take him to the edge, she slid her wet mouth down in one slick, quick slide, as far as she could go. He tasted of salt and need and Colt.

His legs trembled. "Ahh!"

She clasped his knees hard and tightened her lips as she slid farther down his shaft. There was no way she could take him all; he was a tall man and his cock was in proportion. After three more quick slides, she looked up at him and smiled. His hands cupped her head. He was catching on.

She wanted to lick his balls, but they were still hidden. "We need to be naked."

He needed no more encouragement. They stripped and stretched out on the bed. She went to bend over him again, but he rolled her to her back and clasped her wrists over her head. Trapped in an ancient four poster with a man intent on her. Finally!

Colt pressed her knees together with his and looked his fill of Stella's heavy breasts. Her nipples were full, the size of silver dollars, and dark, delicious red. He flicked one with his tongue to see how sensitive she was. She sucked in a quick breath and arched, her hands happily pinned over her head. She wrapped her fingers around the wrought-iron supports in the head board, leaving her helpless to his exploration. Her contusions were healing nicely, but he'd seen her wince in pain when she hopped out of his car.

He kissed a light bruise on her throat, over her carotid artery. "I've never had a woman stretched out naked for me before. May I look you over?"

"You're a doctor, Colt. You've seen—"

"Not like this. Not alive and warm and wanting me. Not completely naked, either." His heart swelled in his chest at the knowledge of her surrender. He had her permission and cooperation to do whatever he wanted with her, to her. His cock throbbed against the softness of her thigh. If he wasn't careful, he'd let fly before he brought her to full pleasure, and that would be a difficult beginning.

Because beginning was the only word for what they shared. A beginning would lead to more, would lead to a future. He was as sure of that as he was his own name.

Her nipples tasted like ripe blueberries, a burst of flavor on his tongue. He sucked her entire aureola into his mouth and rolled the tip with his tongue. She squirmed, wanting her legs free, but he kept her knees tightly closed between his.

Her pubis was covered with dark red swirls of hair that hid her deepest feminine secrets, her waist flared, wide and comfortable, into hips meant for riding. Every thought, every muscle and sinew in his body strained toward her.

He'd dreamed of kissing the back of her neck, sliding his hands into her wet cunny, and rubbing until pleasure overtook her and she collapsed against him. In his dream, he'd bent her over at the waist and rammed himself into her from behind, deep and thrusting, like an animal. But that was a dream, and penetration was impossible. She was right. They had to be cautious.

As he trailed his mouth and lips down to her navel, he didn't think she'd mind his taking her from behind. She was a generous woman intent on exploring him as much as he wanted to explore her.

He dipped his tongue into her sweet bud of a navel, the scent of her wet mound coming to him, in an enticing aroma of need and womanly musk. "You're beautiful," he murmured.

A lift of his hair told him she'd let go of the bedstead, but she didn't tug him away from his target.

Mouth play. He'd dreamed of it, wondered about it.

And now it was his to enjoy.

"I'm going to make you work for it," she said on a huff. She slid her hands over her curls, fingers closed tightly. He chuckled.

"A challenge you'll lose, Stella." He set his mouth to the apex of two fingers and pressed. "Are you going to be shy now?"

She nodded, her face pink, eyes bright. "Work for it. Make me so ready I can't resist."

He saw her game now. If she could tell herself he'd convinced her, driven her mad with passion, then she could forgive herself for her womanly desire. He set himself to the game wholeheartedly.

He started by sliding his mouth down to her inner thigh and licking the warm flesh. She sighed and her muscles tensed under his ministrations.

Tantalizing minx.

He nuzzled against her soft hair, rooted his tongue between her tightly closed fingers. A taste of her juices burst on the tip of his tongue. Sweat heaven, she was delicious!

He pressed his palm on her covering hand firmly so her belly could feel what it would be like to have his weight covering her. As expected, her fingers loosened on a sigh. He took full advantage and slicked his tongue deeper between her guardian digits.

Her sweet juices flooded through her cupping hand. Then he remembered what she'd done with her mouth on his finger and copied the motion. Sliding low, he slid his mouth over her forefinger and sucked it deep, moving it aside while he milked it. With a deft movement, he slid his other hand close and speared a finger into her slit. He released her forefinger while she writhed, and stabbed his tongue between her pink, juicy folds.

Her clitoris rose, plump and rubbery, to his mouth, and he'd won the battle of wills. Now, he could carry her away on a passion so hot she could never deny him.

He set to work and lapped and kissed her intimately. Her fingers fell slack to her inner thighs, and the pot of honey that was Stella opened to him.

What was left of this civilized man deserted him as her legs opened to his gaze. Wet, plump lips popped open, and her secrets revealed themselves to his questing tongue. He pressed his cock into the bedclothes, willing himself to control.

But it was a hard-fought battle.

He growled and worked his way between her outer lips until he'd exposed the small bud of her pleasure center. Wet, glistening, the bud peeped out at him.

He wasn't sure what she wanted, so he lay the flat of his tongue on the bud and pressed up. She bucked and the bud stiffened against his tongue. He tickled and swirled it, felt her tension rise as her hands fell away completely.

Her legs opened wide in the sweetest offering. With no control left, he reared up and grabbed her hips while she splayed herself to his view. With a growl of appreciation, Colt buried his face in the cradle she offered and tasted the wine of her inner beauty.

She gushed moisture for him, as his tongue delved as deeply as he could go. He lapped and played and tasted and sipped as she bucked and lunged, pressing her pussy high toward him. She needed more, needed deeper, wider.

"You need a cock, Stella. My cock," he said, as he experimented by sliding two fingers into her wet slit. Her lips opened and bloomed as he slid in and out of her. "So wet! Hear yourself? You're slick and slippery and greedy for cock."

"Fuck me, Colt."

In appreciation, he slid a third finger into her and she bucked wildly, straining for more. He plunged more rapidly. "Is this enough?"

"Harder, faster!" she begged. "Fuck me!" Her plea made his cock weep until he couldn't take it anymore. He pulled his hand free of her and slicked her moisture along his shaft until he was wet and gleaming.

He straddled her backward and offered his cock to her mouth, while he slipped his fingers back into her weepy, needy cunny. Her hips bucked and rolled. Her mouth, wet and hot, played the head of his cock until he feared losing control. If he snapped, he'd plunge into her throat and cause an injury. He shook with holding back.

Her mischievous fingers found his sac and diddled and played. When she squeezed him, he groaned. "I'll come if you do that again."

She stopped. "Let's come together."

She pressed her pussy up toward his face, while he felt the low, hot slide of her mouth take his cock gently. With control within reach again, he pumped and retreated into her mouth, in a slow mouth penetration that shook him.

She clasped his head and pulled him to her waiting need.

He slid three fingers inside her again, marveling at the juiciness he found. He bent his head to her and licked around her clitoris, lapping at the cunny juice glistening just for him.

His cock throbbed in her mouth while she sucked and swirled and milked him. He mimicked her mouth action on her cunt, while he kept up a steady pressure in her channel. He sucked gently on her clitoris until it stood straight out; then he used his thumb and lips and tongue on the valiant bud.

He crooned and moaned with each pass of her tongue across the tip of his ready cock.

Suddenly, she groaned and went stiff. Her pussy gushed against his fingers, and instinct took over as he pressed into her, wishing his cock was buried deep, deep, deep. Deeper than his fingers, deep enough to bury his seed in her grasping womb.

"I'm coming!" she screamed, and bucked and held while he suckled and took her higher.

His orgasm built in the depth of his balls and rose like a

geyser through his shaft and into her mouth. Her wet, sucking, greedy mouth.

He cried out with the sheer pleasure, sure he would die of it. Felt sure he didn't want to live if he never had it again.

Three hours later, Blue watched as Colt lifted his hat in a good-bye salute and drove off. He hadn't wanted to leave her, but a young boy had knocked on her door looking for him. His father was in pain and he'd been sent to find Doc Stephens.

She'd offered to help, but Colt shook his head and frowned.

Luckily, they'd already been dressed when the knock came. Colt had blushed red when the boy showed up. Redder still when she'd kissed his cheek at the door. She supposed that was forward and too public for the good doctor, but she felt wonderful and didn't care if the world knew it.

There hadn't been time to discuss when they'd see each other again, and Blue knew it might not happen at all.

Maybe she'd go back to her own life before he returned.

But she still couldn't see why she was here at all.

Colt's car putt-putt-putted away down the lane. She had to get her own car back, but the idea of driving it again gave her the creeps. Bart Jameson had taken the damaged wire wheels to be fixed and put the chassis on blocks in Belle's front drive.

Belle had made noises about the car sitting there because Perdition House was supposed to be the perfect retreat. No reminders of life outside the grounds were permitted to interfere with her gentleman callers' good time.

Sooner or later, Blue would have to pick up her car. Stella knew how to drive and so did Blue. But a Model T? Sure, it might have simple controls, but Blue was used to power steering and brakes and all the modern conveniences. Like windshield wipers and shock absorbers, and especially seatbelts. She rubbed her neck.

Maybe she could tell Colt she was too afraid to get behind

the wheel. Maybe he would offer to teach her to drive with confidence again.

Although he'd made a comment about women not being suited to driving. Hmm. While Blue could happily let him think that way for the time being, she had the idea that Stella would bristle.

She had no choice but to drive again, and soon.

The bump on her head gave her ready excuses for any missteps she took while adjusting to life here, so she'd best use it to her advantage.

She watched until Colt was out of sight, on his way to his house call. Wow, that was a shock. A doctor who made house calls.

For the first time in days, she was completely alone. She could be Blue again. She cupped Stella's full breasts, felt her heart beating strongly in her chest, filled her lungs with fresh air, and closed her eyes. Blood rushed every which way through her body, streaming life.

Her orgasms had made her feel powerfully feminine and alive again. Colt was a fabulous lover. Once she'd pointed the way toward oral sex as a good way to avoid penetration, he'd taken the lead like a master.

She cupped herself, gave her mound a shimmy, to feel the aftereffects of coming. Sweet release from being with a sweet man.

With a happy spin, she went into the bath to fill the narrow tub. The apartment had all the modern conveniences. A copper water heater in the kitchen provided plenty of hot water. She indulged and found some Epsom salts to pour in. No scent, but the mineral soak eased her achy muscles. Stella's body hadn't had sex in way too long, and the days in bed following her accident had left her weaker than she'd been the day Blue had woken up here.

She found a new block of ice in the icebox. The milk was cold, and there was a fresh loaf of bread in a breadbox on the counter. All in all, the kitchen was well stocked, and Blue felt more at home than she imagined she would. No electrical appliances, but she recognized a lot of the kitchen gadgets from trips to the museum.

She headed down to the store and found a box of breakfast cereal she recognized. She knew corn flakes had been around forever, but this was way cool.

While she paid Jed for her purchases, the bell over the shop door rang. At the sound, she turned and saw Belle, dressed in a slim skirt and long-waisted coat. Her hat, a brilliant crimson number, was velvet, with a wide brim and long ties that fluttered over her ample breasts. The color emphasized her white-blonde hair and reminded Blue of Faye again. The women were obviously related. Aside from their appearance, the women shared one other thing that made them stand out.

They'd both been kind to Blue McCann.

Jed and Belle exchanged greetings, but Belle looked drawn and unhappy, in spite of the slight lift of her lips that she mustered into a fleeting smile.

Payback. Time to offer a kindness in return.

"I was about to make some coffee, Belle. Care for a cup?" If she could figure out the old-fashioned coffee percolator, she'd be fine.

5

Belle's expression didn't lighten until she dropped her hat and gloves on Stella's kitchen table. She relaxed and settled into a chair. Blue filled the coffee percolator with water and the basket with grounds. She set it on the stove, mentally crossing her fingers that it turned out all right.

When she faced Belle again, the other woman was worrying at her bottom lip and staring out the window.

"Belle? What's the problem?" She'd been so kind to Blue at Perdition, Blue had to offer whatever help she could.

"I'm pregnant." Belle lifted wet eyes to her and blew out a breath. "There, I said it. I feel so stupid!"

"But, how?" More importantly, "Who?" Blue asked.

"The usual way, with the usual culprit: a man I thought was a trifle but turned out to be far more. Love makes us all fools," Belle said through a tired smile. She waved her hand. "His name doesn't matter, and he can't know. No one can know."

"You need a doctor to be certain. Have you seen Colt?"

"What woman needs a doctor to know about a baby?" she

scoffed. Her brows knit into a frown. "And do you think I'd see him over my own sister?" Belle's eyes went sharp with anger, as if Stella should know better. As if Stella would understand the need for secrets.

Stella was Belle Grantham's sister! Blue sank to her ladder-back chair and put her hand over Belle's in comfort. As much for herself as for Belle. "But, you're sure?"

Belle moved a comforting hand across her flat belly. "I'm sure." For the first time since she'd seen her downstairs, a shy joy showed in Belle's expression, and Blue needed no more confirmation. She'd seen the look many times while she'd been in classes.

A burbling, popping sound came from the stove top and the air filled with the scent of fresh coffee. Belle stood and got down cups, saucers, and the sugar bowl, obviously comfortable in Stella's kitchen. Naturally she'd be at home in her sister's kitchen. She found a pie that Hope had left for Stella on the counter. "Apple, my favorite," she said, and started to cut wedges.

Blue watched and blinked back a tear. She'd never had a sister, but her heart swelled with some emotion she was afraid to name. "Apple's my favorite too," she said, full of questions that had nothing to do with pie or coffee.

Belle went to the stove for the coffee, but Blue stood and stayed her hand. "You sit. No caffeine for you. You'll have a glass of milk." Her voice was firm and steady, which amazed her because her hands shook.

This must be why she was here. Stella was a midwife, and her sister needed her.

Belle gave her an odd look when Blue guided her to her seat. "Coffee's not good for the baby," she explained.

"Nonsense," Belle snapped. "I'll drink what I want. Nothing passes to the child, everyone knows that."

How could she tell her that old information was wrong? "No alcohol either," Blue said sternly, holding her gaze. "I'm serious, Belle. Pregnant women need to eat well, sleep well, and get exercise and fresh air." Not to mention vitamins, massages, and regular checkups. She could just imagine Belle and Colt's expressions if she mentioned any of those modern ideas.

Belle made a noise through her teeth. "Ridiculous." But she slid her cup and saucer to the far side of the table, in a gesture meant to mollify Stella.

"I suppose you think I'm here to ask you to get rid of it, but I'm not."

It was a sad fact that women had practiced abortion as birth control for thousands of years. Some of the home remedies were deadly. "You're not?" Blue asked, keeping her face clear of relief. She didn't know how Stella would react to a statement like Belle's, so she opted for neutrality.

"I've thought about this ever since your accident. Life's precious, and I want to give this child a good home," she said in a matter-of-fact tone. "We'll go to Europe for a Grand Tour where you'll deliver the baby. We should leave next month."

"I can't deliver the baby!"

"Why not?"

"Well," she blustered, "what if the delivery goes wrong? I'm your sister, Belle. I might get too emotional, too upset to think clearly." She had the overwhelming urge to wring her hands at the idea of Belle putting her and her newborn's life into her inexperienced hands. This couldn't possibly be right. This couldn't be why this switch was made.

Anyone would think it common knowledge that they were sisters, but the more she thought of it, she couldn't recall anyone mentioning it.

And Stella looked nothing like Belle, except for their hourglass figures. They both had big boobs and trim waists.

"What are you staring at?" Belle asked.

"I'm looking for . . ."

"A maternal glow? Forget it, Stella. You won't see it."

She rolled her eyes and patted her hand where it held the forkful of apple pie. "I've already seen it."

Belle blanched. "Well, fine, I do feel a . . . certain attachment," she admitted. "But I won't keep this child. I can't keep it and expect to stay in business. No one knows we're sisters, and no one can know I'm a mother. You and this child can be used against me. My loving you both—" Her voice broke off suddenly and tears welled. "Don't look so surprised. I am capable of tears. I am capable of—" She broke off again and gathered her strength. "I am capable of love."

"Of course you are!" Blue rose and went to her *sister.* She knelt by Belle's chair and wrapped her arms around her shaking shoulders. "I love you too!" She wasn't sure if the sisters said it much, but the words were needed now. Her chest warmed with affection, and she enjoyed a glimmer of hope that maybe she could be of help here.

"The baby, Stella. Will you raise it?" Belle whispered against her hair. She went on, "It's a lot to ask, but what else can we do?" She ended her sniffles, dabbed at her eyes, wiped her nose, and the breakdown was over. Gone, as if it had never happened. Blue leaned back and watched in awe as Belle Grantham's backbone straightened and her eyes glittered hard. "If I were ever blackmailed into revealing secrets, there's no telling the damage that could be done."

Politicians, captains of industry, they all found their way to Perdition House sooner or later. Belle was right to keep the baby a secret. If her child was threatened, Belle would do whatever was necessary to save it, even bring down a government.

With the First World War on the horizon, America needed stability. An unstable America at this point in history could mean a different outcome for the world. Even though America didn't join in until 1917, their support was essential in winning the war to end all wars, as it was called.

"I'll help you, Belle. Just tell me what you need me to do."

"How involved are you with Colt Stephens?" Belle leaned in as if it were a rare occurrence for the sisters to share confidences. Which appeared to be the case, because apparently Stella hadn't known about the man in Belle's life.

No one had any knowledge of Belle's private life, and it had to stay that way.

Blue wondered at all the secrets Perdition House held. "Why do you ask about Colt?" She was entitled to a secret of her own.

"Please, it's clear as glass he's mad for you, and the moment you woke up after that bump on the head, you looked at him differently."

Blue shrugged. It was on the tip of her tongue to pass him off as a fling, but the memory of the way he held her, his expressive face full of true affection stopped the comment. "I like him. A lot."

"Have you taken him to bed yet?"

Blue felt heat rise from her neck to her hairline.

Belle laughed, low and husky, a woman who knew the signs. "I thought so. Is there talk of marriage?" Her eyes went sharp again, the consummate businesswoman.

"He's mentioned it."

She frowned. "Make certain to marry him. Promise me again."

Again? This was dangerous ground. "Why marriage?" she shrugged. "You don't care about all that."

"But our father does. And since he raised you with his wife, and not like me with Mama's wild influences, he'll expect you to marry. You shouldn't disappoint him. The scandal would probably reveal me as his daughter too. The whole thing is a house of cards, Stella. Our lives will be ruined." She stood and paced the wide floorboards.

"Marry Colt and he'll come to Europe with us. When we come back with a baby, they'll think it's yours."

Blue could only hope to stay here that long. An adventure! Intrigue! Her heart thudded faster, and she felt almost as alive and excited as she did in the sack with Colt. Delicious man.

Blue's body had been so ill for so long, she'd never considered having a child. She wouldn't have lived long enough to have a family. This chance to raise Belle's baby with a good man at her side seemed like an offer from heaven itself.

"Next time he asks me, I'll accept. It shouldn't be difficult, he's a good man." She raised her eyes to the ceiling and sent up a silent prayer that this charade among Stella, Blue, and whatever force, for good or evil, could continue forever.

"Papa will be pleased one of us will make good. And this will keep his name clear of scandal, will allow me to see my child as it grows, and keep me in business."

"If I didn't have strong feelings for Colt, I would have to refuse."

Belle slammed to a halt. "Which reminds me. Why have you changed your mind about him?"

Blue tilted her chin in a gesture that seemed right for the woman she'd learned Stella to be: fearless, adventurous, and kind. "He's proven to be a much better man than my stubborn mind allowed me to see at first glance."

Belle eyed her shrewdly. "All right. We're agreed, then."

"How soon do you want to leave?"

Belle slid her hand across her belly in a common gesture of maternal love. "No later than next month."

"Fine. We'll tell Colt about the baby after a wedding date is set. He'll have to know about our father, and all the reasons for keeping our secrets, or he won't agree. I think I know him well enough to know that about him."

She only hoped she could find a way to guarantee she could live out Stella's life. She eyed her "sister." Belle would be devastated to learn the woman she knew as Stella wasn't actually Stella. If Blue did manage to stay in this time, she had a feeling it wouldn't be long before she felt true sisterly affection for the madame of Perdition House. Maybe that would be enough for both of them.

"How can you leave the business for months?"

"Felicity will take it over for me. She's the only one I'd trust to keep the house running smoothly. The gentlemen like her and the captain's not the jealous sort. Besides, we've been friends since we were children together in Galveston. The captain knows more about me than you do." She smiled softly, the picture of maternal wisdom.

"Will you tell Felicity why you're leaving?" It was a test to see how secret this baby would be.

"No one but you, Colt, and I will know."

It should be simple enough to have Colt deliver the baby when the time came. With that out of the way, she felt a stirring of excitement. She rose and hugged Belle. "We'll raise this baby together, Belle. You'll be the most loving auntie any child could have."

Then they had a sniffling good cry together.

Two days later, Colt rushed through the checkup on Mr. Henderson's appendectomy. Satisfied with the way the incision was healing, he returned home, only to find Howard Jones in the examination room there. His cheek was swollen.

Colt took one look inside the man's mouth and sent him to the dentist for a tooth extraction. He could have done it, but he had a gentleman's agreement with the local dentist, and Colt always kept his word. As soon as Jones stepped outside into the cooling evening air, he locked the office door.

The half-dozen prophylactics he had in his medical bag called to him. Two days of being with Stella without being inside her was killing him.

In spite of his recent lamentable behavior with an unmarried woman, he was a gentleman. Stella was a lady, well-bred and raised by one of the leading men in industry. He had to do right by her.

He wanted to do right by her, in spite of her forward-thinking ways. She was an odd combination. For a midwife to come from her background and standing was rare. Unheard of, actually. Most midwives these days were from immigrant families, and a concerted effort from the medical community was afoot to rid the country of all of them.

He slipped into his coat, grabbed his hat, and stepped out into the gathering gloom with nothing but Stella on his mind.

All in all, she had been lucky to establish herself with the women in Perdition House. He supposed it was the measure of respect he'd seen between Stella and Belle Grantham that allowed for the easy rapport Stella had with the women who worked in the house.

He and Stella had agreed on no penetration, but he already found that agreement untenable. Preparation was the only sensible way to handle their attraction.

He wanted Stella, in ways he'd never wanted another woman. The thoughts that ringed his mind were like a band of hedonistic pleasures that tightened every hour and made his blood heat to boiling.

It wasn't just physical release he craved. He wanted so much more. He wanted her love, her kind thoughts; he wanted a life with her and children! The thought of children with Stella made his footsteps falter and halt.

With one hand on the door of his automobile, he stood stunned at the vision before his mind's eye. Stella with a baby in her arms and a toddler clutching her skirt.

It was all a man could wish for, as he saw the imaginary Stella raise her eyes to his with heated promise.

He climbed into his automobile and headed with determination to her apartment. They had much to discuss.

6

The apartment over the store was as busy as a train station. Blue swore that anyone who had ever met Stella McCreedy had stopped by in the last couple of days. She had a pantry full of fruit preserves and pickled beets, and an icebox stuffed with a chicken, butter, and eggs. A burlap sack full of potatoes sat on her kitchen floor. She planned on dragging it into the pantry as soon as she caught her breath.

Blue had never had so many friends and well-wishers. Her life as Blue McCann had been lonely from birth. Left in a back alley by her mother, she'd been blue with cold when she'd been found. The nurses had given her the name, and no one had seen fit to change it. Blue she became. McCann had come from the head nurse, who'd called child services that first day.

In this life as Stella, she was flummoxed by all the attention and good wishes. Stella was well-liked and appreciated by friends and patients. It seemed that Stella was a proud woman, and every-one who stopped by was prepared to push the food at her. So when Blue stumbled through the thank yous, no one seemed to notice that Stella wasn't her normal self.

As for Blue, she held every moment of appreciation to her heart and let it warm through her. There was even a point where she felt a tiny bit jealous of Stella. To have a life in 1913 where she was her own woman, in charge of her own affairs, was remarkable.

And yet, Stella was no longer living her life, Blue was. So it was up to Blue to live Stella's life without doing any damage. She was a guardian of Stella's existence, and the responsibility weighed more heavily with every passing day.

Colt would be here soon, and she dug out fresh sheets and found some lavender water to sprinkle across the bedding.

Seduction.

She sighed and heated. Colt would love this. The room looked pretty and fresh and inviting.

As for cooking, she now felt comfortable lighting the stove. A stew that had been left by a grateful new mother bubbled in a pot. The scent was delicious.

She had no idea if Stella could cook, but the lack of ingredients in the house when she'd arrived made Blue doubt it. Either that or she survived on her patients' grateful contributions. Her own lack of skill in the kitchen seemed to be another way she and Stella were similar. She ignored the mental reminder that Stella was an artist in her spare time, while Blue had been addicted to renovation and real-estate shows on television.

Her interest in decor had already brightened Stella's apartment and decluttering was well under way.

The putt-putt of Colt's car came to her from the back alley.

He climbed down and reached onto the passenger seat for his medical bag and a bouquet of wild flowers. She dug a vase out of the cupboard in the second bedroom and filled it with water while he bounded up the back stairs.

When he stepped into the kitchen, she drank in the sight of him. He slipped his hat off his head and grinned while he held out the flowers for her. She took them, gave them a sniff, and remarked, "And what payment would you expect for these?"

He flushed and crowded her against the table, then leaned over her. She dropped the flowers to the table at her back. "Much the same payment I'll give you for that delicious stew I smell."

Something dangerous and delicious shifted behind his eyes. He'd gone dark and exciting. He wanted sex, hungered for it, for her. She edged along the table to the end, then fled out of the kitchen. Her long skirt made her stumble, so she lifted her hem to her knees with a whoop.

Barely able to contain her giggles, she led him down the hall to the living room, correction, she thought, it's called a parlor. His feet pounded behind her slowly and with great, thundering thumps. The man put on a show that made her laugh harder and toss in a sexy squeal every few steps. She felt his hand brush her shoulder, so she sped up and danced on the far side of a round table.

His eyes gleamed, while his teeth flashed with every phony growl he produced. She wanted to collapse with the giggles, but she was having too much fun.

It was Stella having fun. Blue couldn't remember ever playing this way. Not for the sheer joy of it! She covered her mouth to contain her laughter, while he flung off his jacket and tossed it over an ornate chair in the corner.

He dodged left; she ran right and scooted back down the hall, unbuttoning her dress as she went. He'd get a great shock when he discovered she wore no underwear! She didn't think Stella would have been so bold, but Blue was up for anything.

As long as it was with Colt Stephens.

She glanced over her shoulder and saw him with one foot up while he unhooked first one boot, then the other. While he concentrated, she slipped into her bedroom and hid in the closet.

He ran past the bedroom door, feet sounding much lighter now that he was in his socks. She contained another giggle and heard him blunder about in the kitchen, growling like a bear as he searched in vain.

She stripped naked as she waited for him to track back to her room. It didn't take long. The closet door flew open, light poured in, and she jumped into his arms all in one motion.

He caught her naked backside and fell back onto the bed with her.

"Caught you!" she said.

"But I was the hunter," he managed to say between nibbling kisses.

She worked at his shirt buttons while straddling him. "Hah, little do men know. Men chase us until we catch them. That's how it really works."

He chuckled and feigned surprise. "Well, then, I've been had!"

"Not yet, you haven't," she said on a sultry note, but his wicked finger had found her wettest secret and plunged in to the first knuckle. *Tease. Please.* She gasped and closed her eyes.

Now it was his turn to chuckle. She rose up to give him more room. He took the hint and set his thumb against her achy clit and rubbed. She shuddered and trembled while he watched her face.

"You are so lovely like this. Open and giving. Stella! Look at me."

She did. His expression was avid, seductive, and oh-so-needy.

He slid his finger out and trailed it across her mouth. Salty.

"Colt, I need you."

"Be mine, Stella."

"Yes," she crooned as she leaned down to his hot neck. She nibbled the skin under his ear, felt the rasp of his bristles at her cheek. "Love me, Colt, any way you want."

Suddenly flipped to her back, she laughed up into his face. His eyes warmed to affectionate as he started a string of kisses that began at the tip of her nose and moved down her body. When he reached her navel, he growled and flipped her over again. He pulled at her hips until she was on all fours.

"Here, now I can get to you the way I want to," he said.

"Are you—" Oh! He wouldn't, would he?

7

Colt was tempted to test the exposed knot of Stella's backside. He palmed her cheeks, opened them. Like the bud of a rose, it was closed tight. Beneath lay a pot of delights, honeyed with her ambrosia, open and ready. Her labia spread, releasing the aphrodisiac scent of her, showing her dark pink opening.

He put his mouth to her, opened wide, and drank, suckling lightly at her clit, then dragging his tongue front to back.

Her belly clenched as she moaned her enjoyment. He slid his hand along the bed under her to clasp her wrist. He tugged and she allowed him to drag her fingers to her clit. Watching her pleasure herself made his cock throb harder. Her feminine fingers rubbed and plucked. The clues to her pleasure were clear.

"Do that," he said. "Make yourself come so I can watch your cunny drip when it happens."

She glanced down through her legs, her eyes gleaming with desire. She spread her mons wide and tapped at her clit with a tat-a-tat rhythm he memorized. Moisture filled her slit, and he obligingly licked it clear, sharing some with her massaging finger.

"If I do this," she said as her panting grew labored, "I want to see you do it too!" Suddenly overcome, she closed her eyes and sighed in a hearty gasp that made her belly clench. The cheeks of her ass shook and her dark red hole opened while she trembled with her orgasm. Dew sluiced down the side of her leg as she cried out.

His hand found his shaft, aroused beyond bearable, and started to pump and slide as he worked his dry flesh. Gathering her moisture, he slicked it over his penis and rose to fall on the bed beside her.

She flopped, prone and spent, until she peeped one eye to watch. It took only a moment for her to roll to an elbow and prop up to murmur encouragement. Periodic swipes of her wet mouth across his nipple helped take him closer.

"Look at how hard you are," she murmured. "The head's dark purple now and there's dew at your little slit. May I taste it?"

"Please do." He raised his hips off the bed to offer himself. The sight of her lips opening wide to encase his bulbous head sent sparks to his eyes. Two quick, hard sucks were all she gave him.

Then she scampered to the side of the bed and settled where he'd been only moments before. "I'll watch from here if you don't mind. I want to see your balls contract as they shoot."

"Liar!" he cried, as he felt her hot, wet mouth encase each ball in turn. She worked one, then the other, drawing and holding them one at a time. The heat from her mouth sent his temperature soaring as he roared into an orgasm and shot his seed up his chest.

She nuzzled and sucked at his balls while he came. Stars burst behind his eyelids as he emptied himself and fell even more under her spell.

"Vixen," he called, and laughed at the odd sensation she created by licking clean his empty shaft and head.

A burning smell entered the room and alerted him to a waft of smoke. "Did you leave the stew on the stove?"

"Oh! I'll never get used to cooking with that thing," she said before she ran naked from the room.

"You can't parade around your kitchen like that," he called. She was gone, though, so he slammed into his pants and took a robe off the hook on the door. He might allow his dignity to disappear when they were about to indulge in intimacies, but he'd be damned if he let her parade around naked!

The stench in the kitchen smelled strongly burnt. The stew ruined, she looked sad enough to cry. "I've burned it." She wrapped her hand in a tea towel to lift the pot, but he stopped her.

"Here, let me," he said, and handed her the robe. He lifted the heavy pot to the side, while she slipped her arms into the dressing gown.

Stella was different from other women. More than forward thinking, even more than Belle Grantham, he realized. Belle had been raised in the Free Love Movement and lived her life accordingly. Stella simply did exactly as she wanted, when she wanted. Colt found her fascinating as she fretted, ties open on her gown, about their burnt supper. On the one hand, she was a fully sexual wanton, on the other, exactly like any other woman when it came to domestic duty.

"I burned the stew," she said, distressed.

"I had a hand in the ruination too."

She slanted him a glance. "You had a hand somewhere," she said with a husky tone. Taking that as an invitation, he slid both hands down her belly and cupped her mons. The silk of her robe felt cool and delicate, and smelled of lavender. He spread her outer lips and began the rhythmic tapping he'd seen her use on herself. "Yes," she murmured.

She opened wide for him and let him slide his fingers in and out of her in rough play as his arousal came back hot and hard. "Do you like that?" His words sounded guttural and dark as night, even to him. He wasn't sure where this demand in his voice came from, but he needed more.

Colt wanted everything she could give. He wanted to know she felt the same need to suck him dry, use him up, and hold him to her forever.

"I need you inside, Colt. I can't take this anymore. I'm so empty. Fill me, please."

He nuzzled at her neck, bit the light flesh of her lobe, and tugged. The packet he'd brought back with him was still in his jacket pocket. "I brought a prophylactic."

"Oh! Thank you!" She moaned and rocked against his hand in a signal he knew all too well. She was close to her pinnacle, and the power he had over her delighted him. But teasing her felt cruel at this point and he took her over the edge into bliss.

"Oh! I'm coming!" She shuddered and came on his tapping finger. Moisture slicked his fingers as he worked her in her frenzy of release. She stood glorious with abandon in his arms, wracked with orgasmic delight.

Stella McCreedy was the most glorious creature he'd ever encountered.

As she weakened in his arms, he gathered her up and carried her back to the bedroom. "We'll eat later, after we've filled every other craving we have," he said.

She nodded weakly. "Thank you." She palmed his cheek and turned his face so she could look into his eyes. Hers were moist and filled with deep affection. "I'm glad you brought the rubber, I must have taken my entire stock to Perdition."

"That's where I got it." He felt heat rise in his face. "Actually, I took six."

She chuckled. "You wicked, wicked man."

Blue's sexual heat cranked up to inferno by the time Colt

carried her back to bed. Stella's body was obviously making up for lost time, while Blue was making up for lost love. Too many to count, she realized.

So many that she was ready to latch on to Colt Stephens and keep him close to her heart for the rest of Stella's life. When Stella came back into her body, Blue hoped there would be some sensory memory of these days with Colt. There had to be!

No one could feel this kind of love without leaving a trace, a signature behind. Stella would know, Blue was sure of it.

And yes, she loved him. Crazy, but true. Colt was kind, gentle, and considerate. Smart and sexy as hell. Not at all like the doctors she'd met in emergency rooms and clinics. They were so overworked that they hardly looked at her. She was only a case. Just one more in a long line. Not the doctors' fault, but the pressure had reduced Blue to a set of symptoms. Her short life had been full of them.

Colt was different from every man who'd crossed Blue's path. With him, she felt safe, complete, and cherished.

"I love the way you make me feel, Colt. Like I'm important. A somebody."

"You're an odd woman, Stella. Smoking cigars, driving that automobile! One would think you had an unseemly amount of confidence for a woman, not a lack of it. And then you say things like this." He settled her on the bed. "I've wanted you since the day I set eyes on you. You're a magnificent woman. An opinionated, forward-thinking, modern woman who treats her patients with respect and a gentle hand. I've learned a lot from you this past month."

"What could you possibly learn from me?"

"Kindness and consideration for the state of a woman's mind. It's commonly thought that women are unstable, have periods of hysteria." He tapped the tip of her nose. "You've made me think otherwise."

"You haven't been a doctor long, but it pleases me very

much that you have such an open mind." Her chest glowed with his praise, and yes, she sopped up every word, like bread in gravy. Poor man had no idea how *modern* she was. "You are sweet to say that I've taught you some things," she said, hoping she wasn't doing damage to Stella's life by behaving so freely with Colt. But she was helpless in her desire and love, and she could only hope Stella would forgive her.

"I'm not being sweet, it's the bald truth. I've learned from you."

She slid to the head of the bed and watched as he dug into his jacket pocket to pull out a small square. The wrapper was different from modern ones, but she felt relieved he'd come prepared. The day had turned to a cool evening and she lifted the covers to slide between the sheets.

His eyes heated. "You're lovely with the bedclothes tucked up under your chin. You look like a virginal miss who's never done this before."

She chuckled, then flipped up the sheets on the other side of the narrow double bed. He slipped beside her and gathered her close. His hair tickled her thighs, and his scent was familiar and warm. She nuzzled the hair on his chest. The beat of his heart under her ear reassured her this wasn't a dream, that Colt was real, she was real, and their love would grow.

Night darkened the window while he ran his hands to her breasts and tweaked her nipples into stiff peaks. She had an amazing response. Her deepest belly clenched in need, and she set his head to her chest, offering each nipple to his seeking mouth.

Each draw of his suckling mouth pulled at her womb and deepened her need to desperate.

She cupped his cock and balls to check for readiness. He groaned against her tits, cupped them, and buried his face between the mounds.

"I need you," she whispered. "Inside." Having him completely would be a step from which she couldn't turn back.

He fitted himself over her, chest to chest, hips to hips, his hard cock to her soft emptiness. Everything felt so right, so true, that Blue couldn't hold back, not her body, not her heart. His head found her entrance, slick and ready. "I'm empty, Colt, so, so empty. Fill me now. Fast!"

His hips rose and she clasped his shaft to guide him. She needed quick penetration, the full slide in to the hilt; then she planned to rock his world. His head entered slowly, probing, splitting her folds and teasing the walls of her channel.

She raised her hips, took more . . .

"What the hell?" she said, as he pressed against a barrier. Stella wouldn't have any kind of birth-control device in place. There was nothing to slip out of place or block the way.

Stella was a virgin!

Colt slid back a little, his expression confounded. "Stella! You're—" But her hands grasping his ass made it clear he wasn't going anywhere but straight in.

"Take me, Colt. All the way. Please," she pleaded. Colt's fingers had been in as far as they could go. But his long cock went deeper, found her maidenhead again, and eased through, opening her channel.

Freeing her!

Only to hold her captive. Blue had betrayed Stella in the most elemental way. Until now, sex with Colt had been fun and good for Blue's battered spirit. But this had changed Stella's body forever.

Wherever she was, did she know? Did she feel the change? Did she know Blue was in love with the man who'd taken Stella's virginity?

8

Blue had lost her virginity years before, but Stella's was way easier. Maybe because she wasn't a teenager. Maybe because she was so damn horny she could scream. Maybe because Colt's fingers had stretched her earlier. Maybe because her heart was already in his snare. Soon, she let all thought slip away, and let Colt draw her back to the moment, to the realness of being here with him. Like this.

Deep between her legs, Colt pumped in and out of her like a steam piston. Her sticky clit sought the base of his cock, and when she arched, she felt the incredible surge of tension she craved.

"Stella," he crooned into her ear, his lips finding her shoulder, nipping her gently. He plunged deeper still and she shuddered when he flooded her, the force of his orgasm taking her into her own. "My love, my life. My own."

"I can't promise myself to you, Colt. Not yet." She picked at the soft cotton tablecloth. They'd rescued the top half of the stew, but it sat in their bowls, untouched.

He sipped at a stiff drink. Having a dutiful marriage proposal turned down could do that to a guy, she supposed.

After a round of some of the best sex she'd ever had, everything passionate about their encounter fizzled when Colt had proposed.

Actually, that wasn't quite right. Everything had fizzled when she'd refused him. "But, it isn't that I don't want to continue in this relationship. I want to be with you. Let's just see how this works out." Twenty-first-century conversation with a twentieth-century man didn't translate well.

"I'd heard that Belle was raised by a mother steeped in the Free Love Movement, but hearing this from you is a shock. You've cleaned up the messes from illegitimate births and seen the devastation they cause. Women thrown out of the family homes, discarded by the men who've mistreated them! I don't know how you can be cavalier about something so serious."

"The prophylactic didn't break, Colt. We're fine."

"But—"

She put up a hand to stop his wild talk. It was wild to her but perfectly sane to him. No one got married because they'd had sex in her time. No one.

She ached for him. He was so confused. She'd made it clear she felt strongly for him, and now, here she was denying those very feelings. Not to mention that Belle would be furious if she found out he'd proposed and she'd tried to put off her response.

But how could she do more damage to Stella? It was wrong, no matter how she looked at it. Stella was innocent in this whole mess, and she was the one who would have to live with everything Blue left behind.

If only Blue could sort out why this switch had occurred, and whether it was permanent. If it was permanent, then she could happily marry Colt and raise Belle's child as theirs. Everything could work out. Colt was magnificent, generous in spirit and loving. In her real life, Blue would never find a man like him, she was sure of it.

"Any woman would be pleased to have your proposal, Colt. I just can't say yes right now. It wouldn't be right. Not yet." She had to be certain she could stay in this time.

With Stella technically out of the picture, it seemed that she should be able to stay. But she had no way to know what was happening with Blue's body.

If this was a soul switch, it seemed feasible to Blue that she'd be able to live out her life here.

Colt finished his drink, put the stopper back in the bottle, and slipped the bottle back into his medical bag. He stood, and after an awkward hug, with no kiss between them, he walked to the door. His face was set like stone, and while she wanted desperately to reach out to him, she wouldn't, couldn't prevent his leaving.

Faye watched as poor Blue McCann's chest rose and fell with shallow breaths. The nurse had been in an hour ago to give her the sorry news. They hadn't found a single living relative for Blue McCann.

No friends had called Blue's cell phone, and there were no numbers in her contact list. Faye couldn't believe anyone could be so alone in the world.

She'd gone to the room Blue rented and found out just how sick and poor she was. With a week left on her rent, fifty-three cents in her wallet, and no bank card or statement anywhere, Blue looked destined for a homeless shelter.

If she'd just wake up, Faye could take her home. Perdition House had plenty of room, in spite of being full of ghosts. They were, for the most part, kindly souls who would allow Blue to recuperate in peace.

But there would be no recuperation, not with a chronic lung disease. And certainly not for a poor woman alone in the world.

Her ghostly great aunt Belle had told her about the corset's effect on Blue. When Faye had pressed her for more information, Belle had shut down and drifted off into wherever she spent her time when she wasn't pestering the life out of Faye.

She lifted Blue's chilled hand and slipped it under the thin flannel sheet. Leaning over the young woman, she reached for her other hand and warmed it between her palms. "Blue, if you can wake up, you'll have a home with me. A job, when you're well enough."

But the disease had nearly run its course, and the harried doctor that had been in that morning had given his patient next to no time. "But if you want to move on, it's all right to let go. Be at peace. There will be no more pain, no more loneliness."

Especially if Belle had anything to do with it.

And Faye suspected that Blue had been a person of interest to Belle since the day she'd been born. The spirits of Perdition were an interesting crew, a blend of self-serving sexual nymphets, greedy for the only physical sensation they could still feel, and warm, caring selflessness.

Somewhere, somehow, this young, failing woman was a vital key to their continuation on the spiritual plane.

She kissed Blue's forehead. "I'll be back in the morning, Blue. I promise," she said. The other patients in the ward weren't in much better shape, but at least Blue's privacy curtains were intact. Faye made sure to close them on her way out.

She stepped into the front foyer of Perdition House an hour later, emotionally spent. A young woman passing away and never having made a mark in her life saddened Faye. "What can I do to help her, Belle?"

"That's beyond the living, Faye." Her voice rose all around Faye, then settled on her shoulders, a comforting shawl.

Belle had been the one to encourage Faye to dig through the trunks in the attic for inventory for TimeStop. She couldn't recall who had discovered that particular corset. They'd found piles of well-preserved clothing and had doubled the store's income in no time. Internet sales had also gone through the roof. "The living may not be allowed to do anything, but is it beyond your ability?"

Belle clucked sadly. "It is now. I helped her make the jump back to nineteen thirteen, but the rest is up to her."

"Can you check in with her? See what's happening?"

Her aunt appeared, sitting on the third step of Perdition House's grand staircase. She propped her chin in her hand and looked mournful.

Unlike her, thought Faye, to seem helpless.

"It's painful for me," Belle explained, "for reasons I didn't understand at the time." She swiped at a tear on her cheek. "But Blue's discovered many things in the past. Love among them."

"I didn't think spirits could feel pain, just orgasm."

"It's not physical, Faye. And before you say more, I will not explain. Not even now, all these years later."

"If Blue dies today, will she live in the past? Or move on?"

"The path she took to go back to when the house was new is there for her to follow."

"But she put on the corset! She took the path already, how can she follow it now? It's already behind her." Maybe if she tried on the corset again, she would come back to this time. But nothing waited for her here. Nothing but death. Distress filled her. "There must be some way to reach out to her, to help!"

"Blue's a smart, resourceful woman, Faye. Have faith." With that, her great aunt faded to nothing.

"There must have been a good reason for arranging this, I just hope you know what you're doing."

"I have faith, Faye. You should too. Haven't I always brought things to rights?"

Blue spent a sleepless lonely night in Stella's bed. She wanted to do what was right, but she had no way of knowing what that was. If she promised to marry Colt and they went off on a Grand Tour of Europe with Belle, Stella could return to an ugly mess.

But if she didn't do all she could to help Stella's own sister, Blue would feel guilty forever. She'd already made a mess of things by having sex with Colt. She'd been greedy and selfish, and Stella was the one who would pay the price.

It wasn't right. It wasn't fair! But life wasn't fair. Blue understood that at an early age, had lived her life with the knowledge that, in spite of trying hard and working toward her dreams, life could kick you right back down.

How was it, then, that she cared so much for Stella's life? Because Stella was an innocent victim in all of this, came the instant reply from her conscience.

She rose at dawn and opened the top bureau drawer. The corset sat folded on top. If she tried it on, would she still be here? Or would she go back to her own time? If she went to her own time, would Stella return before any more damage was done?

Terrified to try, feeling responsible for what would happen to Belle and her baby, Blue waffled.

The corset was as lovely now as the first time she'd seen it in the window of TimeStop. It seemed like weeks ago, but it had been only a few days.

The bump on her head had mellowed down to no more than a knot, and the color had faded to yellow. Her headache had disappeared within hours, and her recuperation had amazed her.

She wasn't used to feeling healthy. She hadn't felt sexual in at least two years. Food tasted good again, the air filled her lungs, fresh and clean. Her heart thumped along steadily, and her mind was never foggy from drugs.

She loved Stella's life.

And she loved Colt Stephens. With no way of knowing Stella's real feelings for the man, she only hoped the other woman wouldn't mind the relationship. Although being a virgin meant she'd been saving herself for marriage, an old-fashioned notion that had never crossed Blue's mind.

She traced the laces of the corset from the bodice to the bottom. Sexy laces, hand stitching. No wonder it had called to her.

As fantastical as this event was, she had to wonder if she'd been called to this piece of clothing for a reason. If her coming back to this point in time had a real purpose, then she needed to find that purpose.

She decided to look at the facts. Like a detective in a television show, she would make a board with every bit of information she knew.

Once the details were laid out in a logical fashion, she hoped to see a pattern or a clue as to what her next step should be.

If nothing came to her, she'd do what she dreaded most.

She'd put the corset back on and see if she went back to her own life. If she didn't at least try it on, she'd feel as if she were stealing the life that Stella had been meant to live.

In spite of knowing that Blue McCann's time on this earth was severely limited, it would be wrong to stay here and take Stella's.

Her narrow closet door looked whitewashed on the inside. Using a pencil, she listed the events as she recalled them. She even jotted the date she first saw the corset in the store window.

Once everything she knew was listed in an arc with plenty of room between the spokes for ideas to be added, she sat back on her bed. Dressed in a soft cotton floor-length nightie, she tucked her knees up and covered her chilled toes with her hem.

Then she stared.

And she thought.

And considered.

9

Blue considered the events as she'd chronologically listed them on the inside of the closet door. But it wasn't until she considered the emotional connections that she could make some sense of things.

She had to combine her knowledge and understanding of everyone involved in this event. From both lives!

Once she figured out that the interconnections couldn't be dismissed as coincidence, her ideas began to take shape.

She'd been abandoned as a baby. Then when her real mother had been found, she'd been left a ward of the state anyway. Her mother hadn't wanted her. The drugs she was addicted to had won out over maternal love. Or maybe, her mother loved her too much to keep her in that lifestyle.

Whatever. The end result was that Blue raised herself within the foster care system. By the time she was diagnosed with her lung disease, she'd already decided life was short, so her teens were one wild tear after another.

Too many boyfriends, too much meaningless sex, and too many parties had further weakened her.

It hadn't been until her friend got pregnant that Blue found her calling. She'd worked and scrimped and saved and taken out loans in order to pay for her education as a doula.

She'd wanted to ensure that babies were born into peaceful, happy environments. She wanted to support mothers so that their children had the best possible start in life. If she'd had the time, she'd have been a good doula, she just knew it.

Stella's strong hands had delivered children. Her fingers were long and narrow enough to reach in and help if necessary. She flexed her fingers, felt the strength in them. Stella had been a competent midwife, a confident woman, and Belle's sister.

A sister newly entrusted with a child's life. A hidden child.

The situation related to this unborn baby. Belle couldn't raise it, not when a thriving business depended on her.

Especially important were the secrets Belle kept. Blue didn't want to know them, and she saw the sense in Belle keeping her sister a secret as well.

She'd asked around, and Belle was known for living an emotionally isolated life. How that must burn! Belle was a warm, caring woman and was forced to deny her natural bent.

She'd created a lovely home in Perdition House, where only the best would do. The girls who lived there deserved to work in a safe environment.

The responsibilities loaded on Blue's shoulders landed heavily. A child's life, the secrets of a nation's leaders, and her love for Colt warred for dominance.

In the end, she knew she had to protect all three.

Blue McCann had been fated to this life. Fated to take over Stella McCreedy's body and raise her sister's child.

There were two people she needed to speak with, but she wasn't sure how to reach them. A telephone hung on the kitchen wall, but it wasn't like any one she'd seen before.

Still, she had to try. Five in the morning seemed too early to call, so she put the corset away and bathed and dressed. By seven, she stood in the kitchen and cranked the phone.

An operator! "Hello, can you tell me how to put a call through to Perdition House? I need to speak with Belle Grantham."

"One moment please." The voice was tinny but efficient. After a series of clicks, she heard a ring and Belle answered.

"Good morning, Perdition House." She sounded sultry and businesslike, a good combination for a madame.

"Belle, I need to get in touch with Lizzie and Bart. Where are they?"

"Stella?"

"Yes, I'm ah, trying to get hold of Lizzie. Do they have a phone?"

"No, but they're due for a visit today. They're coming for lunch, would you like me to send them over? Or would you care to join us here? Your car's ready to go, and I'd like it out of my driveway."

"Maybe Bart could drive it over here? Just as soon as they arrive?"

"Lizzie can drive. Bart's not convinced automobiles are safe, and with your accident, he wears a smug expression whenever the topic comes up."

They chatted about a couple of other details, but when Belle said nothing about the baby, or Colt proposing, Blue followed her lead. Maybe operators could listen in without customers knowing.

Blue hung the mouthpiece back on the hook and dug out a box she'd found. Inside was stationery and a pen and ink set. It was time to write Stella a note.

She had something to explain, just in case she and Stella did another switch. An hour later, she thought she'd gotten the details right. At least she hoped she had.

Shortly before noon, a knock sounded at the door. The

looming hulk of shadow at the window told her it was Bart and Lizzie, the couple who'd rescued her from the car wreck. There was one thing she needed to know, and Lizzie was the woman to tell her. She went to the door and opened it.

Lizzie's face lit up in a happy smile, while Bart stood back with his hat in his hand. "Hello, Stella. Feeling better I see."

They were a mismatched pair, he a giant and she a tiny delicate slip of femininity. Mismatched until a look into their eyes showed the love they shared. It was almost painful to see because she'd given up on ever finding anything similar. Her mind skipped to Colt, but she shook her head. It wasn't safe to think of Colt and love in the same moment.

Not when she had no idea how long she might have with him.

As for Belle and the baby, she prayed that Belle's plan would work out for everyone involved, even if it meant that Stella would return and Blue would go back to her living death.

"I'm much better, Lizzie." She waved them to chairs, pleased to see that Lizzie smiled at Stella's improved memory.

Bart's chair squeaked a protest but held up under his weight. "Thank you for being so quick to help me that day. I don't know what would have happened if you hadn't been there." She touched her scalp to remind Lizzie of the bump she suffered. "I may have wandered off confused. But, forgive me, I meant to offer you coffee and cake."

Bart's eyes lit up, and she got him a heavy china mug and a slice of pound cake. He accepted the food with a shy, grateful smile. Lizzie patted his hand, pleased that Stella remembered how awkward her husband could be with fine china. He was literally a bull in a china shop.

"I still can't recall all the details of my accident and I hoped you could tell me what you saw. You know, immediately before I hit the ditch, and then when you first saw me on the ground."

"Surely. I don't think I'll ever forget it, will you, Bart?"

"No, it was like it all slowed down. Like I could see it comin' before it happened. Never seen nothing like that before."

Lizzie nodded like a bird about to sing. "You were ahead of us on the road and then the car started skidding sideways, and suddenly, you ditched it and slammed into a tree. All I saw then was you, flying up and over the front of the car."

"I went through the windshield?"

"You don't have a real windshield," Bart explained. "You replaced it with that monocle glass to reduce the weight so you could go faster. Got rid of your wooden wheels too. You told Doc Stephens about all that the first time you met. Don't you recall?"

"No, I don't." She patted her hair. "I guess I've lost more memories than I knew."

"That's to be expected considering when I first set eyes on you," Lizzie explained, "I could have sworn you were a goner." She looked closely at Blue's neck. "Seems strange there's no bruise or anything."

Melted ice trickled down her spine and set off tingles of apprehension. She covered her neck with both hands. "Why?" She'd had a bruise on her neck, but it had disappeared faster than any others. She remembered Colt kissing it once. It had been gone the next day.

"I got to you first, but we both thought your neck was broke," Lizzie explained. "Your head dangled like a straw doll that's lost its stuffing."

Bart nodded his agreement. He spoke in a rumbling baritone. "All twisted up, you was."

Blue's belly dropped with the weight of a boulder. Stella had died! There hadn't been a switch at all! Stella had died and Blue had been given the chance to live this life. Stella's life.

The room went watery as tears filled her eyes. Distressed,

Lizzie rose and patted her back. "There, there, you're fine now. Right as rain, just like always. In no time, you'll be back taking care of all the women who need you."

She nodded, unable to sort out all her thoughts. All her feelings.

Colt hadn't said a word about a neck injury. As a test, she rolled her head from side to side. She felt fine, not a crick or a creak anywhere. "See? Good as new," she said to reassure the other couple.

Badly shaken, Blue did her best to hide the effect of their news from her guests. But they were due for lunch at Perdition House, so they climbed into Bart's carriage and left. Lizzie had driven Stella's car, slowly and carefully, and under Bart's watchful eye. After Lizzie and Bart left, she swept the kitchen and tidied the bedroom.

Like every other major event in her life, she had to handle this alone.

She couldn't tell Belle her sister was gone forever. She couldn't tell Colt the woman he'd cared for was dead. No one would believe any of this, so she had to slip into Stella's life like a hand in a glove.

Even her training as a doula had been destiny. Cursing her stubbornness, she recalled the school counselor's suggestion that Blue take the midwifery classes. She'd assumed the old lady was just after the higher tuition. Her low-paying job convinced her to stick with the less expensive doula option.

She'd bucked destiny that day and didn't want to try it again; there was no saying how she might mess up.

Another side reminded her she'd done her best. That's all anyone can do, she told herself. *And that's all you can do now.*

She tore up the note she'd written to Stella and burned the fine paper in the stove's firebox. Then she sat and had a good cry for the woman whose life she'd taken. Stella McCreedy had

had good friends, family who loved her, and a fine man who'd been interested in her. And not a one of them would ever know she was gone.

Blue had a lot to live up to, and she was very grateful to have the chance.

But she had to make certain that the future would unfold as it should.

She considered the next step of her plan and stood at the kitchen door staring at the automobile that waited at the bottom of the back stairs. She could see the attraction. Stella had had it painted a bright yellow, rather than black, the windshield was tiny and oval shaped and would offer no protection from wind or rain, but it looked cool. The heavy wooden wheels she saw on all the other vehicles had been replaced by snazzy metal spokes.

Afraid she wouldn't be able to drive the thing without sending it into another tree, she caught a ride to Perdition House with Hope's husband. Jed had to deliver a couple of dresses one of the girls had ordered. Blue told Jed she felt too nervous to get behind the wheel, and he kindly refreshed her memory on the simple controls.

If she took it slow, she could probably learn how to drive one of these things, but the bouncy ride was hell on her backside. It would be years before roads were paved. There were many changes coming to the world.

She was excited to live through them. It came to her that she'd have an insider's knowledge on up-and-coming inventions and where to invest her money, if she ever earned any.

Hope's husband kept up a steady stream of conversation about his children. Jed's excitement over being a father again with Hope cheered her. He was everything Hope said he was, a great husband and father.

Colt would be equally awesome in those roles.

As soon as they stopped in front of the house, she climbed out of the delivery van with her wrapped package tucked under her arm.

The van had a bench seat for two with a large box in back. Painted a deep green, Jed had the sides painted with the name of his store in fancy script. The red lettering edged in gold leaf reminded her of old signs in museums. He gave her a tip of his cap and went to the back of the truck to get his delivery.

Perdition House loomed before her, three stories of Victorian glory. Somewhere, there was a trunk in the attic she had to find.

Belle opened the front door and stepped out onto the wraparound veranda. "You missed lunch by two hours!" She looked past Blue at Jed's truck. "You didn't drive yourself?"

She shook her head. "Not yet. I'm not ready. My stomach rolled when I saw the car. All I see is me flying out of the seat, over the hood."

Belle's expression went soft. "It'll take time. You'll be ready soon."

"Could you sell it for me?" The idea of having some cash felt right. "I may invest in something." Like the *Ford Motor Company*. When they got back from Europe, she could buy another car. Something slower that had a full windshield. And somehow, she'd find a way to strap herself in.

Her *sister* pursed her lips. "I wondered when your father's blood would win out." Her eyes lit with humor at the in joke, and Blue recalled that their daddy was a force to be reckoned with in business. As was Belle. She relaxed and knew that whatever investing Stella did would seem natural to anyone who knew her.

"What brings you out here?"

"My apartment was closing in on me." Blue figured Stella was not much of a homebody, so the excuse sounded right.

"Not surprised." Belle assessed her with a sharp eye. "You

look remarkably recovered. There's a glow in your cheeks I haven't seen in some time."

"Thanks! I'll tell you how it got there over tea." She mimicked Belle's inspection. "And I could say the same about your glow."

Belle chuckled and led the way into the house. They settled for tea in Belle's office. At two in the afternoon, the house was quieter than usual. Most of the girls were resting or shopping, the gentleman callers, as Belle preferred to call her clients, were still at work.

"A party from Washington left yesterday," Belle said. "A couple of senators and an ambassador or two." The smile on her sister's face was content.

A fresh crop of secrets, went unsaid.

Belle poured the tea and prepared it the way Stella preferred. Two lumps of sugar, no milk. Blue drank it and pretended satisfaction. She missed her cappuccinos.

Belle leaned in over the tea table. "You haven't reconsidered our agreement, have you?"

The fear she read in Belle's gaze tore at her heart. "Of course not. I haven't discussed it with Colt, though. That may take a few days." She couldn't promise anything to anyone here if she wasn't destined to stay in Stella's body.

Belle nodded and studied her over her fine china teacup. The gold rim was unmarred by use. The pattern was new, but was antique and elegant to Blue's eyes. She'd seen it before in shops filled with collectibles and estate sale items.

More proof she'd always been meant to be here. Why else would she have been born with an interest in old things? She always loved museums and junk shops. She hadn't been able to afford to buy antiques, but she'd always liked looking.

Her arrival here must be a correction. If a mistake occurred when Stella had been killed, she was the replacement.

"Belle, do you believe in destiny?"

She rolled her eyes. "I believe we're meant to look after ourselves and our families."

"And the women you employ?"

Belle blinked several times. "Before you found me, they were my family. So I take care of them, invest their savings, if they're smart enough to have any, and make sure they're healthy and safe."

"You have no idea how rare you are, do you?"

Color suffused her smooth cheeks. Belle and Stella hadn't been raised together. Their connection was more of the heart than any familial bond. And Belle was a crackerjack businesswoman with socially liberal leanings.

Blue liked her immensely. "I'm honored that you'd ask me to help you with your situation. If Colt refuses to agree, I'll do it alone." Blue's opinion of fathers, especially stepfathers, had been formed early. But those times were looser when it came to family ties.

"Colt Stephens will understand and accept the responsibility. He's a good man," Belle said with a wistful smile. "And good men are rare. And I'll be right here, always." The simmering fear behind her expression eased.

"He is a good man." She felt heat rise in her cheeks. She wanted more than anything to have Colt agree to this plan between the sisters, but if he didn't, she'd have to buck society and be a single mother. For Belle's sake.

"Colt cares for you, Stella. Deeply." Belle patted her hand in comfort. "Have no fear. Things will work out as they should. You asked if I believe in destiny. Perhaps it was destiny that helped you find me when you decided to look."

"I think you're right." Belle had no idea how right she was!

No way could Blue let Colt think she was committed, then disappear on him. She wouldn't do that. She wouldn't continue the cycle of abandonment. Belle's child needed her.

* * *

"Thank you, Dr. Stephens," Billy Walker said after a poke on the shoulder from his mother. She nodded and tugged the boy by his suspenders until he followed her out the examination room door.

With luck, his fever would break tonight and he'd be better by morning. His mother had no other children, so she tended to panic at the first sniffle. A more experienced woman would have tossed the lad under the covers, given him soup, and kept him at home.

He'd tried all day to set aside thoughts of Stella and her refusal, but he'd failed miserably. The wonderful independent streak that he appreciated in the woman might ruin whatever chance he had with her. He'd offered marriage because he wanted to marry her. If he'd wanted to dally with her, that's what he'd have offered, a dalliance.

A woman like Stella couldn't possibly prefer an affair over the joys of marriage. She confounded him completely.

He opened the door to his office with too much force, startling Mr. O'Reilly, who perched on the edge of his seat facing Colt's desk. "What can I do for you today, Mr. O'Reilly?"

"Nothin', it's the missus, she thinks I need seein' to, and she won't let up."

Colt took his seat behind his desk, determined to put Stella out of his mind. But O'Reilly had the same color eyes as the wayward midwife, and Colt had the devil's own time to keep his mind on his patient.

Damn woman! He had a mind to retract his proposal and to hell with her. "Won't let up, eh? Women can get under your skin, now can't they?"

"Nags, that's what," O'Reilly said. "But truth be told, Doc, I have occasions where my left arm tingles. I recall my father having similar before he passed."

Colt nodded as he threw himself wholeheartedly into the conversation. He couldn't allow thoughts of Stella to interfere any longer. One way or another, he would settle his thorny problem with Stella tonight.

Come hell or high water.

At Perdition House, the telephone on Belle's desk rang. When Belle answered, Blue motioned that she'd be back in five. She tucked her paper package under her arm and slipped out to the hall. No one else was around, so she belted it up the stairs as quickly as she could. Oh, this body was healthy.

The dash up the stairs felt wonderful. Her lungs heaved by the third floor, but she couldn't recall ever being able to work her own heart and lungs this way.

At the top floor, she searched the ceiling for a way up into the attic. At the back of a short hall, she found a square hatch built into the ceiling. Embedded at one end was a brass ring.

In the corner, she spied a pole with a brass hook at the end. She hooked the hook into the ring and pulled. A set of stairs smoothly descended to the floor.

With one more glance around to see that no one watched her, Blue climbed the stairs into the attic.

There were beds up here! Alcoves in the windows held single beds with washstands and basins. Narrow closets were set between the beds to give the appearance of privacy. The windows were wide open to catch the breezes.

She hadn't considered how many staff would be needed to keep a house of this size running. She didn't see any insulation in the rafters, though. Maybe these beds were used only in the busier summer season.

But with people using these quarters she needed to hurry, in case she was discovered.

On the opposite wall were trunks and boxes and racks of clothing and accessories. Racks of old shoes, dressmaker's forms, and huge hats with long feathers and wide brims took half the space. One of the dressmaker's forms sported a bustle. Thanking her stars for the change in fashion, she shifted her way to the back of the trunks. Anything toward the front of the stacks was likely to belong to some of the newer arrivals.

She had to find something that looked like it had been here a while and wasn't likely to leave.

Against the wall, she found exactly what she needed. A heavy royal blue travel trunk with brass corners and a locking latch. The engraved letters *IG* on the lock flap told her the trunk belonged to Isabelle Grantham.

She lifted the lid and inhaled the scent of cedar. Wow, she'd spared no expense.

But with a tour of Europe coming up, the trunk would be used soon. She had to find something else.

An older box with a crooked homemade lid caught her eye. The name carved into the lid was familiar. She'd seen it in Stella's files. A young woman who wouldn't need the box again. Colt had reviewed the case with her, and they agreed Stella had done all that it was possible to do for the woman.

This was the trunk she needed to use.

When the luggage for the tour was sorted out, she would be here to make certain this trunk was shoved into a corner and forgotten. Not that Belle would want to use it, but she might decide to throw it out.

When she'd first tried on the corset in TimeStop, Faye had told her it had been found in perfect condition in a trunk in the attic of her home.

This trunk. This home. Perdition House.

The corset and the whorehouse attic were her only connection to the future.

She untied the string on her package and brought out the corset, wrapped in soft linen. Inside the trunk, she found a diary written by the owner. She flipped through and knew she had to leave the diary with the corset. Perhaps Faye would assume the corset belonged to the diary's owner. She covered the diary with the corset and laid both to rest in the bottom of the dead girl's trunk. On top, she set the note she'd spent hours composing.

This corset is for Blue McCann. She'll understand it's for her when she sees it.

And she *had* understood it was hers. Blue had wanted the corset at first sight. The fine hand stitching had called to her every time she'd walked by TimeStop.

Until, as destiny would have it, Faye saw her looking through the shop window and stepped outside to bring her into the warmth. She realized now that Faye had merely been waiting for Blue to show up, and that Faye likely understood that Blue had to try on the corset. She remembered how Faye had known things she had no way of knowing: like how Blue took her coffee and how there wasn't anyone waiting for her to get home that day.

The whole atmosphere of the shop had been warm, welcoming, and encouraged her to feel safe.

To bring her here.

To this time, and to this version of perdition, which had turned out to be heaven itself as far as Blue was concerned.

Blue McCann was finally in the right place at the right time for the first time in her life.

10

When Blue settled the corset into the trunk that would hold it for over eight decades, a sense of rightness settled in her soul.

She was now Belle Grantham's secret sister, a midwife, and Dr. Colt Stephens's lover.

Blue McCann had climbed into this attic, but it was Stella McCreedy, reborn, who climbed back down. The stairs folded up into the ceiling and her secret was safe—as were all the secrets that Belle held dear.

The hall clock chimed three times, and the new Stella felt a searing heat in her belly. The world dimmed to gray as she fought for consciousness, but the pain seared through her gut and she leaned on the wall to stay upright. It was no use, the gray deepened to black as she doubled over with pain, then collapsed in the empty hallway.

The hall clock on the third floor chimed three times. Faye barely heard it because she was in the kitchen. A glance at the kitchen clock confirmed the time. As long as she'd lived in Perdition House, that hall clock had not worked. She'd tried setting it countless times, but with the cost of other repairs, she'd had to set it aside until the cash flow improved. She shrugged, used to the odd noises in the old house, and took her tea and settled on the side porch. She enjoyed reading e-mail in her antique wicker chair. Today was chilly and damp, so she draped an afghan across her knees.

Fifteen minutes later, the phone rang and she ran to answer in the kitchen. When she heard the serious tone in the nurse's voice, she stepped back outside and braced herself against the support beam.

The head nurse on Blue's floor gave Faye the sad news she'd been waiting for. She kept a tight hold on her emotions, while her heart pounded in her chest. How could it be that a total stranger would get this call, that there would be no one else in Blue McCann's life that would get the news of her passing?

She thanked the nurse for letting her know and stood awash in guilt. She never should have invited Blue into TimeStop, never should have encouraged her to try on that corset, no matter what that damn note had said. She knew better than to trust anything that came out of Perdition House.

"Don't be ridiculous, Faye," Belle murmured in her ear. She had the most annoying habit of reading Faye's mind. "Nothing happens in Perdition without good reason. Blue's the one who left the note with the corset."

Faye's knees gave out and she slid into her wicker chair again. "You knew Blue would go back to nineteen thirteen. And you knew she would die because of that corset."

"No, Blue was ill most of her life. A chronic lung disease. With money and decent care as a child, she might have lived longer, but Blue wasn't born into a strong family, Faye. Not every child is."

Faye nodded but didn't feel any better for her hand in this. "There was a reason for her to go back there, I hope. It wasn't just some whim of yours?" Bitterness tinged the words and Faye didn't care. Just because Belle was dead didn't mean she had the right to be cavalier about the life of a young woman in need of help.

"Of course it wasn't a whim. My sister, Stella McCreedy, had an accident and died before her time. She drove like a madwoman, over hill and dale, racing like the wind. She was usually exhausted, too, which probably made her more reckless."

"I'm sorry, Belle. I didn't know." How odd to offer sympathy to a woman dead for decades. But Belle was more alive to Faye than her own parents, and she cared deeply about the sorrow of her loss. "Wait a minute! Stella was the midwife here!" She remembered dreaming about a woman who smoked cigars and drove one of the first Model T's ever modified for speed.

"No one ever knew we were half sisters. We didn't look at all alike. At the time, I didn't know she'd been replaced by Blue McCann."

"So Blue went back and stole Stella's body?" She must have been so confused!

"You could call it that. But it wouldn't have happened if the fate of the world didn't depend on Stella." She sighed. "And, therefore, on Blue."

"But Blue was alone in the world. The nurse only called me because there was no one else to claim—Oh my!" The enormity of the events caught up to her.

Belle clucked her tongue and settled into the settee across from the wing chair. She conjured a teapot and poured herself a cup. "Since you're incapable of being polite and offering something more substantial, I'll make do with this."

"Help yourself," Faye said dryly. Belle making busy spelled more of a disaster coming. "What else?"

Belle raised her hand to Faye's face. "Sleep, child, and you'll see the rest for yourself."

"I'm tired, mind if I curl up out here and take a nap?" Faye pulled the afghan over her shoulders and tucked her feet up as her head fell back and sleep claimed her.

Henry, the cook's son at Perdition House, barreled into Colt's outer office as he finished his afternoon clinic. He was just restocking his medical bag when the door banged open. "It's Miz McCreedy, Dr. Stephens. Ma says to come quick! She blacked out in the upstairs hall and you need to see her."

He didn't need to hear any more. Colt grabbed the rest of his instruments, threw everything into his medical bag, and ran out to his car. Henry climbed on his horse and took off at a gallop with Colt close behind. He ran through every possible reason for her collapse and came up with nothing.

Her head had healed, her memories were not complete yet, but she was making progress. What he didn't know was why she'd been at Perdition House. If she'd pushed herself to visit a patient there, he would give her a stern warning.

But he was at fault. He never should have had relations with her. The activity with him was clearly too much, too soon. Her heart had raced, she'd strained herself. He'd taken his pleasure without a thought for her.

He'd allowed his base nature free rein with an injured woman. His knuckles squeezed tight on the steering wheel as he bounced and lurched around a bend in the road. Dead ahead was a huge boulder, but he kept to the far side of the road and bypassed it. As he careened around the boulder, he remembered the way Stella had flown out of her car and into that tree. He managed, barely, to keep his car on the road.

This was his fault! As a doctor, he should have known better, as a man, he was a failure at keeping the woman he loved safe. He should have known she'd get back to work too soon. The entire trip was one berating thought after another, until all he could see was Stella, pale and worn, slipping away from him.

Blue woke to the worried expression and love in Colt's eyes. "I'm here," she said, and she *really* was. It may have been Blue McCann who'd hidden the corset in Perdition's attic, but Blue was Stella now and here to stay.

Here.

To stay.

In this time, in this healthy body, and in love with this man.

"Yes, you're here. In Perdition House again. Why?" he asked.

She pulled her body to a sitting position. She was in the same room she'd had when she'd woken up from the accident. This time, though, she remembered everything she needed to.

Taking his hands in hers, Stella lifted them to her lips for a kiss. "I came for tea with Belle. I'm fine. I ran up the stairs at full speed, just to see if I could, and when I got up three floors, I fainted."

"Where was Belle?"

"On the phone. I know it was silly, but . . ." She shrugged. "I wanted to test my limits now that I feel well again."

He frowned and shook his head. "You overexerted yourself? That's all? You're sure?"

"I won't do it again, I promise." Not today at least. She wasn't about to tell him of the sudden pain, the blacking out of all light. The way a pinprick of brilliance called to her to come back.

The way she knew that Blue's life was over and had begun again here. She accepted Stella's life as her own now, fully and completely, and felt blessed to do it.

"Speaking of testing limits. You are testing the limits of my patience." The relief in his eyes nearly tore her apart. She leaned forward and gathered Colt to her.

"I don't mean to test you. I just had to be sure that if I promised we could have a future, I could keep it. I know now that I can. If you still want me."

"Want you? My greatest fear was that you might want to continue as we've been." He ran his long elegant fingers through his hair so that it stood on end. The slick of pomade he used wasn't heavy enough to withstand the furrowing. "Because, Stella, that's the wrong thing to say right now."

"You don't want to continue the way we've been?" She found it hard to maintain a serious expression. "You don't want to make love anymore?"

His hands clenched into fists. "Of course I want that. But I don't want to have you outside of marriage. I'm a proper man who wants a proper wife."

"I'll be your wife, Colt Stephens, but I can't promise to always be proper."

"Thank heavens," he said, and dragged her into his chest. The kiss he devoured her with curled her toes.

Thank perdition! she thought. "Thank heavens for what? The acceptance of your proposal or my refusal to be proper?"

"Both! We can be wild with each other, but to the world we'll be properly wed. Let no one tear us asunder."

"How do you feel about children?"

"Once we're married, we can do away with rubbers. I'll not have speculation about the timing of our nuptials."

"Not *our* children." She tiptoed her fingertips up his chest. "Exactly."

"Explain." His brows dropped into a furrow. "And I have a feeling this will be anything but proper."

"I will, but first, I need you."

"No, I can't take you so soon after a fainting spell. I've pushed you to the limits, and I won't do it again."

"When it comes to loving you, Colt Stephens, I have no limits." And she proved it.

* * *

Faye woke from her dream aroused. Everything was normal on that front, she realized. Whenever Belle sent her a story from the old days in the house, she woke ready and wet.

"I've already called Liam for you," her great aunt said with a soft smile. "He'll be here soon to take care of you. The man's as randy as his grandfather."

Faye slid her hand across her pussy, combing through her damp curls. Liam. Yes. Her lover and best friend. "What happened to Stella and Colt?"

"Colt agreed to take my child as his own, so he and Stella raised my son, William."

Her expression set alarm bells clanging in her head. "Your son? William Grantham Stephens?" A rock the size of a baseball slid down her throat and landed with a lump to join the dread in her belly. "He was your son?"

Belle took a sip of conjured tea, then let the teacup hover by her shoulder, while she clasped her hands in her lap. The look on her face was bland while she waited for Faye to make all the necessary connections.

"He was my great grandfather! You're not my aunt at all. You—you're—"

"That's right. I had to keep quiet about having a child. If anyone found out, they might have harmed him in an attempt to blackmail secrets from me. State secrets that would have affected the whole world. I knew far too many things, Faye."

"You've always said Perdition was a house of secrets."

"Senators loved the place! They brought ambassadors, governors, even a couple of presidential candidates spent time here." She smiled, the picture of serene pride. "Gentlemen of commerce and politics need a place to retreat, need to rest and recoup. I kept all their secrets safe."

"I'm the last of them, aren't I? You knew when I visited as a child that I would be the only one in the family who would care enough to keep this place going instead of selling it off."

"Without you, Perdition House and all the spirits who dwell here would have been destroyed." Belle's chilled hand smoothed her cheek. "You are Perdition's last secret. And the best one we've ever had. Thank you, my dear, for everything you've done."

To Die For

Prologue

1964
Las Vegas, Nevada

His brand-new black Chevy Impala SS with the snazzy red bucket seats sat between them and the far distant road. He and Lenny were in a deep gully. Deep enough that the car would never be seen by the travelers heading for the strip.

Frank LaMotta stood while Lenny sniveled on his knees in the dirt by the left front fender. "Move away from the car." He gestured with his pistol.

Lenny crawled like the maggot he was. When he got far enough from the Chevy, Frank leveled the gun again—right between Lenny's bulging eyes. "I don't wanna have to wash your blood off it. Not when we just drove it off the lot."

Lenny's gaze flicked to the car. "You fuckin' bastard, you knew I'd want to see it." Cars and women had been a reason to compete for years.

"Where are the diamonds?" The boss didn't like the idea of his goods being heisted. Lenny should have known better.

"What diamonds?" But Lenny's lips twitched and Frank wanted to laugh as piss ran into the dirt. Lenny always was a coward. Worse, he thought he was better than everyone else.

"You pissed yourself," Frank pointed out, enjoying the moment. "If only Loretta could see you now."

Lenny narrowed his eyes, trying to look like a man again. "You leave her out of this."

"Tell me where the diamonds are and maybe I will." He raised his gun hand to indicate the fullness of the broad's tits, while his other hand held his bulging crotch. "Maybe I won't."

Lenny roared and made a lunge for the gun. Frank saw the move coming and smashed the pistol into the stupid bastard's temple. Lenny sank back, dazed, onto the hard-packed gully floor. "Tell me where you stashed the haul and I'll leave her be." He shrugged as if fucking Loretta was the last thing he wanted.

They both knew he was lying. He'd wanted that broad since he'd first seen her onstage. But she'd chosen Lenny first. Frank had been patient long enough.

A wild cunning entered Lenny's gaze. "I won't tell you where I stashed the diamonds, Frank." He put his hands up to implore. "You know I won't."

"You'll tell me or Loretta's next." After he fucked her good and hard, just to let her know what she passed up by taking Lenny into her bed.

The stupid bastard still shook his head. "Nah, you wouldn't hurt her. Not when she told me how she feels about you."

His cock twitched to life. "Whadda ya mean?"

"I came back for her and she told me. Damn broad! I came *back* for her. If I hadn't, I'd a been in South America by now. You never would'a found me."

"What'd she tell you?" Any red-blooded male would focus on Loretta. That woman left him speechless. He almost hated her for it.

"She wouldn't leave with me because of you." Lenny shook his head sadly. "Fuckin' broad. Can't trust 'em. Never could."

He and Lenny had talked once about getting out, what it would be like, but fuck it, that dream was as dead as Lenny.

"We've known each other a lot of years," Lenny whined. "Do me one favor."

Frank nodded, pleased at the idea of Loretta waiting for him, wet and ready. He nodded. "For the sake of the years."

"Loretta. The boss might figure she knows more'n she does. I never told her anything, I swear." The knowledge of his death sat clear in his gaze. "I got the feeling the last few weeks there was someone else, so I never told her nothin'."

Stupid bastard good as told him she'd been thinking about Frank. He stopped a moan at the thought of all that female flesh quivering for him. He could taste her now. He'd keep her name out of it. He'd keep her for himself. "When I'm banging her tonight, I'll think of you."

The bullet hit clean. Least he could do for a friend. Lenny slumped, life draining into the dirt, following the track of piss. They'd run together for fifteen years. But now, Frank had a new Chevy and Lenny's woman.

1

Today
Seattle, Washington

The phone call he never expected to get came at 4:40 PM on Saturday. Tawny James. Hallelujah.

He tried like hell to keep up with what she said, but images of Tawny flashed into his mind. He saw her legs, breasts, incredible hips, all smooth and lush with those dimples just below the small of her back where her ass filled out her bikini bottom.

Which was exactly what she expected would happen. Which was why she'd quit working for him in the first place.

He pulled his head back from where it wanted to go and shoved it back into the conversation. Something she said raised every one of his protective instincts. She was in danger and he'd been doing the teenage fantasy thing about her body. He was such a shit. And she knew it. "A stalker?" he asked. "You're sure?"

"Some creep's just gone through my laundry at the Wash 'n' Suds, Stack. What would you call it if it isn't stalking?"

"Sick? Perverted?" Stalking, why hadn't he thought of that? This guy was probably another ex-boss who lov—wanted to get her into bed.

"Me, too, except this is the last straw. This guy's been in my house."

"What? When?" And the all-important question: "Where?" He jotted her address, but he memorized it as she spoke. Each syllable stood emblazoned in his skull.

"I'll come get you," he said, "and bring you here. If he's watching, he'll see you've reached out for help."

"Once he gets a load of your size, that may be enough to make him back off." She chuckled, low and breathless in that husky way she had that made him think of her breasts, jiggling, and her ass, all soft—

Pull it back, Stack. Now.

"I have a sense he's some weasel of a guy that I'd never notice in my daily routine," she explained.

"Not an ex?" Which was the way these things usually went. But the underwear angle didn't seem right for a love affair gone wrong. Not unless the guy shredded her clothes. Most of Tawny's clothes deserved to be shredded.

"I don't have any exes, Stack. Just you."

"Finish your laundry at my place. I can be there in fifteen."

"Fine. I'll be outside."

"Inside," he insisted. "I'll come in for you." No point putting her on the street where she could be snatched.

"Will do."

He didn't replay the fantasy of having Tawny James in his bed until he was sure she'd disconnected. Thirty seconds later, he shook free of the teenager that had him by the 'nads and shut off the office lights as he locked up.

On the way to get her, he thought of a stranger, a man, going through her home, her clothes, her lingerie, touching things he had no right to touch. Learning about her, knowing things he didn't. The whole idea made him furious. The fact that she'd been scared enough to call him, when he should be the last man she'd want in her life, made him livid.

Someone had scared Tawny James, shaken her sense of security.

Stack Hamilton would make him pay.

Tawny flipped her phone closed and piled her underwear back into her laundry basket. "Damn pervert," she muttered with a disgusted shiver. She'd have to wash every pair again.

She felt better now that she'd called Stack. He would find this guy and set him straight. She didn't want any trouble from a weirdo, and she didn't think the police would be any help.

Not at this stage. She hadn't been threatened in any way. No odd phone calls or actual proof of anything, but a woman knew when her things had been moved. When her clothing had been pawed.

Tawny kept her drawers neat, her makeup put away. Her thongs and panties were sorted by age and wear. She tossed out the oldest ones before using a newer pair.

The police would need far more evidence of a crime than her gut feeling or the fact that her pile of thongs had been flipped over so that her newest ones were on the top.

But most importantly, Tawny was a nip-it-in-the-bud kind of gal and preferred facing her troubles before they grew.

Unless that trouble was Stack Hamilton, she reminded herself.

Stack.

She'd tried to put him out of her mind months ago but had come to accept Stack Hamilton would always own a piece of her, and that she would always miss him.

Too bad he was such a jerk.

A sexy, desirable jerk. A jerk she wanted so bad she could taste the need.

They'd had a good thing going while it lasted. For the three years she'd worked for him, she had found the job an interesting challenge. For a while it seemed Stack had actually noticed her mind. Together, they were a great team. He was all action, while she kept the office together, the accounts in order, and provided tissues to weepy female clients.

She and Stack had had an easy camaraderie, been friends even.

Then, in a fit of stupid, she'd agreed to go on a stakeout at a public swimming pool. She should have known better, especially after what she'd witnessed the night before in his office.

But the James women weren't smart when it came to men, and when decision time had come for her, she'd gone the way of her mother and grandmother. Her flapper great-grandmother had been widowed young when her rum-running husband had been shot during a smuggling job.

Oh yes, Tawny came from a long line of gullible, love-struck women. She'd been stupid that day at the pool because she was angry, jealous, and blinded by the idea of vengeance. Stack had come to her, desperate for another pair of eyes at the pool, a woman's pair of eyes. Tawny, angry with him for what she'd witnessed the night before, had wanted Stack to understand what he'd been ignoring all the time they'd worked together.

Hadn't he seen her humor, her brains? Her devotion to his business, to him? Apparently not.

But once his eyes had set themselves on her, that had been the end of Stack liking her mind. One look at her in her bathing suit and he'd gone all male need, and their friendship had gone down the tubes.

She was out of there, heartsore and tired. She'd been jealous and all kinds of stupid. She'd known her logic was flawed, but what did a woman's heart know of logic?

Just like all the generations of James women before her, as far back as they could track, the women she was descended from had made bad choices in men.

She'd hoped she'd broken free of the curse, but obviously

falling for Stack was as bad as any other choice a James woman had made.

The man was a hound when it came to women, and she had the evidence, the memory. She shut her eyes, but it only brought the images to mind again.

She deliberately placed a sunshine-dappled meadow scene over the images of Stack and the blonde. She sighed deeply, drinking in the serenity she conjured. A buck and doe wandered into the meadow, increasing the pastoral beauty. The buck nuzzled the doe and she nuzzled back. Very sweet. The buck swept his nose along her side, down her flank. He was gentle, caring, and she turned her head to give him a lick with her long dark tongue.

She lifted her tail to offer the buck the chance to sniff her there too. His ears pricked up at the action, and he moved to the rear and covered her back. When the humping started, Tawny popped her eyes open, back to the laundry and the chatter of the women around her.

It was no use; the moment she thought of Stack, she thought of sex. Even now, months after leaving his employ and his easy friendship.

She could never forget the way he'd stared at her when she'd walked out onto the pool deck. He grabbed a towel to cover his crotch without a moment's hesitation as his eyes had gone wide, then dropped from her face to her chest and stopped there for a long moment. She'd seen the flush on his neck from where she stood ten feet away.

By the time he'd taken a full inventory of her body, she'd known there was nothing left of the friendship they'd enjoyed. From that moment on, she was a woman to be conquered. Like all the others he'd had, Tawny would be another woman to brag about.

As soon as she got the scratch together she was going for a boob job. The smaller the better, she thought as she tucked her bras under a couple of towels in the basket. She didn't want to remind him of what she kept under her long, heavy dresses. Firing up Stack's libido was the last thing she wanted. It would be wrong.

It would be stupid.

Encouraging Stack would be just what her mother and grandmother would do. Going with her feminine instincts, letting her libido rule her actions, was what had created this chasm between them.

When she'd walked out of Hamilton Securities, she'd walked out on one of the best friendships she'd ever had.

She twisted her fingers together in an old habit she hated. Untangling her hands, she slipped her palms beneath her thighs and kept them there while she waited.

She glanced at her laundry basket again and noticed the tag on one of her bras was hanging out of the open plastic weave. She wedged her bras farther down in the pile. Across the top she spread a dishtowel with the picture of a rooster dead center.

Another word for rooster was cock.

Sheesh. It wasn't Stack's libido she was afraid of.

It was hers.

She turned the dishtowel over.

She took her seat again and waited for her knight in tarnished armor to appear. She didn't need rescuing, and she could probably handle this weasel on her own, but instinct told her this was more than your average pervert. A real pervert would steal her panties or worse, use them to masturbate into and leave them behind for her to find. But to paw through it all and do nothing made no sense.

A squeal of brakes announced Stack Hamilton's arrival. He climbed out of his Escalade and rounded the hood, eyes scanning every direction as he moved with determined strides to the front door of the Wash 'n' Suds.

She stood and watched his approach. Man, he was big. Bigger than she remembered. Bigger than she liked, she lied to herself. Broad shoulders, long black hair under a black cowboy hat, Stack Hamilton was sin on two legs.

The kind of man to ruin a woman's best intentions. She'd hired on with him because he'd been desperate for help. Bills and his unpaid invoices had cascaded from his desk when she'd walked into his office. He wasn't much for paperwork, he'd said, and he'd soon be in deep shit if he didn't get some of this cleared.

Cash flow had all but stopped because he was too busy to collect his accounts receivable.

"I'm good at that," she'd said.

Stack had said, "Good is what I need. 'Cause I'm all kinds of bad."

She should have heeded his warning. But then that's what the James women had done whenever their good sense warred with desire. Good sense lost to bad boys every time.

But not this time. Not with Stack. This time, Tawny James would break the cycle. She pinched her tongue between her teeth to keep it from lolling out of her mouth as he pulled open the Laundromat's door and stepped into the scent of detergent, bleach, and fabric softener.

He slid his shades to sit just above his brows and swiveled his head to face her. His eyes cut down her body and flared with humor. Of all the things she liked about him, his sense of humor was the one thing she'd never been able to resist.

"Ready?" Two strides brought him to her filled and stacked baskets. He picked them up, arms bulging, and turned for the door.

"Nice to see you too. How you been, Tawny? Goooood," she snarked. "How you been, Stack? A jerk you say, how nice," she muttered as she followed him to the waiting SUV. "This thing must be killing you at the gas pumps."

He opened the back door, then slid her baskets in one at a time. "Get in."

"Wait, my bike's there." She went to the bicycle rack and unlocked her bike. It was a new commuter bike and she couldn't leave it. "It's my only transportation."

He snorted and stood guard over her while she unhitched the trailer. His shades were back down to cover his eyes, but she knew they weren't on her. He watched the street for signs of the pervert. That's why she'd called him.

His total focus on a job was the *only* reason she'd called him. In the time they'd worked together, she'd never seen him distracted from the job at hand. Stack was the ultimate professional at what he did. He was tough, knowledgeable, and a straight shooter.

He offered security services and detective work. He could blend in, or not, intimidate people with his sheer bulk, or sweet-talk a child into giving clear eye witness statements.

The man could do it all with a clarity of focus she appreciated. Had come to depend on.

The only time she'd ever seen him shook up was when he'd seen her in that damn bathing suit. When he'd tracked every line and curve of her body with his eyes, she'd melted into her panties and run like hell out of his life.

She'd hoped she'd finally found a man who appreciated her mind rather than her body. She'd thought she'd found a friend.

If she hadn't been freaked at seeing him the night before *hip deep* in some other woman, she'd probably still be his right-hand gal.

She'd still be dressed in a sack and hoping he'd finally notice her warm eyes, competent hands, and bright humor.

But in the end, Stack wasn't a friend, he was a man.

A big, bad-ass, shit-kicker of a man.

And he'd wanted to fuck her, just like every other big, bad-ass, shit-kicker she'd ever known.

He picked up her bike trailer and slid it into the back of the SUV, then took the bike from her. "Climb in," he said again.

She hoisted herself to the passenger seat and buckled up without a word.

He pulled out into traffic. "So, what's going on? Full detail."

"Yes, I know the drill. I guess I should have taken notes when I first felt someone's eyes on me, but I shook it all off."

Just like all the other people she'd run across during her time with Hamilton Securities. She, like their clients, had waited until the situation could no longer be ignored.

She felt foolish. With a sidelong glance at Stack, she saw his agreement in the set of his hard lips and the tilt of his chin as he focused on the road. He thought she should have known better.

"I should have known better," she admitted. "I saw it often enough when I worked for you."

He shook his head. "Don't be hard on yourself, Tawny. These things start so subtly it would be a miracle if you'd noticed. It's a door held open for you, a glance held too long. The itchy feeling at the back of your neck when you're walking to your car. Individually, it's nothing. Put events together, it's still nothing. Just a feeling."

"Exactly. When I saw people come into the office all shaken up and weirded out, I'd think they were just paranoid. But after this last week or so, I'd be offended if someone thought the same about me."

"Did something happen to you recently that changed things in your life? Win a lottery? Lose a job? Get a job? Drop a boyfriend?"

She recognized the questions. He often began a stalking investigation this way. "You believe me."

He turned his head and the muscle in his jaw jumped. "You wouldn't have called *me* if you weren't scared. I'd be the last person you'd call." She'd hurt him by running away the way she had. It was there, in his eyes. He'd missed her.

Her heart did a rhumba and a fine warmth stole up her back, but this was not the time to be distracted.

"I am scared. But, actually, you were the only person I wanted to call for help." He blinked at that, then slid his eyes to the road ahead. "The cops will blow me off, and even though I've met a few of your competitors since we worked together, I think you're the best at what you do."

He turned to face her again. She saw smile lines bracket his mouth. She refused to look at his lips, they tempted her too much. "I appreciate your trust," he said on a roughened note.

She pulled down the visor to get the notepad and pen he tucked up there. A picture fell out of the square of papers. It was her, at her desk, smiling and happy. She was mugging for the camera with her only claim to fame. "You've still got this?"

"You're the only woman I know who can touch the tip of her nose with her tongue without crossing her eyes. I would never part with that evidence." He changed lanes suddenly and took the freeway ramp. "Now jot down the answers to those questions."

"Right." She looked at the blank notepaper. "Six months ago, I got word that my Grandmother Loretta died. She was in a nursing home."

"You inherit enough money for someone to want it?"

"No, she'd been there for a few years. There was only enough left to pay for her funeral. Which was kind of bawdy and raucous. Ever been to a former showgirl's funeral?"

The corner of his lips twitched. "Can't say that I have."

"Retired strippers and barkers come out of the woodwork and relive their glory days. The stories out of Vegas forty or fifty years ago are enough to make a girl blush. Sin City doesn't say the half of it."

"I can imagine. They say there are bodies in the desert that'll never be found."

She shivered. "I bet there are."

"Let's get back to your answers. How did your grandmother's death change your life? You said there was no inheritance to speak of."

"It didn't really change my life. It was just sad. I didn't know her well. My mom, Pansy, moved us around a lot. But I wish I'd known Loretta better." Mostly because Loretta's mother had been the start of all the emotional dramas, the men, the messes. Loretta had been raised in a home with a succession of men trooping through, and she'd been marked by all of that. Then she married Frank LaMotta. Some of the things Pansy had told her about Loretta and Frank's marriage was enough to curl hair. Tawny would have loved to get some advice on how to avoid what Loretta and, eventually, Pansy had fallen into.

Loretta had been in a loveless, violent marriage with a truly despicable man. Lust, jealousy, and a sick kind of hatred had ruined whatever decent relationship her grandparents might have had. Rumor had it Pansy's father had been connected back in the day. Apparently, he was a Las Vegas henchman, a thug, and a serial philanderer. When Loretta's looks had faded, he'd taken on multiple mistresses and flaunted them all. Some of the stories told at Loretta's funeral should never have surfaced, but Tawny had put most of them down to faulty memories and senility.

As a teenager, Pansy had run off with the first biker who had crooked his finger at her. Ten years later, she and Tawny had been left behind at a truck stop south of Seattle.

Three months later, her first stepfather appeared. That one had married Pansy.

In an effort to avoid the same kind of life that the previous generations of James women had suffered, Tawny had shut down her feminine needs and shut men out of her life.

By twelve, she was taping down her breasts. By eighteen, she wore nothing but baggy sweats and loose jeans. Ugly, heavy shoes helped shorten the look of her legs, and a certain shade of yellow turned her complexion sallow.

"Okay, enough about your grandmother, I can't see a reason for you being stalked out of all that. No lottery win, either?" Stack's voice dissipated the old memories.

"And no job news," she said. "When I quit working for you—"

"Ran away like a child, you mean," he interrupted.

"When I quit my job with you, I was approached by several of your competitors. Some of them asked about your client list, wanted to know why you're so successful and they're not. It was disgusting. I had no idea Bill Forrester was such a whiny skunk."

"Stinks out whatever room he's in. But I'm glad you told me. He closed shop. Last I heard he moved to Boston."

She made a good riddance sound in her throat. "I should have called you right away when he asked for the inside scoop on your client list, but I didn't want to talk to you."

She'd been afraid if she heard Stack's voice, she'd have gone running back to him.

Even now, his velvet-covered rumble rolled down her spine like a massage wheel, easing her muscles, tending to her sore spots, soothing her. Making her wet.

He'd had this effect on her since day one. As much as she'd tried to resist him, he could charm her with nothing but a look.

She was one messed-up James.

If Loretta were alive, would she recognize this feeling? Would she tell Tawny how to make it stop?

2

Tawny jotted her notes on the other questions Stack had asked about her life in the past six months. No big changes. She worked in a cubicle in an insurance company now. Some of the insurance investigators were pretty good at their jobs, but none had the skill that Stack had.

None of them would dirty their hands or take time from their caseload to help her find out who was following her.

"It's gross that someone's pawing through my underwear. They don't take anything, so I don't understand it."

"Not cutting the crotches out of your panties?" Stack asked as he pulled the Escalade into the parking lot of his new location. This one was in a nondescript strip mall that had seen better days. Literally.

"This place looked good for all of thirty days back in nineteen fifty-seven. You trying to restore the chi-chi element?"

"You always had a mouth," he said. But it was only half a snarl. The other half was close to, but not quite, but may have been, one quarter of a chuckle.

Not bad considering his earlier surliness.

"No, my underwear's intact. I don't know if a thong counts as an actual crotch, though."

His jaw jumped and he turned his head to face her squarely. He shoved his shades to just above his brows again. She could almost hear the tension pop in his neck as he forced his muscles to move. "TMI on that, Tawny. Too much information. I don't need a visual of you in a thong."

Time stopped. No breath stirred the air between them. His eyes burned like coals until she closed her eyes against the blaze of heat, want, and plain old lust that filled the vehicle, from both of them. But she couldn't run from him this time. She didn't have the strength. He'd worked his magic already. "I'm sorry I goaded you. I shouldn't have, um, mentioned my thongs."

His eyes flared hotter.

The need to be near him, the relief at seeing him after all this time had scrambled her brains. "I'm just stressed, scared, weirded out. It won't happen again."

"See that it doesn't." His eyes burned through her clothes as he dropped his gaze to her belly, then up to her chest and settled on her eyes. "Unless you want me to act on what I still feel for you, shut the fuck up about whatever you're wearing under that shapeless sack of shit you call a dress."

She swallowed, but all the moisture was gone from her mouth and throat. "I'll shut the fuck up."

He grunted and climbed out, slamming his door behind him.

She sucked in a breath, then blew it out slowly. "Get a grip. Taunting the man is the stupidest thing you've ever done."

But a soft voice in her head disagreed. *Leaving him was the stupidest thing . . .* She figured the voice must belong to Loretta.

She followed him out into the cooling evening air. He pulled her laundry baskets out and set them on the pavement; then he reached in for her bike and trailer. "Thanks. Which one of these illustrious storefronts is yours?" She eyed the set of six run-down shops but didn't see his sign.

"Second floor over the bakery, and my apartment's directly above."

In gold scroll letters, she read the sign on the window of his office: HAMILTON SECURITIES. "You realize the name of the company sounds like an investment firm." She'd had to field a lot of comments about that.

"Since I offer different types of security, I pluralized the name. Besides, you know I don't have to advertise."

Stack had great word of mouth. His clients appreciated his discretion and professionalism, and sent their friends.

"What's with the cowboy hat?" It looked great, especially with his black hair flying loose to his shoulders. She lifted her stuffed laundry baskets and followed him to the door wedged between a closed bakery and an open convenience store.

"A bar owner in Texas hired me. I needed to blend in." He unlocked the door and stepped into the narrow hall. A set of stairs went straight up to the next floor. The foyer was too narrow for them to stand in at the same time.

"We're not in Texas now," she quipped, as she began the climb. He left the trailer at the foot of the stairs but carried the bike on one shoulder. She put some sway into her hips just for fun.

"I got back an hour ago," he said. "I haven't done anything but catch up on messages. When I got your call, I was waiting for another or I wouldn't have answered. I'm dog tired."

"And you like the look, admit it." Normally he was in a suit, his hair tamed by a thong at his nape. She'd often wanted to see it loose but would never ask. She didn't even know how silky it felt, and a stab of female pique made her shoot him a barbed comment. "The women must have loved it in that bar in Texas."

"I wouldn't know. I didn't notice."

She let out a huff. *Right.* As she climbed higher, the quiet warmth of the narrow staircase provided enough intimacy that her breath caught. She *wanted* to know the texture of his hair. She needed to know the temperature of his skin, the way his bristles would feel rasping down her belly. How his lips would feel, his mouth would taste. How hard he could get, and whether she could make him gasp. "It's stuffy in here," she said, wondering how in the world she would keep her hands to herself.

"Left here," he said as she reached the first landing. She turned and faced the entrance to his office.

"Why did you move from the last place?" She looked inside for strength and came up empty. Her lower belly warmed in need and she licked her lips. One more floor and they'd be in his apartment.

"The downtown location was too public. My clients are happier driving out here where there's less chance of anyone recognizing them."

"Of course." The truly wealthy didn't live anywhere near here. This area was strictly middle class and hard working. The kind of neighborhood where both parents worked and the streets were quiet during the day. She shuffled out of his way to allow him to squeeze by her to open the door.

When he moved, his arm brushed her breast and she sucked in a breath. Her nipples pebbled and rose under her heavy denim jumper. He was right, she was wearing a piece-of-shit dress. One of her standard cover-ups.

He froze for a heartbeat when he heard her sudden breath. Then he smoothly unlocked the door and held it open for her. "The convenience store and bakery provide the cover of lots of cars coming and going. No one pays attention."

She slipped inside, set down her baskets, and pulled her bike into the reception area while he dashed back down to get the trailer. In thirty seconds, he'd be back. She needed every tick of the clock to gather her wits and decide what to do about Stack Hamilton.

Stack settled behind his desk to finish with the rest of his waiting messages. If he didn't deal with them right away, the whole mess would get worse and he'd be further behind. Tawny was in the outer office making a pot of coffee and clucking about all the dead plants. He'd told her when she started working with him to get some phony ones, but did she listen?

Listening to her putter and mutter about lazy-ass bosses who don't water plants put a goofy grin on his face. While he'd been out picking up Tawny from the Wash 'n' Suds, a completed file had come in from a freelance operative he used on occasion. "I need to handle a couple of urgent messages and some calls before I take you upstairs," he called to her.

"Okay." She leaned into his doorway and pouted. "You could get a cactus or two. You probably wouldn't kill those."

"Yeh, yeh. Would you like the key to my place? You don't have to wait here."

"If I leave you alone, you'll work all day." She disappeared again, doing whatever feminine thing she'd do to spruce things up.

He handled some calls, fielded questions from some of the guys in the field, and smelled the scent of Tawny's coffee. He'd forgotten how bad her coffee tasted. No matter, he was glad she was willing to make it. She brought him in a mug and set it on the desk, well away from his keyboard.

He nodded his thanks and continued with his call.

Tawny wandered to the window to peer out to the parking lot. He noticed she moved the blind carefully and stood to the side. Smart girl, seeing but not being seen.

He opened the manila file folder on his desk and glanced at the top photo. A wayward wife going down on her girlfriend.

His client suspected she was sleeping with his male partner. Poor bastard had no clue his wife swung this way. It wasn't his partner his wife was cheating with, but his lawyer. Ugly business all around.

The image was first class. Clearly, the women were accomplished and comfortable lovers. The ecstasy on the girlfriend's face wasn't easy to fake. Hands clenched into the sheets that covered the hotel bed, legs spread open to receive her lover's mouth and tongue.

The next photo was much the same, but her legs were pulled higher and this one zoomed in, clearly showing the client's wife in profile. Her tongue was out in a spear and aimed directly at the open pussy. Her hand had moved between her own thighs.

Beside them on the bed, he saw what looked to be a strap-on dildo. He wondered which of them would wear it. Before he could find out, he heard Tawny gasp. She was good at reading upside down and he'd forgotten her skill. This image would be easy for her to make sense of from where she stood.

"Hot, isn't it?" He wondered if the client would agree or be appalled. He couldn't tell. The guy seemed too straitlaced to get off on the sight of his wife with another woman, but he'd seen stranger things.

Tawny's cheeks went pink, but she nodded gamely. "I see business hasn't changed much."

"Human nature never does. When lust rears its head, people lose their minds." He flipped the file closed and set it aside. "Just a couple more messages to deal with."

"Drink your coffee, you look tired."

He took a sip, covered his reaction well, and grinned his thanks.

The phone rang and he answered. This was the call he'd been waiting for. Tawny perked up at his tone and realized the call was important just by watching his reaction.

She waved to get his attention and slipped out of his office.

Next, he heard the outer office door open and close, and her footsteps heading down. Damn it! She'd left the office and was going outside.

He ended the conversation abruptly with a quick apology and dropped the phone. By the time he stepped out onto the landing, he caught sight of the door at street level swinging closed.

Damn that woman, she knew better than to leave his protection. He'd been careful not to be followed, but he was tired and anyone could make a mistake.

He bounded down the stairs after her, wrenched the door open, and slid to a stop outside. The door to the convenience store was just closing. He stepped up and saw her through the glass, heading toward the back of the store.

His heart stopped just looking at her. Everything they'd ever shared rushed back. They'd laughed a lot in the office, had grown comfortable with each other, sometimes they could even finish the other's sentences. Like now, with the message. She knew his body language so well that she'd left him alone to deal with his call. She read him like a book.

He still needed to handle the nervous client, but that could wait. His priority was keeping Tawny safe. He stepped into the store and she didn't turn around to see who'd come in behind her. With a nod to the clerk, he moved silently down the aisle toward his quarry.

"I know it's you," she said without turning around. "Finished with your call already? I assumed you'd be on the phone a while."

"How'd you know it was me?" he growled, ticked that she'd be cavalier about her safety. She knew better, damn it!

"There's a mirror on the back wall. I saw you the moment you showed up glaring at me through the door."

The crazy urge to grab her by the hips and wrap his arms around her nearly made him reach out, but he quelled the feeling. She wouldn't appreciate the gesture, and she might go so far as to take off again.

To keep his itchy fingers occupied, he grabbed a pack of toilet paper and squeezed it. "What did you need from here?"

"Toiletries. A toothbrush and paste. Things like that."

He nodded and squeezed harder. "Good, okay."

She gave him the once-over, took in the mangled toilet paper, and grinned at him. "Take it easy, Stack. We'll get through this."

He grunted and trailed her through the store, toilet paper in hand.

"Convenience store prices on toothbrushes and paste are enough to gut a bank account," she said when she picked up a tube of paste, put it back down, and reached for a bargain brand.

Ten minutes later, at the cashier's counter, he shoved all her purchases into a white plastic bag with the store logo on the side, then dropped a twenty on the counter and ushered her outside.

"You didn't have to pay for my things," she hissed.

"I wanted to. You don't know when you'll be able to return to work."

"The only time I've ever been broke is when I worked for you."

Stunned, he froze with his hand on the open door. She gave him a saucy, humor-filled grin and slipped past him. "What are you saying? I'm cheap?"

"When it comes to paying me, you were. I make close to one third more now."

He frowned and considered. "I had no idea. I would have paid you more if you'd asked. You were fantastic at your job." He felt like a heel as he trudged behind her up the stairs to his office landing.

She stopped and turned to look down at him. His face was at breast level and his body felt energized at the thought. "You could have told me a time or two." But her eyes still held the humor this conversation had started with.

"Rub salt in the wound, why don't you? I feel bad about your salary, and now you're saying I never told you how great you were at your job. I don't know why you stayed with me for so long."

"Don't you?" She did an about-face and quickened her pace. He followed her bouncing ass to the landing.

"About those photos you saw earlier, you're still under your agreement of confidentiality."

She shook her head. "That agreement was null and void when I quit." They'd reached his office door.

"No, it wasn't." His tone was firm and brooked no argument. She made a face.

Her taste in clothes needed serious help. She wore a heavy denim dress that had one of those low waists and a hem that rested at her ankles. Some hideous yellow T-shirt buttoned to her neck. "There's a ladies' store at the end of the plaza. You could pick up some clothes there."

"I just got the essentials." She pointed to the bag in his hand. "And I brought clothes with me, remember?"

"What's up with that?" He couldn't resist asking. They'd fallen right back into their old familiar friendly roles. But this time, there was an edge to everything they said, a friction that had never been between them before. He liked it.

A lot.

But still, he had to ask. "You dress like a refugee from a religious cult, yet you're nothing like your appearance."

She bit her lip but strode into his office with a determined gleam in her eye.

"You hide behind that shit, Tawny, and I can't see why." Why any woman would hide the kind of body Tawny had been blessed with was out of his ken.

"My business, Stack." But she looked uncomfortable with

the line of questioning. A nice guy would let up. A nice guy would let her settle in upstairs while he dealt with the backlog on his desk.

Stack had never seen himself as a nice guy.

Pity.

"You know you changed your life by choosing to dress that way. With a body like yours—"

"What?" She spun to face him, agitated. "I could get laid once in a while? Some man would rescue me from a life of drudgery? Run around on me or give me a kid or two and leave me to raise them on my own." She crossed her arms over her chest in a classic protective stance. "Hey, yeah, that'd be following the family tradition."

"Okay. I get it, life wasn't fair. It rarely is."

She turned toward the door. "I'll go upstairs and put this stuff away. Thanks for the use of your spare room."

"No sweat. Here's the key." She made sure to avoid touching his hand when he passed her his key ring. "You'll find fresh sheets in the linen closet in the hall. One of the team used the apartment while I was in Texas. This isn't the first time we've housed a client who needed protection."

She nodded and walked out. He tracked the sound of her footsteps for as long as he could hear them. If he had his way, she'd be changing the sheets on *his* bed and sliding in there with him.

What he couldn't figure was why, when they worked together for three full years and she dressed to kill any hint of male interest, she would suddenly expose her spectacular body to him in the middle of a job. She wore a bikini, at a public pool, where he couldn't do a damn thing about it.

He'd never lost focus on a job before that day. He hadn't been able to see anything but Tawny in all her glory. Luckily, the client hadn't noticed at the time, but he knew he'd lost focus, and so had Tawny.

Ten minutes after they caught the peeper at the exclusive country club's pool, Tawny quit the agency and took off like a bat out of hell. He felt like a fool for having never been aware of what Tawny had been hiding under her clothes for three full years! A stupid, aroused fool, who'd had a great relationship with a woman and was too blind to see that it could have been more. It could have lasted.

He'd wanted many times to track her down and talk. Try to explain how good her disguise was. Then, he got angry. She'd set out to make him feel like an ass and succeeded. But why she chose that particular day to expose herself, he didn't know.

He hadn't seen her since. Instead, he'd gone back to work and waited, hoped, for the phone to ring. He'd wanted her to miss him the way he missed her, every day, every time he unlocked his office door and walked into the emptiness.

In the three years they'd worked together, Tawny had been standoffish and undemonstrative. She was bright, gifted with a wicked sense of humor that he loved to play off of, and drawn tight as a violin string.

When the conversations had turned remotely personal, she'd pulled off a forbidding stare that had iced him but good. Her friendliness had been a cover, a blind that had fooled him.

Stack didn't like to be fooled. Not by a woman, and never by a friend. Tawny had played at being a friend, when all along she'd been all woman.

To the best of his recall, they'd never even touched. He couldn't remember ever slapping palms in a high five, or otherwise showing appreciation for a birthday gift or holiday bonus. Hell, he'd never even bussed her cheek with a perfunctory kiss.

And now, all he could think of was seeing her body again. That day at the pool, he'd finally understood why she'd been given her name. Her skin was tawny as a lion's fur, smooth and creamy.

Spectacular from her head to her toes, Tawny was a living,

breathing sex goddess. Lush and shapely, her curves had drawn the attention of everyone at the pool that day. The women had shot daggers with their eyes, and he could swear the men were ready to shoot their loads.

But the question remained. Why that day? Why choose to bring herself into the light, let him see her as a woman for the first time, then run away?

He cast the ceiling a glance, heard her light movements in the kitchen area, and decided it was time to find out.

3

Tawny slipped the last of Stack's dishes onto the dish drainer on his kitchen counter. The window over the sink looked out to the back alley. She felt Stack's arrival before she heard him step into the kitchen. "There were dishes left in the sink, I washed them. I've got to keep busy or I'll go crazy wondering if he's out there staring at your office window."

"We weren't followed here, and no one watched us when we went to the store. I'd have seen them." He leaned on the doorframe, his shoulders broad enough to hold up the whole building.

She'd felt his concern and protectiveness like a cloak drifting over her from head to toe. Warmth stole from her chest, down her arms, and along to her fingertips. "I shouldn't have left the building without you. I forgot for a moment why I was there. It all seemed so familiar and comfortable that I slipped into my receptionist role and just . . . forgot that someone's been following me." A thought crossed her mind. She straightened and faced him squarely. "It hasn't been you, has it?"

He went red as a stoplight. "No, not that I haven't thought

about you." His lips firmed. "I've wondered how you've been. I've considered calling, but you didn't seem to want any contact and I had to respect that."

"Thank you." While she appreciated the respect, it also grated on her that he hadn't acted on his impulse to call. She probably would have spoken to him. If she was in a good mood. If she was vulnerable at that particular moment and wanted to talk to him. If she was lonely. *Who was she kidding? She'd been lonely for Stack since the day she'd quit.*

He shrugged. "I respect women, and you especially. Now, tell me everything that happened today."

Respect. It was one of her main priorities in a relationship, and the thought that he would offer it to her so easily made it difficult not to throw herself at him. She gripped the counter at her back. She needed something solid to hold on to.

He'd asked about the details of her day, and she needed to focus and recall. He was so broad, so focused on her, so *familiar* that her nerves settled. "I've been running everything through my head and I can't figure out who this is. Or why they're doing it."

"Just talk. Close your eyes, walk through your day again. Let me hear what you're seeing as you recall."

She'd seen him use this technique successfully many times. Maybe if she'd tried it herself she'd have remembered something useful before this. She'd been right to come here, right to put her faith in Stack. If she let her heart slip farther down the slope toward loving him, she could deal with the fallout later.

She let her eyelids drop and slowed her breathing. Three long, slow breaths later, she realized he hadn't moved. He waited on the other side of her eyelids, watching her chest rise and fall, allowing her to "see" the events of her day.

She walked herself through her morning, noting how humdrum and boring her life sounded. Eventually, she got to the

Wash 'n' Suds. Against the dark screen of her mind's eye she saw herself opening the dryer to put a load of her clothes inside. Settling in, she spoke of every detail as if it were happening now for the first time.

"I need the washroom, so I close the door of the dryer, set the timer and heat setting, and leave the clothes to tumble. Other people are to the right and left of me."

"Men or women?" He spoke softly, and she knew this meant he didn't want to startle her. His voice gentled her, let her relax.

"Moms with family clothing. Men's work clothes, children's clothes, their own."

"Do you see the women?"

"Yes."

"Are they your size?"

She shook her head. "One is pregnant, the other is painfully skinny. Bony, like she's forgotten what a meal tastes like."

She heard his gentle hum, as if he'd nodded at her description, but she kept her eyes closed. "You're in the ladies' room," he prodded.

"Yes, I have to hurry because my first dryer is close to finishing its cycle. It's a busy day, with lots of people waiting for dryers. I step back out of the restroom and see my newest dryer has stopped before the cycle's ended. I check the door and it's open. I swear and look all around, but I don't see anyone watching me.

"The pregnant woman says a man opened it, tested the clothes to see how dry they were, and then walked out. She thought he was waiting for me and was checking to see how much longer he'd have to wait in the parking lot."

"She was lying."

"No, I don't think so. She walked to the window and pointed to a car parked under a tree on the far side of the lot. Since the car was in the shade, I couldn't make out if anyone was inside."

"That's when you called me."

"Not right away. I decided the guy was just a pervert who staked out the place to get his jollies looking at underwear."

"You thought he waited for you to leave your dryer unattended, then pawed your clothes."

She opened her eyes, feeling stupid all over again. Maybe that was exactly what happened. Maybe she was here for nothing. But Stack's expression was serious and concerned. "That happens, right?" She looked for confirmation.

"You wouldn't have called me unless something felt off. You're too smart to dismiss a gut feeling, Tawny." He stepped closer and she wondered if, just this once, he would touch her.

He never had, not since they'd briefly shaken hands when he'd welcomed her to his firm. As often as she'd wanted to reach out to him, she never had. She'd been so firmly set in her decision to be friends, to hide from his view, that she'd never let him see that she cared.

Now, he stood not four inches from her, close enough that she could feel the heat from his chest, smell the scent of his aftershave. He'd used the bottle he kept in his glove box, probably on the way to pick her up.

She knew so many intimate details of this man's life that she could hardly believe she didn't know the feel of his hands, not on her shoulder in a comforting pat, or on any other part of her body, including and especially on her erogenous zones.

"Close your eyes again and take me back there with you. Tell me why you called me. Tell me why you got scared."

She closed her eyes, licked her lips, and allowed herself to go back to the Wash 'n' Suds again. "I closed the dryer so it could finish, then took the rest of my laundry out of the first dryer. A woman rushed to use the machine the minute I emptied it. I heard a couple of bitchy comments about pushy women, but I didn't want to get involved, so I moved toward the window. I folded my towels while I kept an eye on the car in the parking lot, but the shade never shifted enough to let me see anything. When the second dryer buzzed, I pulled everything out."

"You're sure nothing was missing."

She envisioned her whole process. "I'm certain. As I folded my tees, I flashed on what had happened at home last week. I ran back to the window, but the car had left. I dashed out to the walkway, but I couldn't see it anywhere. That's when I got creeped out and called you."

"Go back to what happened at your place and tell me why you think someone was there." His breath danced across her face. He'd had coffee and something minty. She wanted to taste his lips, to feel the pressure and moist heat of his mouth, but she had to continue. She was on the verge of an important memory and she couldn't mess it up. She couldn't afford to be stupid.

Keeping her eyes closed, she said, "I keep my thongs sorted by oldest on top with my newest on the bottom of the pile. I didn't see anything wrong with my room until I went to pull out my underwear. The pile of thongs had been flipped so that my newest were on top. I'd never do that." When she got no response, she peeped one eye open. Big mistake.

He had that look again. That hungry male need thing that set her heart to top speed. Tension coiled around him like a spring. She stood four inches from a dark panther on high alert.

Tawny had never wanted to be pounced on so badly in her life.

Had she moved closer to him? The counter no longer pressed into her back, and he seemed near enough to kiss. His eyes went dark as they scanned her face. Up close like this he was too hard to resist. He was just plain hard.

He was bad.

He was hot.

He was what she wanted, and his touch would be to die for.

"Why did you wear that bikini that day? Why did you wait so long to show me who you are under those god-awful clothes?"

Typical male, deciding that a woman was nothing but a body. In one fell swoop he'd done away with the jokes they'd shared, the conversations they'd had, the friendship they'd built. Touching or no touching, they'd shared a lot of good times and a lot of stress. They'd seen each other at their worst and their best. He'd made her laugh many times, while she'd returned the favor. He'd always said he loved her sense of humor.

And all that had been wiped away when she'd walked out onto that pool deck and dropped her towel.

She'd seen his cock rise like a trumpet in a solo, his eyes drink in every inch of her curves, and saw the light of friendship dim to nothing. She hadn't thought of that when she'd donned the suit. Stupid. Stupid James girl.

Still, she should be honest now. He'd come for her immediately when she'd called, no matter that she'd left him high and dry, no matter that he'd just gotten off a plane and felt bone tired.

"I saw you," she blurted. "With your little friend. The night before. Fucking in your office."

He'd been pumping into some woman on the desk and she'd been rapturous. Tawny could still see his buttocks hollowing with each thrust, see the way his naked back glistened with his efforts, smell the musk of their passion.

It had enraged her, made her stupidly jealous, and she'd done the unthinkable. She'd behaved like every other James woman who had ever lived. She'd gone after her man.

Her man! He'd ceased being her friend, her boss, her buddy. Her secret desire. She'd wanted to make him notice, to let him know there was a part of her he'd never seen. A part of her that he might want.

Fuck! She was one messed-up woman.

The next day at the pool stakeout she'd shown him what he

was missing. She'd strutted and preened and turned him on. She'd had no idea she felt that possessive about Stack. It shamed her now, that stupidity, made her feel like such a chump.

She knew all along he had lots of women. But to her knowledge, he'd never had one visit the office. She'd never had to see him with another woman.

She'd lusted for him for so long she'd gone a little crazy.

Maybe if he'd had a real girlfriend, someone who swung by the office to see him at lunch, or chatted with her when she answered the phone, she wouldn't have reacted on such a visceral level. But none of his women had behaved like girlfriends. He hadn't bonded with anyone.

It hurt to see him be so cavalier as to fuck some slut when she, his friend and confidante, was right there in front of him.

His brows knit as he tried to make his brain work. "Fucking in my office? Who?"

He didn't even remember! "A blonde, I think. Small and thin. Different from me. I, ah, kind of went nuts, and the next day I showed up at the pool wearing a bikini. I shouldn't have. Our relationship was strictly professional. You were my boss."

"Yes, but you were the first woman I've ever been friends with. The only woman. That meant a lot to me." He raised his palms in supplication and melted her heart with one tilt of his head. His expression was ingenuous. He had no idea that they could be anything more than friends. He'd never, not ever, thought of Tawny the way she thought of him.

Not until he'd seen her body.

That hurt.

She remembered the pump, pump, pump of his ass, the strength of his back, the way he'd held that woman. The way her own body had reacted at the sight, sound, and scent of Stack Hamilton making love.

A shiver ran through her at the memory. She closed her eyes and used his trick again.

"What are you seeing now?"

"You, with your back to the door, her legs wrapped around your waist. She'd left her shoes on. Bright blue stilettoes. She had muscular legs, and she kept crooning for you to fuck her fast and hard."

"How did you feel when you saw that?" his voice went gravelly, aroused.

Her breath rose and fell faster, her eyelids fluttered open until she looked directly into his eyes.

"Answer me, Tawny. Go back there and tell me what you see."

She kept her eyes open, stayed brave or stupid, she wasn't sure which. "I see you grinding into her. I see me, wanting that too."

"Do you still want what you saw that day?" He held her gaze, hot and hard and needy. His lower body brushed lightly, once, twice, against hers.

Her hips strained toward his of their own volition.

4

"Yes, I want you grinding into me, hard, hot, and fast." Tawny's words sent him over the edge and he obliged her. He pressed his hips deep between her thighs, but her ugly-ass dress got in the way. Miles of heavy denim wrapped her in a cocoon solid as a chastity belt.

"Take this off." He pulled and tugged and yanked the yards of cotton up and over her head. "I hate these things you wear, and, babe, it's gotta stop."

She tugged her T-shirt off next. The look of her skin went from sallow and sickly to rosy and flushed when the yellow material no longer framed her face. "You must be color-blind," he said, "to wear such an ugly color."

"No, just determined not to be noticed."

He stood back to see her from head to toe. "Magnificent," he murmured, but she looked cautious at the word.

No way would he say another word. No way would he frighten her into running again.

The scent of her rose to him and he lost his mind as he allowed his need to take over. The need for sex, his need for release, need for touch, his need for Tawny overcame his caution.

He slid his hands to her lower waist, felt the heat of her soft flesh, and tugged her close. He pressed his cock against her thigh, desperate for the feel of her there against his sensitive skin. He wedged himself between her legs and slid back and forth along the crease between her leg and her pussy. If he felt her wet channel graze him, he'd slam into her and pop like a teenager, so he kept away from her inviting wetness.

"We need to move to the bedroom. I don't keep protection in my kitchen drawers." His voice was guttural with need, but he didn't care. She had to know she had the upper hand here. He was lost and he couldn't hide it.

"Yes, thanks," she said, foggy and unmindful. The idea cheered him. He wasn't alone in this sexual fugue. "I nearly forgot about protection." She bit her lip; then she said the words he'd waited to hear: "I want you so much, Stack. I'm dripping."

"You are," he said as he set a fingertip to a warm trail of moisture on her inner thigh. So soft. He slicked his finger along the moisture, savoring the flavor. Her eyes flared as she watched him lick his finger. Salty-sweet need slid across his tongue, inflaming him.

He hadn't seen her body since that day at the pool, but his memory had served him well. Caution stopped him from speaking. He didn't want to remind her of his reaction that day. He might break if she walked away from him now. In this moment, there was nothing he needed more than Tawny.

So, he looked his fill but said nothing. Exactly as he recalled, her breasts were full, high, and heavy, and overfilled her plain cotton bra. An image of her bikini top overlaid the ugly cotton.

This bounty of lush female flesh was all Tawny. She wore no push-up pads. There was no silicone. Nothing but what her great genes had given her. Mountains of warm, soft flesh and feminine sexuality that called to arms everything sexual in him.

She was completely female to his male. Her waist was narrow and firm, her belly flat but softly giving. He smoothed his hands up from her pubis to cup her breasts, warm and pliant. He ran his hands down her sides, feeling the flare at her hips that said she was wide enough to take everything he wanted to give her. Inside his head, he roared with possessiveness. His blood pounded and his cock stiffened to a thick spike of need.

He tugged her thong away from her lower belly and looked down. She squeaked and he chuckled. "Beautiful," he murmured. "You look delicious, Tawny." This time, the roar in his head settled in his throat and he growled his need. Her scent, fully aroused, moist and female, bloomed in his nose. Unlike a lot of women, Tawny hadn't shaved. She was lush with soft curls that shone with her juices. "I'm going to have to taste you, you know that."

She squeaked again, and glory of glories, her legs opened and he knew he'd been right. She knew what she wanted, knew what he wanted, and was willing and even anxious to let him get his mouth on her.

All the blood in his legs had gone to his cock, and he wasn't sure he could stand much longer.

Tawny James was a helluva woman: built for loving, built for sex, built for babies. He slid his hand to her pussy, combed through her curls, felt her wet and full in the palm of his hand.

His legs started to shake as he lost himself in the scent and feel of her. He tapped her slit and felt her lips open.

"Oh, shit. I'm in over my head, Tawny." And he didn't care. He wanted Tawny James for every reason a man could want a woman.

"Not yet, you're not," she murmured, and pressed her hands on his shoulders to ease him to the floor.

For the first time in his life, a woman made him fall to his knees. Happily.

He pressed his face to the curls at the top of her legs and

breathed in her musky desire. His heart stopped beating, his hands shook, and his mouth watered. His dick wept with the drive to enter and take and fill her. His balls ached for need of release, and all he could do was open his mouth and seek the glory she offered.

Tawny opened for him, ripe and plump and juicy. No thong that he'd ever envisioned could compare with the reality of this thin, red line of material that did nothing to stem the tide of juices he found.

He'd need his tongue for that.

Her clit peeped out at him, firm and rubbery. He laved and suckled at the delicate flesh, while her thighs trembled and shook with each stroke. He was in heaven, buried chin deep in Tawny James.

He braced her knees on his shoulders to help her stand while he burrowed and worked at her pussy. Her folds opened like a blossom in the sun when he slid his finger along her trench.

Inside, she was slickly hot and ready for deep penetration. He obliged with two fingers and pumped hard to prepare her for more.

Her delicate clit got harder with each pass of his tongue, while her juice flowed over his chin. She moaned and rocked against his mouth, urging him deeper, needing to come.

"Oh! I'm coming." The words were throaty, guttural, and came with a gush of moisture so creamy he wanted to drown in her.

Her quaking shudders continued until she was lost in a haze of sensation. Soft cries rained down on him as he held her still against his mouth and tongue. He swirled his tongue, let her rock against his firmed lips until she quieted and her shudders eased. His heart pounded so loud she must have been able to hear it.

He wanted to let loose an earsplitting yell of triumph, but that would only spook her. Instead, with the last ounce of control he possessed, he stood and lifted her into his arms. All he wanted was to carry her to his bed with some measure of grace. She fit against him perfectly. Her pert, luscious ass rubbed his cock as he moved. Beyond all reason, his bloodless legs worked the way he needed them to.

Tawny gloried in Stack's attention. She was tall, solid, and had never been lifted and carried by a man in all her adult life. When he set her on the bed, she slipped her thong off and waited while he undressed. She wanted to cover her face, but she was too desperate to see him for shyness to ruin things now.

He was stupendous. His black hair flowed to his shoulders in abundant waves. Body, his hair had body. And his body had hair. A glorious mat covered his chest in a manly V that narrowed to his groin. Black and lustrous, it matched the thick hair on his head.

Stack Hamilton was perfect, absolutely perfect.

"You're so beautiful," he said, his voice suddenly rough and worshipful. He'd said that in the kitchen, too, but now he sounded desperate to convince her that what he said was true.

She flushed hot in the face and patted her cheeks. "Stack, you don't have to—"

He raised a hand to cut her off.

She fell silent. What more was there to say? She'd already let him eat her into a raging come. His mouth had been on her, his tongue inside her. She could think of nothing more personal, more intimate than that.

Except . . .

"Lean forward," he said. His request was rough, earthy, and she didn't hesitate to follow through.

She leaned ahead so her forehead rested on her raised knees. His hands went to her bra catch. "What the hell?"

"Oh, yes. Sorry," she said, and reached behind her to undo all three catches. "Guess you haven't seen this much support before."

"This is one ugly-ass bra," he said as he slipped the straps down her shoulders.

The bra fell away and she tossed it off the bed. It was ugly, that much was true. But she'd never worn bras with seduction in mind.

"If I don't use decent support, I'll have boobs to my knees by the time I'm thirty. And those pretty lacy things you think look so good will not hold up these babies." She supported her breasts to show him and his eyes widened at the gesture.

"Flick your nipples," he said, his voice a throaty hum.

She did, surprised by the urgency in the sensation—urgency and disappointment. She wanted his fingers, not her own, *his* hands cupping her, *his* mouth drawing her deep.

"Pull them."

"What?"

"Like this." He slid two fingers over the tips of her breasts, wedging her nipples in the apex.

She sighed with the heated intimacy, the quiet surge of sensation. Stack Hamilton was good at this. Very, very good. For three years, she'd hidden from him, from this.

He tugged gently to create an edgy shaft of sensation that zipped to her low belly.

She let her head fall back, her eyes close, better to enjoy the rocketing spasms as he tugged and released. "It's so much better when you do it."

He chuckled. "You're big and soft, and your nipples are perfect." He bent to suckle and she arched toward him, needing more. He cupped her breasts, made a trench between them, and licked her there while playing her nipples into hard hard need.

When his mouth captured her and sucked deep, she felt her womb contract with each suck. She watched his face firm, his cheeks hollow with every intake of flesh. His tongue swirled and his teeth scraped lightly, teasing her into a frenzy.

His knees braced hers on either side so she couldn't open

her legs. She shifted and tried, but he wouldn't budge. The suckling went on and on while she melted into a pool of achy need at her core, unable to open for him, as much as she needed to.

He *knew* damn well she was flexing her legs. "Let me open my legs. Stack! Let me move!" She made a strong attempt, but he only opened his eyes and stared at her face, his mouth full of her right breast. The suck he gave her was the strongest yet. Seeing his eyes on her as he suckled made her moan. She rode a surge of excitement and arousal.

His cock rose stiff and proud between them, daring her to claim him. She set her fingertip to him, felt the dew drop of need. He jerked in a spasm and she grinned. "Gotcha," she murmured, as she wrapped her hand around his shaft.

He released her with a soft pop as he straightened so she could get a better grasp on his cock. "Torture, that's what you're in for now," she said, then lowered her face to run the tip of him across her forehead, down her nose to her closed lips.

She licked her lips to get them extra wet. Then she tap-tap-tapped his head against her mouth while his knees flexed and his belly clenched. She liked this. Loved the anticipation of the taste of him, waiting for the feel of his heat inside her wet mouth.

She licked the sticky essence of him off her lips and studied his expression. Hard, demanding, but thrillingly silent, he waited, completely tensed, coiled and ready to spring.

Tawny considered dallying. "Want me to tease you? Or make you pop the way you did to me?" The come she'd had had blown her mind, and she wanted to return the favor.

He reached to smooth a tendril of hair behind her ear. "It doesn't make much difference, we'll be at this all night long anyway."

"If I'd known how this would be, I never would've run from you."

He stilled, then held her cheek with delicacy as if she were a blossom and he a Renaissance lover. "I never would have let you go."

"Will you kiss me now, please?" That was the intimate act she craved. The one thing she needed in this moment.

He cupped her face in his large, heated hands and held her still. The need, the desire, the affection in his gaze thrilled her beyond anything he'd done to her physically. She was his, completely.

"I can't believe I haven't yet. But there's nothing more I'd love to do. Give me your mouth, Tawny James, and I'll give you mine."

She shuddered and shook and settled back down on the bed, while he covered her and fit her to him. Their legs entwined, his chest weighed on hers comfortably, his chest hair brushed her nipples into hard buds. Her belly felt the weight of his hips comfortably between her own. She felt nakedly female, open, willing, while he felt hard and manly and ready to claim her.

She sighed and her breath caught as she gave herself over to him completely.

Tawny's scent took Stack over the top and he eased her legs open. He settled against her wet cradle. "You smell wet and womanly and ready." He slid his hands under her soft ass and lifted her against his aching rod. She was wet and open, and he wanted to drive into her fast. But she'd asked for a kiss and the lady deserved to get his best. He gathered the tattered remnants of his control and fell into her eyes.

Fear settled inside him as he watched her. Tawny had seen him with Lila, a woman who called on rare occasions for some down-and-dirty play. Lila was fun and hot, but empty when it came to anything more than a quick ride.

Tawny had shown him over three long years that a woman could be much more. He wanted that *more* that he'd felt with Tawny, he wanted it all.

In a weird way, it came down to this kiss. This personal, intimate, mouth-to-mouth kiss. He didn't want to mess it up. He wanted her to love kissing him.

A kiss. A nothing little press of lips to lips. A buss. A peck. A meeting of mouths.

The idea of kissing Tawny James made his heart skip several beats. Christ, he'd had his tongue buried in her pussy. Had felt her cunt gush and muscles clench when she came.

But the idea of kissing her felt as if his fate was sealed. His fate bound to hers.

If kissing Tawny meant blending his life with hers, he'd be a happy man.

He held her still and looked into the eyes that had swum with humor and intelligence for three years while he'd ignored them. He looked at the mouth that had cajoled and joked with him, and encouraged him when he'd been worried about clients, business, and overdue accounts. His thumbs brushed the eyebrows that she'd knit in concern for him when a job turned dangerous.

"This kiss? This kiss means a lot," he murmured as he drank her in.

"Yes," she breathed. "Kiss me, Stack, make me yours."

And he slipped his lips across hers, once, twice, hesitating, drawing out the blurred heat, the want, the love.

He settled on her then, let his cock wedge along her opening, let his hands hold her head, let his lips coax and his tongue tip inside her eager mouth.

She tasted of love and forever, and he wasn't scared.

Not at all.

This was hot. Hotter than anything he'd ever done before. A kiss. Who'd have thought it? Her body was soft and giving under his, her legs smooth and open. She kissed him back with power in every tongue stroke, with greed and female need in every response.

He lifted his head, saw her eyes gleaming in the gentle light, and dived into her mouth again. She was sweet, demanding, female in every way.

And now, finally, he was scared.

"You never touched me before," he said. "You never let me touch you. Why now?" She shifted under him, opened enough that he could feel the wet entrance of her, the labia resting, wet and slick around his shaft. Half an inch and he'd be in her. He arched back, ready to slide, needing to bury himself and touch her from the inside.

"You can't, we're not protected," she said as she slid a little to the side. "But I want you skin-to-skin so much it hurts."

He tore open the package he pulled out of his bedside table in record time and sheathed himself quickly.

The need to drive into her consumed him, and all thought fled as he gave in to the primal need of man for woman.

She was tight and wet and lusciously ready, and he'd never felt so welcome. Tawny sighed when he seated himself in perfect alignment, in quiet reverence, and in tumultuous joy.

She rocked.

He rolled.

She bucked.

He pressed.

She came.

He groaned and let his heart pour into her as he joined her in the leap over the precipice.

5

"I can't recall ever touching you before," he said after he'd exhausted his supply of condoms. He snugged Tawny close and petted her long, lean body from sternum to pubis. Soft, smooth, giving, he loved the textures of her, the scent, the taste. He nuzzled her hair, kissed her ear. "I don't know that I'll ever get enough of just touching."

She pulled his head down to hers for a kiss. "I know what you mean."

Dawn had edged into the room by the time the kisses ended. They were heading down an unsafe road, so he rolled her to her side and spooned instead. This way he could cup her breasts and feel her ass pressing into his crotch. He slid his mouth to the nape of her neck and nipped lightly. She turned with a sexy chuckle and he growled into her ear, turning the chuckle into a throaty laugh.

Tawny rocked her ass against his rock-hard cock. His hips strained to within an inch of sliding deep. "Stop moving or I'll be fuck-deep inside you again. And I'm out of protection."

She moved so fast away from him, he wondered if she'd fall

out of bed. He chuckled. "Glad to see you feel the same way about a baby as I do."

"Bad timing. I'm not having anyone's baby until I'm sure daddy's sticking around. Which means I'll likely die childless."

"You've got a hard line to walk on that."

"It's only fair. I won't bring a kid into a world without a real father. The kind they write about in books. Those authors sure know how to spin a tale."

He chuckled. "My father stuck around. I had a great childhood. Steady, reliable parents. Got a brother and sister I see regularly. My parents have been married for close to forty years."

"Hmph. So I guess it's possible."

Her doubtful tone ticked him off, made him defensive. "I'm not making it up, Tawny. Some men are happy to stay. Some men stay in love with their wives and take an interest in their children too."

She rolled to her back. "That so, big man?"

"That's so." A sharp edge of panic cut its way through his belly. He didn't like the feeling.

She patted his cheek, then slipped out of bed. He watched her leave the room. A couple minutes later, he heard the shower running. He couldn't remember the last time he'd been so easily dismissed.

Her phone rang inside her purse on the dresser. He plucked the phone out and checked the number, but it wasn't one he recognized. He let the call go to voice mail. He walked into the bathroom and called to her that she had a message on her phone.

Then he hit the kitchen to put the coffee on. He considered joining Tawny in the shower but changed his mind. There would be more time later, after he stopped at the drug store.

Now that he'd had her, he wasn't about to let her go anytime soon. In spite of her thoughts to the contrary, he wasn't the kind of man to walk away from women he cared about.

The implied insult about being a walk-away father still stung, but it was way, way too early to tackle that one.

"We shook hands once. When I accepted the job," she said when she walked into his kitchen fifteen minutes later. She gently patted her long hair with a towel, squeezing out excess water. "You said you couldn't recall us touching before. That handshake sent me on my butt, so I made sure not to touch you again."

He didn't recall the handshake. He swallowed hard. Damn, but his fingers burned to skim her cheek, to hold her still for his kiss. But a deep fear kept him at bay. Tawny was different from his other sexual partners. Correction, his previous partners.

He didn't see a time when he'd go back to any one of them.

He *liked* Tawny. Affectionate appreciation for a woman was rare. He had it once for a buddy's kid sister. She'd been in the fearless freckles and braces stage, and he'd corrected her assumption that all boys wanted sexpots. He'd been her friend when she needed a shoulder and couldn't talk to her big brother.

But this thing with Tawny had him twisted up. He had burned his retinas on the sight of her in that bikini. She'd read his sudden rush of desire and lust, and had run as far and as fast as she could.

No way could he afford another mistake with her. Not now, not when he'd had her all night long.

Under the scent of shampoo and his deodorant soap, she held a fragrance that was all Tawny. The scent lured him close, made him want to drive into her and cosset her at the same time. He didn't know which way was up anymore.

Which way was right.

If he touched her now he'd be lost, and without another condom, he had to wait.

The sheen in her eyes, the way she licked her lips after each sip of coffee told him she was ready and wanting more too.

The want of her was so fierce it scared the piss out of him.

"About Lila," he began, "I need to apologize for engaging in sex at the office. I thought you'd left for the night, and she's not—"

"Please. Stop. I don't want to think about you and her." She closed her eyes and shook her head as if she wanted to erase an image in her head.

Regret burned for giving her the image in the first place. "I'm sorry you saw anything, if I could go back and undo it all, I would."

She looked at him again and waved a hand in dismissal. "I'd been hoping, . . . never mind. It was silly."

"Hoping what?"

"That you'd like me for me. Not just this—" she waved her hand down her spectacular body, once again hidden by baggy jeans and an oversized tee. "Like I said before, I got a little crazy."

The bikini was beginning to make sense. She hated that her body made her a target of lust. She was a man magnet, and that day at the pool he'd behaved exactly the way other men had.

Too bad.

She'd shocked the shit out of him. After three years of working together, her standoffish behavior and the ugliest clothes he'd ever seen, it was no wonder he'd nearly had a stroke. He *would* have had a stroke if there'd been any blood left to run through his body. One look at Tawny and every drop had raced to his cock.

Hardest woody he'd ever sported until last night.

"I'm sorry you saw me that night, but I won't apologize for being a man. I don't know what else to say. But at the pool the next day, you waved a red flag at a bull. You show off a body like yours, cocks sit up and take notice. There's nothing new there."

She raised her hand. "I'm not the first woman in my family

to make stupid mistakes. This body has been a curse for generations."

"So you hide it."

She nodded.

"And when I reacted like any red-blooded male would, you ran."

Another nod.

Which meant she didn't want the same reaction from him that she'd had from every other man. "You've put me in a bind here, Tawny. You think we hit the sack because I'm in lust. You need to know it's more than that."

"It is?" Her eyes went wide, softened into "come love me," and he very nearly did.

"Oh, yeah."

"Oh. So what do you want to do?"

"I want to fuck you until your eyes roll back in your head. I want to hear you moan and scream. I want to feel your soft, wet pussy suck me in and hold me there, tight, until you come."

"You've already done that, and more," she whispered, heated response in every word. Her pretty face flushed pink. She blinked at the memories he'd brought to her mind. With any luck at all, he'd replaced the old image of him with Lila with new ones.

He swallowed. Not a drop of moisture wet his throat, but he'd made his point. "We need to get moving. I'll take my shower."

Tawny was funny, smart, and capable. The kind of woman any man with a brain would want. Tawny was the kind of woman a man held on to. Too bad she didn't realize that for herself.

Half of him wanted her to follow him into the shower, to take charge and reach for him. He heard the musical notes of her cell phone from the bedroom again.

"Your phone's ringing," he called as he headed into the bathroom. "I'll be out in two minutes." He couldn't spend his day smelling of sex, but he wanted to hear the quality of her tone when she answered the call. If she sounded agitated, he'd put off his shower to find out what upset her. Her footsteps sounded down the hall.

The ring tone ended, and her soft voice sounded calm. "Hi, Mom."

Not her stalker, but this was rare. Tawny and her mother had little contact except for family emergencies. Raised the way she'd been, Tawny had an independent streak. A streak he'd admired, much the way he'd admired everything else he knew about her. Leaving her to her conversation, he jumped into the shower and prepared for the day.

Tawny was safe for now. If not from him, then at least from her stalker.

"Sorry," Tawny said to Pansy, "I haven't been in touch. I've been meaning to call. Things have just been hairy around here."

"Did you get the package I sent?" Her mom's voice sounded urgent.

Confession time. "No, I moved." She winced.

"When?"

"Last month, and I'm sorry I didn't let you know. This place came up suddenly and I had to take it right away."

"Sure. I know how that goes."

Guilt for not calling more often settled in her spine. Pansy didn't ask for much, never had. The men in her mother's life had made sure she kept her expectations low.

The least Tawny could do was stay in touch. "What did you send me?"

"Loretta's Vegas costume. She wanted you to have it."

"Really?" She'd seen a picture of her grandmother in the sixties during her dancing days. The family called her the Queen of Rhinestones on a good day. On a bad day, the name-calling had been ugly. "The bustier alone must weigh what? Five pounds? Ten? I don't know how she could stand up straight." Add that to the weight of her breasts and the woman was a goddess of strength and endurance.

"She worked out. My mother was stronger than you could imagine. Not just physically but emotionally strong." Pansy's voice broke.

"Are you all right?"

"I got a letter from Loretta through the estate lawyer when the will was read. She knew about her dementia so she wrote it while she still could. It explained so much about her life with my father. As it turns out, he wasn't my biological father." Soft sniffles filled the air between mother and daughter.

"What?" The bastard grandfather, the abusive serial philanderer wasn't Pansy's dad. Loretta had had a lover before that old bastard had made Loretta's life a living hell. "Good for her," Tawny cheered. *You go, Loretta!*

Pansy chuckled mid-sniff. "In the letter she said the memories she had of my father sustained her through her rotten marriage. She suffered for my sake, Tawny. I feel like such a shit. I never looked beyond what I needed from her. When I didn't get it, I never asked why. I never stopped to consider what she was suffering at the hands of . . . that bastard Frank. God, it's such a relief to know I'm not related to *him.*"

"She loved you. She put up with Frank for your sake. You did some of that for me too." Please, let Stack be different. Let Stack feel something more than lust.

"She was afraid of Frank. She let him believe I was his child to protect me. And in the end, to protect you too."

"Why me?"

"There's something sewn into the bra."

"What?"

"I don't want to say, but you have to get that package. If I'd opened this letter before I sent the package to you, I'd have delivered the costume myself." She sighed and lobbed a full-out guilt blast. "You still wouldn't have it, though, since you moved without telling me."

"Nice shot, Mom, and I deserve it. Are you done with the guilt thing now?"

"Yes." The silence after the single-word response said a lot. But it gave Tawny time to accept that Loretta had kept a lot of secrets.

She sighed. "I'm sorry. I should have told you about the move." The why of her mysterious pervert seeped into her conscious. "But this is creepy. Someone else must know about the costume."

"Then I'm coming to see you. I need to explain more in person."

Stack walked back into the room, probably in response to her louder, more urgent tone of voice. "Hold on a sec, Mom." She quickly told Stack the gist of the story.

"Get the tracking number for the package."

She did. "I'll call back when I get it, Mom. No worries."

"What's going on?" Suspicious mother's voice rang through the air into her ear. "Will you pick me up at the airport?"

"Sure. Let me know when you're getting in."

"You still haven't given me your new address. In case things get crazy for you, I can meet you there."

"I'm, ah, staying with Stack for now."

"What?!"

"Gotta go!" She hung up on her mother for the first time in her adult life. Teenage angst didn't count. Pansy always said aliens had abducted Tawny then, anyway. They didn't return her until she was twenty and had learned a little about life.

Stack, already on the move, headed for the door, leading with a trail of hot testosterone and clean male. She snatched her purse off the sofa on the way by and followed him out. "I don't know what's sewn into the costume, but my mother's on her way."

They took the stairs down quickly while Tawny filled him

in about her grandfather and grandmother. "Rumor has it, Frank was connected back in the day. He was a vile man and a worse husband. A thug."

"Hmm, so what you're saying is, you come from a line of strong, smart women who know how to survive."

The idea nearly stopped her cold. Loretta was a wily survivor, not just a victim. Her decision to pretend Pansy was Frank's child must have been one born of desperation and fear. "But where did my real grandfather go? Why wasn't he there for Loretta and my mother?"

"You said Frank may have been in the mob back then." He bent the tip of his nose. "You may never know what happened to your real grandfather. Maybe Frank kept that secret. Maybe the guy who fathered Pansy wanted to be there for the woman he loved and their child."

"I'd like to think so, but with Loretta gone now, too, there's no way to know for sure." This all gave Tawny more to ponder. "The creep factor's just gone up a notch, though."

"Whatever's inside that costume must be valuable or dangerous if Pansy wouldn't say more on the phone. And call her back with my address. I moved since you worked with me, she won't know that."

She rolled her eyes. "Not you too. She squeezed tons of guilt into that one call, you don't have to add any more."

"What do you mean?" He opened the outside door and scanned the parking lot before allowing her to step outside.

Standing behind him gave her a moment to feel how broad his shoulders really were. They blocked the light from the foyer window.

"Why did you walk away from me?" she asked. He'd gone for a shower, of course, but he'd left in the middle of a critical conversation, putting an end to the discussion. That wasn't Stack's way. He finished whatever he started, much to her satisfaction.

"Not the time, Tawny." He kept moving, but since he sped up, she figured she had him on the run. A man who ran this fast was scared.

Stack was scared.

Of *her.*

Didn't that beat all? He wasn't afraid of anything that she'd ever seen. He'd walked into bar brawls and come out unscathed. He'd spent nights supervising coked-out rock stars and little-girl pop stars, and even survived depressed soap stars. Nothing fazed him.

Something joyful woke in her chest. Tawny James had Stack Hamilton on the run. Secret glee made her want to laugh, but she couldn't. Whatever had spooked the man, he had to work it out himself.

Laughing at him would be wrong.

Very wrong.

She chuckled to herself as he pulled the Escalade's door open and waved her into her seat. His head turned, neat ponytail in place again, and checked the parking lot, before he strode around the hood of the vehicle like a man barefoot on hot coals.

She might not laugh at him, but she could smile.

Once in the vehicle, she gave him her previous address so they could check with the new tenant to see if a package had been delivered.

The interior of the SUV became comfortably silent. Whatever thoughts were running around in Stack's head, he kept to himself. She was no better because her thoughts revolved around her grandmother's secret love and all the downstream effects the marriage to Frank had on Pansy, and by extension, Tawny. The behavior that Tawny saw as reckless might have been nothing more than self-preservation.

Maybe she came from sterner stuff than she thought. She glanced at Stack. His features looked cut from granite as he drove.

As much as she'd shown him her intelligence and wit and friendship, he'd done the same for three years. The sex they shared last night was spectacular and in no way diminished all the other feelings they had for each other.

A quiet hope grew as she looked at him.

"What?"

"Nothing," she said with a secret smile. But his expression lightened.

"We're here. And I know that wasn't a look about nothing." He climbed out cautiously, looking in every direction for anyone on their tail. When he motioned her to climb out, she sighed in relief. She wasn't built for all this skullduggery.

She was relieved she'd buried her fear and called Stack. No one else would have taken her seriously, nor would they have offered her round-the-clock protection. She didn't want to think of all the other things Stack had done for her, but a blush stole into her cheeks as they knocked on her old apartment door.

Mrs. Jenkins peeked out her door and after some small talk, and some obvious interest in Stack, explained that Tawny and her friend had just missed the new tenant. He was off for a day in his kayak. Thank God for observant neighbors, Tawny thought, wondering how often her own comings and goings had been noted. Not to worry, came the other half of her mind, you lived such a boring life here, Mrs. Jenkins would have nothing to say anyway. Tawny smiled serenely. *What would she say now?*

"Thanks, Mrs. Jenkins," she said. "Did a package come to this apartment for me?"

Her former neighbor shrugged. "You could check with Stanley, see if he knows." With that, she popped back inside her apartment and Tawny heard the slide of a chain lock.

Stack took her hand. "Who's Stanley?"

"The landlord. He keeps a pretty sharp eye on the front door because he's too lazy to fix the buzzers."

He nodded grimly. "That may play in our favor."

However, the landlord gave her a notice from the postal service that a delivery attempt had been made. She could pick up her package from the local post office as soon as it opened in the morning. "But you're not the only one who's been looking, Ms. James. Some guy was here, trying to . . ." he trailed off.

Stack leaned in over Tawny's shoulder. "Trying to what?"

Stanley looked nervous and directed his gaze to Tawny. "He said he was your boyfriend and that you'd sent him to check on a package." He rubbed his balding head. "But, ah, I figured you didn't have a fella, at least, I've never seen you with one before." He flicked a glance at the looming Stack.

Stack relaxed and gave the man a grin. "Glad to hear it," he said, and slipped his arm across her shoulders. "So, what'd you tell him?"

"He came across a little tough, if you know what I mean. All I said was that the post office had left a card for you. I didn't tell him which office, though!"

Stack nodded and backed up. Tawny accepted the notice card and they walked away. When they were out of earshot, she said, "I'm shaking."

"No worries, we'll have all the backup we need."

Tawny laughed nervously. "The good thing is, Stanley thinks everyone looks tough."

Back in the truck, Stack flicked the corner of the delivery notice. "At least now we can assume that this guy's not after your body or your underwear," he said as he frowned in thought. "And where did he learn about whatever's in the costume, if Pansy only recently read the letter Loretta left her." He didn't direct the question to Tawny, more to himself.

"I can't imagine why this person would assume I'd put my grandmother's Vegas costume in with my own underwear, either. I can't think of one good reason for that. It's weird."

He slanted her a glance. "You may find this hard to believe, but men don't understand the workings of a woman's mind. To a guy, a bra is a bra is a bra." He grinned. "Unless it's industrial strength like yours." He waggled his brows.

"Hey, I like my breasts perky, and I aim to keep them that way."

He gave her a salacious look and she warmed deeply.

"Works for me." He settled with his back to his door, facing her. "Maybe he figured you wouldn't know there was anything hidden inside, so he looked in your lingerie drawer. Why wouldn't a woman put it in there?"

"And he thought I'd want to wear a rhinestone-studded bra under my T-shirts?"

"With what I've seen you hide under your clothes, anything's possible."

"Very funny."

She pondered what she knew of the last year of her grandmother's life. "He could have visited my grandmother in the nursing home. Pansy went twice a week: Wednesdays and Saturdays. Loretta got lost in her memories a lot toward the end. Maybe she said something about her secret stash."

"Call Pansy, find out when she's getting in. Ask her if she's got any ideas for us to pursue while we're waiting."

She caught Pansy at the ticket counter in the Reno airport. Her mother had no idea who might have visited Loretta but promised to think about everything on the plane. "Gotta go, Tawny, I've been asked for a drink once we get through security."

Tawny laughed and disconnected. "Pansy will think on it," she said.

As far as Tawny was concerned, she didn't want to pursue anything. She wanted Stack. In bed. She wanted to climb all over him and make it impossible for him to ignore or forget her ever again.

"We can't get the package from the post office until tomorrow. What will we do until my mom gets here?"

He slid his sunglasses up to his forehead so she could read his focused gaze. "We'll go back to bed."

"Oh."

Stack pulled the SUV into a drug-store parking lot and jogged into the store, while Tawny called her mother one more time. As much as she wanted to leave all this behind while she enjoyed Stack's attentions, she wouldn't relax with him until she had more answers.

Pansy's voice went low. "I won't talk about this on the phone."

"Now you're scaring me." She told her mother about having her underwear rifled at home and the man in the parking lot of the Wash 'n' Suds.

"So that's why you're staying with Stack? That the only reason?"

The tone said, *Don't be stupid, Tawny.* Just like it always did when Tawny showed interest in a man. A classic case of "do what I say, not as I do." Pansy had always wanted Tawny to be careful with her heart and stronger than the generations before.

Loretta had hidden so much from Pansy that she'd grown up confused and lonely for attention. When it was Pansy's turn to set an example for an impressionable daughter, she swung like a pendulum and became overprotective. Pansy used dire warnings to frighten her daughter into believing her figure was a curse. No wonder she'd grown up hiding her body!

What a messed-up family. And all for love, Tawny realized. Her voice broke. "Mom, I love you and I know you love me enough to want to protect me. But because of that, I've lived a lot of my life afraid. I can't be afraid anymore. Sooner or later, I have to trust a man. Stack's the man."

"You're sure?"

"Yes."

The man in question abruptly opened the driver's door,

tossed in a brown paper bag with the pharmacy's logo on it, and buckled up. "Well?"

"We'll pick you up tonight at six," she said, as much to let Stack know what was happening as confirming with Pansy. "See you then."

"Love you, Tawny," Pansy said with a hitch. "Stay safe, honey bun."

"I love you too. And I'll be with Stack the whole time. I've never been safer."

His hand slid to her thigh and gave it an easy squeeze to reassure her.

6

Stack wanted nothing more than to make good on the promise he'd made Tawny about spending the rest of the day in bed. But there was one thing they needed to do first.

"I'm betting your guy knows you spent the night away from home. Tell me how your place is set up. Is there a back way out of the building?"

"Out by the garbage bins and visitor parking. Why?"

"We should check out the apartment. See if it's been searched more diligently. You said the only thing you noticed was your dresser drawers being messed up."

"Not messed up exactly. Carefully rearranged, as if he didn't want me to notice. And I didn't, not at first, but yesterday at the Wash 'n' Suds I added things up."

And today, she had been informed this guy had been diligent enough to get her former address. Stack was glad he'd been there for her.

"He was careful because he didn't want you to know he'd been there. But if he noticed you didn't come home last night, he may have broken in for a more thorough search. How's your lock?"

She shivered and crossed her arms over her chest. "The lock's nothing special. In fact, it's old and the handle needs tightening." Her eyes widened with fear. "And obviously he knows that because he got into the place before."

Stack pulled her to him and held her to his chest. Her hair felt soft against his chin; her underlying scent brought back memories of the night before. "He's not after you." He smoothed her back until he felt her muscles relax some. "He's after whatever's sewn into Loretta's bra. If he took advantage of the empty apartment, we may find clues to his identity. Maybe he left fingerprints or something. He doesn't sound like a pro, and it's a good bet he's working alone."

She pulled back to stare up at him. "Are you saying you want to go to my place? Is it safe?"

"I'd never suggest we go together if it meant putting you in danger. I'd go in alone if that were the case. But this is about that package, not about you. I seriously doubt your life's in danger. This guy doesn't want to hurt you." He had to believe that. It would kill him if he were wrong, but he'd go down himself before he let anything bad happen to Tawny.

"I believe you. And I believe *in* you, Stack. I always have."

"I need you to come with me because you're the only one who'll know if anything's missing, especially if you've just moved in. All your belongings have been recently packed and unpacked, so they're fresh in your mind. You can get anything else you need to stay with me and I can take a good look around to see if I can spot the guy watching the place. If there's a possibility of fingerprints, I'll lift them and send them off to a lab I use."

She swallowed and thought for a moment. "You're sure he's working alone?"

"I'd bet on it."

"Me too. He wants whatever's in the package." She nodded and flashed him a relieved smile. "He could have hurt me anytime but didn't. In fact, he's been in more danger of being caught. Let's do this now before we go home and forget everything but each other." She took the pharmacy bag off the dashboard and slid it into her purse. She grinned and looked away from him, out her window. "So we don't forget them."

"They're the last things I'd forget." He smoothed his palm up her thigh. "You're shy about this," he noted. She went pink in the cheeks and still refused to look at him.

"It's not that. I'm just happy is all." Finally, she faced him. "This"—she waved from her chest to his—"this is good, don't you think? It's nice to be with you again."

He stopped at a red light and took the whole time just to look at her. "This is good, Tawny. I missed you more than you know. I missed talking to you, missed making you laugh, missed your lousy coffee, missed that perfume you like."

Her mouth dropped open. "I make lousy coffee?" She put a hand to her chest in shock.

"Ugly truth? It's watery."

"So that's why you always came in with those gigantic travel mugs from that kiosk. I assumed the bikini-clad baristas made you drive through there every morning."

He shrugged. "Hey, I'm a red-blooded male; those bikinis didn't hurt. But I loved the way you smelled. I missed the scent of you in the office, missed your smile too."

Her cheeks went redder, making her look pretty and young. "That was just my shampoo." She refused to mention her smile.

He gave an exaggerated sniff. "You smell even better today and you used *my* shampoo."

"Drive, big man, the light's green." But she smiled, the insult to her coffee forgotten. Almost. "That's why you made the coffee while I showered this morning."

He turned onto the freeway ramp to head north. "I'll teach you. It's not that difficult."

"I like my coffee my way," she grumbled. He chuckled.

From the freeway, she gave him directions, and within twenty minutes they'd parked a block and a half from her three-story apartment building. They walked along the sidewalk, holding hands in a display to emphasize they were in a relationship.

To an observer, it would seem they were returning home from a night out. He slung his arm over her shoulder, pulled her into a brief kiss designed to make her feel wanted.

It worked. Oh! To have the real thing with Stack. "You make us look connected," Tawny commented.

"We are. At least I am," he replied, as he swept the block with his eyes.

His casual admission made her falter, so that he stopped moving and caught her to him. "What?" he said into her ear. "Did you see someone you recognize? Is the truck here from the parking lot?"

"No, ah. You said, ah, you said, you're connected. To me."

"Yes, so?" He cupped her cheek and made her look up into his face. His worried face.

"I am, too, Stack. More connected than I thought I could be." A thrill chased around her belly and settled near her heart.

"That's good, right? Let's move, it's one thing to look like we've been together all night, it's another to re-enact the bedroom action." But his gaze heated her through.

She shivered with need and nodded.

He slid his palm down her arm to take her hand and kicked the pace into high gear.

She quickly led the way into the building. Inside, they took the stairs. Her apartment faced the street.

Tawny opened the apartment door and gasped. "It's been ransacked. Totally trashed."

"He's getting pissed that he can't find what he's looking for." Stack stepped inside, and closed and inspected the locking mechanism. "Jimmied. He's sloppy, but this lock's a piece of shit. Maybe he didn't bother with gloves and I can lift a print." He carried a kit with him and knelt to check the lock mechanism.

She wrinkled her nose. She'd put off installing a deadbolt until her next pay.

"He knows you'd find this mess sooner or later," Stack added. "But obviously he thinks you've already got the costume. He has no idea the package hasn't arrived."

He ran to the front window that overlooked the street. "Just as I thought." He rummaged into his denim shirt pocket and pulled out his notepad. He jotted something. "I saw a man duck behind some trash cans across the street. He just climbed into a rental car. I'll make a couple calls and we'll get his name."

"I want him charged," she said, appalled and chilled by the scene of destruction. The whole living room had been tossed. Her sofa cushions were sliced open, the back of the sofa exposed and gutted. Even her fish tank had been emptied, the colored stones from the bottom scattered across her soaking carpet. Tiny gold bodies glinted in the sun. "He killed my goldfish! What kind of sick prick is this guy?"

She knelt and used a half-dry magazine to scoop up Ariel One and Two.

"He didn't just dump the tank, Tawny. He combed through the stones."

They were strewn around, clear swipe marks from where the man had swirled through the pile that would have landed when he turned the tank upside down.

"I can't wait to find out what my mom has to say."

He made his calls, gave the car information to a contact, and flipped his phone closed. "We need to be quick here and go out the back way. If this guy's watching from a distance, he'll think we're still here for a while." He pulled out his fingerprint kit and got to work quickly.

"Won't he expect me to call the police?"

"If we do call them in, he'll probably figure out that you don't have the package yet. He might up his game and get dangerous. Until we know what it is he's after, it's best to keep this under wraps."

"I've got a clear print here, and here," he pointed to the lock and the door, and dusted lightly with powder. After he lifted the prints, he checked his watch. "He probably came here, tossed the place, then found your previous address and went there. Now he knows as much as we do."

"Except he knows that whatever's sewn inside that bustier is valuable enough to cause all this damage."

She raided her fridge for food that would spoil and watered her plants. Stack took care of her goldfish while she collected her mail. Her laptop was smashed.

They jogged down the back stairs and out the service door to the alley. No one was watching the exit. A trio of boys shot hoops a couple buildings over, but other than that the area was quiet. They headed down the alley to the cross street that would take them to the Escalade, and left her neighborhood and her trashed apartment behind.

If her stalker was watching the front of the building, he'd think they were still inside cleaning up his mess.

Back at Stack's, she put away the food that needed refrigeration while he made more phone calls. Next, she used his laptop and checked her e-mail, thinking that there might be a message from her mother or her mystery man. No luck.

She skimmed her e-mails, found a few pieces of spam mail that promised her the ability to enlarge her penis, but nothing important. Stack set his large palms on her shoulders and gave her a gentle rub when he found the tightness she lived with.

She gave in to the seductive pressure of his hands and dropped her head to let him knead her flesh. She moaned with the heated, gentle pressure. "I thought penises enlarged pretty much on their own," she said.

"Mine does. Wanna see?"

"Sure!" She used a surprised tone, as if amazed at the idea he'd make the offer.

She looked up in time to see his humorous twinkle turn dark as he considered. "Maybe there's a clue in older e-mails. Did your mom ever give you any reports on how Loretta was doing?"

"Of course, I should have thought of that myself." She did a search for all the e-mails Pansy sent from the year previous to Loretta's death. He pulled up another chair and read along with her.

Through piecing together various comments, Stack and Tawny discovered that Loretta had battled a series of infections that left her with a case of delirium. She ranted about the mob in Las Vegas.

"There's a comment about a guy named Lenny who went out one night and never came back. She thought he was still in the desert, trying to find his way back to her." Tawny shuddered at the image.

"Pansy say anything else that was in the letter?"

"Just that Frank wasn't my real grandfather." Grandpa Frank had been one mean son of a bitch, and no one knew why Loretta stayed with him. "My grandmother suffered years of abuse because she had to let her husband think Pansy was his child."

"She must have had good reason to be afraid for Pansy."

"I think he may have murdered this Lenny. Why else would

she have said he was still in the desert? Lenny must have been the man she really loved."

Stack's jaw jumped as he shook his head. "Love can make us do terrible things." He turned and his eyes softened in affection. "Or it can bring out the best in us. Your grandmother sacrificed a lot to keep her child safe."

Tawny's throat closed and she blinked. "If there's any justice where she is, she'll be with Lenny at last."

"Good thought," he said with a nod. "Hold on to it."

"I will." If Loretta and Lenny were finally together, maybe she could hope that love would come her way too.

"The package is safe inside the post office for now. I'm glad she sent it registered." He leaned in close and set his hand at the base of her neck. Warmth suffused her and she turned to find herself nose-to-nose with Stack.

"If your mother knows his last name, we should be able to learn something about Lenny's disappearance."

"So we wait for her?"

He nodded. "But not here."

"Where?"

His eyes flared into a blaze of desire. "I'll show you." He took her hand, then stood.

She rose and let him lead her to his bedroom.

"If I didn't know better, I'd say your bed had been searched as thoroughly as my living room." The sheets were topsy-turvy, torn from the mattress corners, the pillows hung over the edge while the comforter draped a chair by the window.

"You're a wild woman," he said, and tossed her on the mattress. She squealed as he landed on top of her with a bounce that rocked the bed.

She fingered the leather thong out of his hair. Then she arranged his black waves to flow to his shoulders. She skimmed her palms up his chest under his shirt, luxuriating in the silky feel of his chest hair.

Before Pansy called, Tawny had wanted his touch, his kiss, his hands on her. She'd wanted him. But he'd walked away instead. Whatever had ruined his intention to kiss her wouldn't happen again. This time, she'd take charge.

She slid her hands to his shoulders and pushed until he gave in and rolled to his back. "You took me with your mouth before. Now it's my turn."

She peeped at him from under her bangs. The corner of his mouth turned down. His voice, rusty with need, deep with want, scored her flesh as it scraped over her from head to toe. "Thank you," he said. "I'd like that."

Heat flared and she bloomed open for him. She flashed on images of long, slow kisses and delicious mouth work.

Her mouth work. She could hardly wait. "I'm going to blow your mind."

7

Stack arched off the bed at the first touch of her lips on the tip of his cock. He was hotter here than anywhere else on his body. The head of his cock was smooth, so velvety Tawny wanted to dally. Her fingers danced along his shaft, playing him like a flute while she rolled the head along the bridge of her nose and across both cheeks.

She drank in the scent of Stack, musky and male. With deliberate slowness, she slid her mouth over him and down, down, down, until she felt him flex. His belly jerked in response to her liquid softness as she swirled her tongue along his shaft.

"Tawny! Some mercy," he pleaded.

She had none. And showed him the lash of her velvet tongue, the whip of her hair as she draped it around his balls and tugged. He arched again and cried out until she squeezed him at the base and held him in thrall.

In the palm of her hand.

The way he held her heart.

"If you want mercy, I'll grant you some. Come for me, Stack."

She mouthed him deeper, took him harder, wetter, sliding and moving over him, taking him to heights he'd never known. She surprised herself with how much she wanted to please him, how powerful it felt to tease him, how she eased him carefully along the path to ecstasy.

He flexed once, twice, a low moan escaping until he exploded in her mouth. He tasted hot and creamy, salty and male. He flipped her onto her back and wedged his still-throbbing cock between her legs, close, so close, but not quite inside. "I want inside. Fuck, I want to feel the heat of you, the wetness of your pussy all around me."

He slid down her body and lifted her ass, splaying her cradle wide. He was so strong! Tawny was solidly built, and he pulled and lifted her like she was a featherweight. She loved the way he made her feel feminine and wanted. To be desired this much was heady stuff, especially for a woman who'd done her best to deny that she wanted to be wanted. His hair flowed wild, silky, and moved with a life of its own as he set his mouth to her and ate her into oblivion.

His expression focused totally on her. The way his eyes slid shut as his cheeks moved with every lick and suck, proved that he loved this kind of loving. His generosity and gentle attention to detail took her closer to the edge than the physical sensation.

She took everything he gave, every slick slide of his lips, tongue, and delving fingers, until she, too, roared through an orgasm. Her personal pinnacle of wild sensation swept her up, fueled by seeing him loving her.

His cock had responded to his enticements, and while she quieted, he slipped into a condom. He dragged her to his lap and drove into her still-pulsing pussy. She wrapped her legs around his waist and seated herself over him. "Harder, Stack! I'm yours."

He rose to his knees, impaled her to the hilt, then grabbed her ass and lifted her up and down until they came together, soaring and grasping. Deeply entwined, their wracking orgasms began and ended with each other.

Three hours later, they held hands while they waited by the baggage claim for Pansy James. Stack saw her first and whistled low.

"If you ever dress like that in public, I'll know you're tired of me." The woman walking toward them sure knew how to advertise! Pansy James hadn't seen them yet, but then seeing anyone else was not on her agenda. For Pansy, it was all about *being seen*. There wasn't a male head that didn't turn her way. There wasn't a woman who didn't go on high alert. She was sex on two legs and knew it.

He clasped Tawny's hand tighter and drew her close to his side, suddenly pleased by the whacked-out clothes Tawny wore. If he saw men look at Tawny the way every red-blooded male in the building ogled Pansy, he'd be in prison for murder in twenty minutes. Probably mass murder to boot.

"I love my mother, but sensible wardrobe is an oxymoron to her."

"They'll need to mop the floor of drool when we leave."

"Hey, that's my mom you're gawking at."

"I'm not gawking, I'm saying a hallelujah." He'd heard that a man should look to the mother to see what was in store. His future with Tawny was coming straight for them. Sin in high heels. *Bring it on.* "The flight must've been on autopilot the whole time because the real pilot was back in the cabin trying to snag dinner with her."

She nudged him hard with her elbow. When he looked at her, he read doubt and nerves. She wanted this meeting to go well. She wanted Pansy to like him.

He studied the woman moving through the crowd, smiling and chatting with total strangers. Tawny's mother was a lightning rod for attention, both male and female. And she played it graciously. The woman was a natural fox. "I now understand why you're so concerned with how the world sees you."

Tawny came from a line of spectacular females: great bones; long limbs; flowing hair; wide, friendly smiles; and great teeth. Holy Mother of God, these women were to die for.

Maybe even worth killing for, he thought, as he remembered the mysterious Lenny and the vile Frank LaMotta. Had there been a love triangle gone wrong? With a woman who looked like these two James women involved, he could easily imagine two lovers fighting to the death.

When Pansy caught sight of her daughter, she moved like a lioness toward a wayward cub. No one would question the woman's love for her child. Her face turned fierce, protective, and worried.

He hoped Tawny recognized the love in her mother's gaze. He wasn't sure if she saw it, though, not the way he did.

The women hugged and kissed each other, murmuring their hellos privately. He stood back and basked in the glory of knowing them. He was the man here to take them home, much to the chagrin of several men who rushed to grab Pansy's luggage off the belt.

Dressed in a pair of low-slung short shorts that sat atop a pair of shapely legs that began with stilettoes, she wore a halter top that made it clear her breasts were all hers. Wildly tousled hair fell to her shoulders and gleamed with health and vitality, even in the harsh lighting of the airport baggage claim area.

When she spied Stack, her face lit into a smile that rose from her wide, mobile lips to her eyes. In that moment, he saw Tawny's charm, humor, and intelligence shine out of her. "You must be Stack Hamilton," she said with genuine warmth. He felt like the only man in the room.

He prayed not to be tongue-tied. Tawny would hate that, take it all wrong. "Yes, ma'am. That would be me."

Tawny hung back, a cautious look filling her gaze. He reached for her hand and tugged her close again. "I'm seeing Tawny now, even though she worked for me a while back. I had a hard road to convince her I was worth the time." He felt Tawny relax at his side and eased out a breath.

"I know," she responded with an assessing glance, "it's about time too. I knew—"

"Mom," Tawny interrupted, "we need to get moving." But relief filled her glance before she bent to pick up Pansy's carry-on bag. "There's a lot to do tonight."

A man in uniform hovered in the corner of Stack's eye. Not the pilot but a full-bird colonel. Stack went on alert, not sure why the guy lurked on the fringes of their personal space.

Tawny's gaze caught sight of him at the same time. He felt her stiffen at his side.

"Yes, we have a lot to deal with," Pansy agreed. "We'll talk in the car; then I'd like to freshen up, if that's okay. I've brought a suitcase with enough clothes for a week." She tilted her head as if to test her welcome.

"That's great, Mom!" Tawny's happiness was genuine. He knew her well enough to know when she faked enthusiasm.

Tawny finally acknowledged the colonel standing three feet behind her mother. "You have a date," she said with a warm smile. She held out her hand to shake and the colonel looked happy enough to piss himself.

"Let me introduce you," Pansy said, every bit the ingenuous beauty.

They left the colonel at the car rental desk, then headed for the short-term parking lot. When they reached the Escalade, Tawny gave her mother the front passenger seat. Pansy sat sideways to make it easier for a three-way conversation.

"I visited my mother in the home for the aged every Wednesday and Saturday," she began. "With her confused state of mind, it's possible she wouldn't have told me about other visitors."

Stack nodded. "If she had mentioned someone, would you have dismissed the information?"

Pansy sighed. "Likely. When she first moved into the home, a couple of her girlfriends would stop by, but when she started to forget who they were, it became too difficult. The visits dropped off, and eventually I was all she had. So, yes, I would have put down the news about someone else visiting as the meanderings of a lost mind."

"What about the visitor's log?" Stack asked.

"I had no reason to ask about it at the time. It's been six months, do you think they'll have the old sign-in sheets?"

"If they were in a three-ring binder, the staff likely tossed the old pages when they put the new pages in. Doesn't sound like the kind of place to have high-tech security."

"You're right. The home had friendly, helpful staff, but no one worried about visitors. They focused on keeping track of their patients. Some of them would wander off," Pansy explained.

Tawny reached from the back seat to pat her mother's shoulder. "I'm sorry I didn't come visit more often to help you out. I don't think I understood how hard it all must have been." A stab of guilt shot through her as Pansy patted her hand.

"My mother and I had some great talks, and I learned a lot about her. She was stronger than I ever knew. Quite a woman." She chuckled. "But after a while, we had the same talks over and over again." She turned and caught Tawny's eye. "I'll give you one piece of advice, honey bun."

"What's that?"

"Keep your sense of humor if I start to lose it." She tapped her temple. "And don't believe half of what I say. Heaven only knows what I'll tell you." She rolled her eyes. "But believe me when I say I had a blast doing it."

Stack coughed.

Pansy reached into her leather satchel bag and pulled out a plain manila envelope. She passed it back to Tawny, then proceeded to ask Stack pointed questions about how he planned to keep her daughter safe.

With only half an ear on the conversation, it sounded promising. Pansy liked Stack.

Tawny had made the mistake of e-mailing her a picture of him when she'd first hired on with Stack. Pansy had never stopped encouraging Tawny to pursue him. If she thought too hard about *that*, it might make her mad. Hearing her mother dismiss things like employee/employer standards and pitfalls for three years had probably encouraged Tawny's standoffish behavior. As much as Tawny wanted to believe she was an adult and mature enough to think for herself, she still harbored a rebellious daughter deep inside.

Society's standards about not messing where you live meant nothing to her mother. It was all about the man, and Pansy had taken one look at Stack and decided he was the man for Tawny.

She pulled the letter out of the envelope and tuned out the front-seat conversation.

What she read brought a tear to her eye. Loretta loved Lenny to the depths of her soul, in spite of his sleazy connections. It sounded like the feeling was mutual. Her grandparents were two people who'd found each other in a city full of sex and sin and easy money. What were the odds?

Loretta knew a lot about Lenny's business. They were ready to sneak out of Vegas with a cache of diamonds when Lenny got a call from longtime associate Frank LaMotta. Frank had just bought a new car and wanted Lenny to see it. Lenny figured he had to go, because if he didn't, Frank would guess Lenny planned to run off. Trapped, Lenny decided the safest bet was to go and play along. Frank had been evilly jealous of Lenny and loved it when he could rub Lenny's face in his success.

Lenny looked at Loretta and she knew that it might be the last time she'd see that look of love. Lenny told her to hide the diamonds and to protect their unborn child at all costs.

He left to see Frank's new Chevy and never came back.

Pregnant and terrified, Loretta took Lenny's advice. She sewed the diamonds into the bodice of her showgirl costume, praying they'd never be noticed amongst the rhinestones.

When Frank LaMotta showed up at her door a few hours later, she knew her fate was sealed with his. She tolerated his lust, hated his touch, and pretended to be glad Lenny had ditched her. If Frank ever learned about the diamonds she'd hidden, he'd kill her for including him in the plot against *the boss*, whoever that was. Loretta didn't say.

She lived out her married life with Frank, a lust-filled man who saw only Loretta's body. A man only too willing to kill to have her. A man from whom she was forced to shield her innocent daughter.

There were a few photos in the envelope, of Pansy as a baby, another of her first day of school, a picnic with family. A large square black boat of a car sat in the background.

There were no pictures of Frank.

"So you sent me the costume not knowing what was sewn into the bodice because Loretta never mentioned any of this?"

"That's right. Even in her delirium, she held on to the notion of protecting me." Pansy's voice softened. "She kept her secrets to keep me safe. There's so much that went unsaid between us. I'm sorry I was such a pain-in-the-ass kid." Pansy's sorrowful eyes connected with her daughter's.

"If the diamonds were hot before Lenny got hold of them," Stack broke in before the women washed the Escalade in tears, "and it's likely they were, then the statute of limitations ran out years ago. Not to mention we have no way of knowing where the original theft took place."

Leave it to him to stay on the investigative trail and dismiss the family angst. The man had focus.

Pansy nodded. "Which is why someone else must have visited her at the home and got some of this story from her while she was confused. They knew enough of the details to lead her toward sharing some of her secrets. Whoever it is must have decided, or been told, the costume would be left to Tawny. She's one generation removed from Frank, the source of all Loretta's troubles, so in an effort to still protect me, she left the costume to her granddaughter."

"With me living in Seattle and her still in Nevada, she hoped no one would look this far afield." The explanation seemed plausible. With a stolen cache of diamonds that no one knew existed up for grabs, it was a wonder Tawny hadn't been killed.

"We'll see what we can learn about Lenny's disappearance, but from the sound of this, we won't find much. I doubt Loretta would have filed a missing person's report under the circumstances."

Pansy agreed. "Not with his murderer climbing into bed with her."

"And her wanting to save her baby." Tawny patted her mom's shoulder, then gave it a gentle squeeze to show her support. "I'm sorry that your growing-up years were so messy."

"I could never figure out why she turned so cold when I began to develop. She wanted me out of the house and away from Frank, but she was afraid to leave. She wanted me out of Frank's reach, and he often said he'd never let her take me. I blamed myself for not being the son they wanted and looked to men for what I was missing from her. Frank was just a dark, violent mass that terrified us both."

"Any idea who would have visited your mother?" Stack asked.

"Frank had mistresses all the time. Maybe one of them?"

"But it's a man who's been watching me and going through my things."

"If one of his women had a son with Frank, he could be our guy." Pansy's voice sounded distant while she thought. Finally, a realization slipped into place in Pansy's expression. "That sounds likely." She got excited, her voice higher. "Frank came home once with a fistful of cigars and screamed that some other woman had given him what Loretta should have. Then he hit her and chased me out of the house."

"How old were you?"

"About seven, maybe eight."

"Why didn't she take the diamonds and run like hell?" Tawny wanted to know.

"Run from Frank? Not a chance. He moved up the ranks in his organization. He became more dangerous, more powerful. He had connections to the law, and he kept a tight rein on Loretta."

"If he'd killed Loretta in a fit of rage or jealousy, anything could have happened to Pansy," Stack murmured. "Loretta must have been on guard every moment."

"Frank made it plain I disappointed him. If I'd been a boy, things might have been different."

"Yeah, you'd have been a thug too," Tawny said.

Stack snorted. "Or a mob lawyer."

"He finally took notice of me when I hit fourteen or so. He pointed me out to some of the young guys who came around the house with him. Not that they hadn't noticed me already." She laughed ironically. "Now that I think about it, he may have seen some value in me after all."

Tawny's belly sank. "You don't mean . . . ?"

"Pimping me out? No, not even Frank could do that to a girl he thought was his kid. I think he would've arranged a marriage. I would've ended up with a connected husband the way my mother did." Pansy fell silent, lost in her memories.

Tawny eased back into her seat, her mind spinning. She tried to rearrange everything she thought about her mother and her grandmother. No wonder Loretta never looked for Pansy once she ran off with Tawny's father.

She was afraid her daughter might actually come back.

8

"I like him," Pansy said about Stack the minute he left them alone in the guest room. "But then, I haven't proved to be a great judge of keepers when it comes to men." She stripped to her bra and panties.

Tawny shrugged. "Knowing a good man when we find one is not a gene we James women seem to have." She threw open her mother's carry-on bag and let Pansy rummage. She pulled out a short, silky robe. "Remember Dennis? I thought he was a decent man, but he turned out to be a real jerk."

"Dennis . . ." Pansy tapped her chin. "Oh, yeah, you were in college and decided only intellectual types would do. He went on to dentistry, didn't he? Why was he a jerk?"

"I didn't tell you?" She stalled, sorry to have brought her first serious boyfriend into the moment. Pansy tied her sash and dug in for her toiletry bag.

"Aren't these regulations a pain? Who travels with a teeny, tiny bottle of shampoo?" She pulled out a plastic zippered bag that did, indeed, contain a teeny, tiny shampoo.

Just when Tawny thought they could move the conversation

along to a new topic, her mother said, "Go on, what was wrong with Dennis?"

"He liked threesomes."

Pansy froze, her hand half out of the bag, clutching a curling iron. She looked over her shoulder. "Lots of guys like them, especially with two chicks."

"It wasn't just any chick he wanted, though."

"It wasn't?"

"It was you."

That stopped Pansy cold; then she twirled and sat with a *whump* on the bed. "That's sick!" Her face twisted in dismay. "Eeeuww!"

"For about three months before he met you, I felt that Dennis was the one. Since then, I've been leery."

Pansy pouted. "I don't blame you, but seriously, honey bun, that Stack's quite a man." She opened her arms and Tawny moved into them for a long moment.

Tawny appreciated the hug, and she hugged Pansy back. "Thanks, and I'm glad you like Stack. I do too. From the first moment I saw him, in fact. I don't think I could have turned down the job he offered me, even if I wanted to. He's just so easy on the eyes, and he made me feel sorry for him within thirty seconds."

"Seriously?"

"He's so big and he looked so helpless and overwhelmed by a desk full of paperwork. His accounts were a mess and he looked desperate."

"A desperate, gorgeous man is hard to resist. And for what it's worth, sympathy is a gene we James women *do* have! To our detriment. I suspect that's why Loretta fell so hard for Lenny. And that's why I ran off with your father too. He needed me and I felt sorry for him." Tawny's father was a long-gone man who never looked back once he left.

"When did he stop needing you?"

"He never did, not really. But you needed me more. I stayed on the road with him for as long as I could, probably longer than I should have, but by the time you were ten, I could see you needed the stability of a home, a regular routine, and school. All the things your father was running from." She shrugged. "Pecker and I parted ways."

Her father's name was Percy, not the kind of name a biker told many people.

"Are you sorry?" Tawny asked, feeling a daughter's guilt at the confession. She'd always assumed Pecker didn't want them anymore.

Pansy threw her arms around her. "Aw, honey bun, that was the day I grew up. And I've been a better person ever since."

After a lot of discussion, Pansy agreed that it would be all right if she actually went on her date. She'd only half agreed to see the colonel because he'd been so adamant about only having one free night to spend with her.

"But I won't leave unless you have backup here," Pansy said with as firm a tone as she ever used.

"Would you feel better if I call in a favor and have a patrol car cruise by a couple times tonight?"

"Yes." But she looked doubtful.

"Mom, if this guy wanted to hurt me, he had lots of chances before I knew he was looking for the diamonds. For whatever it's worth, I doubt we're dealing with a vicious career criminal. Stack agrees."

Mollified when Stack called the local police and made arrangements for some extra patrols, Pansy agreed to leave them alone. With a twinkle in her eye, she called her impatient colonel.

He arrived within the hour and shared a few moments of conversation with Stack. Each man nodded and shook hands, then turned to the women. With a hug and a whisper not to wait up, Pansy left with her date, in a swirl of expensive cologne.

* * *

The next morning, with Stack's coffee brewing, Tawny took a quick shower with him. They managed to get clean without getting down and dirty, but it was tough. With the clock ticking toward the post office opening, they had no choice but to keep their hands to themselves.

The problem started when Tawny picked up a towel to use on her hair. "Need help with that?" Stack offered.

Her eyes glowed with happiness and the warmth of the look flashed an invitation. "Thanks!"

He gathered the soft cotton and told her to sit at the edge of the bed. Scooping her hair into flat plaits, he patted the shafts, squeezing and finger-combing to get most of the water out of her hair and onto the towel. He massaged her scalp gently while she leaned into his hands. When she moaned lightly, he checked the time on the bedside clock.

"We've got an hour before the post office opens," he said. He rose to his knees and glanced down the front of her body. "And Pansy didn't come home last night. The apartment's all ours."

She tilted her head to one side and he nipped the soft lobe of her ear between his teeth. She sighed and capitulated just like that. No fuss, no pretty words, nothing but his own need was enough to rouse her.

Three wasted years. Damn.

Dressed in her industrial-strength bra and a red silky thong, he had a bird's-eye view down her long, luscious body.

Heat centered in his groin as he rubbed and listened to her soft moans of pleasure. He tossed the damp towel aside.

"You're good at this," she said, "much better than a hair dryer."

"Your personal exotic slave, here to do your bidding."

She froze at his next touch. "Really? You'll do exactly what I want, when I want it?"

"Only for you," he promised. He slid around to suckle on her other ear.

"Scoot back," she said.

He did, giving her enough room to lay flat. He scooped her hair and fanned it out on the hastily made bed.

She pulled up her heels to rest on the edge of the bed and opened her legs. The aroused scent of her, the deliciously open vee of her cradle called to him. He answered and dropped his head between her open thighs, and nudged the string of her thong aside with his nose.

Delicious and ready, Tawny laughed when he speared into her with his tongue. She murmured, "Make this quick, big man, we've got somewhere to be." The sexy witch unzipped him and took his freshly filled cock in one long, open-mouthed kiss.

Both ready, both needy, they lapped and swallowed until they took each other into oblivion.

Slowly, as Stack's breathing returned to normal, the tap-tap of high heels outside the bedroom door told him of Pansy's return.

"Anyone home?" she called. "I smell coffee, so I'm guessing you've been distracted." A light, charmed chuckle drifted away as she walked past the bedroom door and headed for the kitchen.

Stack smoothed his hand down Tawny's soft belly and sighed with the rightness of having her with him in his bed, his home, his life. "I like this."

She rolled and twisted so her face leaned over his. She pecked him on the lips. "I love this with you," she said. "I never much liked oral before, but you've got a talent, big man."

"You know what they say about talent, don't you?"

"No, what?"

"It should be exploited at every opportunity."

"Well said. I agree."

He slid both hands into her hair and held her so he could

kiss her, share the tastes of themselves. He wanted more, right away, but he squeezed the soft flesh of her bottom. Gave her a light tap to roust her out of the bed. "We need to get moving. The post office will be opening just as we get there."

"Right." She rolled off his bed and he wondered if she'd want to come back once she had the diamonds. He hadn't considered that she might want to take off with the money, start somewhere fresh. A new life.

Without him.

Blindsided by the idea, he fell into a dark silence, buried in his thoughts. Life without her. He flat out didn't want to go back to living without Tawny James.

They found Pansy in the kitchen, drinking a mug of coffee, with two more steaming on the counter for Stack and Tawny.

"You look happy this morning," Tawny said through a grin. She was dressed in her shorts again, topped by a peacock blue tank top. The spaghetti straps slipped down her shoulders, and her lips were puffy from kisses, her skin rosy. Her eyes were lit by a fire Tawny recognized. "You're in love again," she said as she took one of the filled mugs.

"I, um, don't want to talk about it." But her eyes were alight with something like fear. Fear? Pansy?

Fear of men didn't compute when it came to Pansy. She was a no holds barred romantic who threw herself into new relationships with her entire being.

Stack must have noticed her underlying edginess as well. "He okay with you, Pansy? Because if he needs a lesson or two on how to treat a lady, I'd be—"

"No! No! He's wonderful! So masterful and manly." She blushed.

"Okay, I've got to sit down. If my mother's blushing, this is big." Tawny pulled out a stool at the sandwich bar and sat. "Fess up, Mom. What kind of man is this colonel?"

"Jeff's a widower who liked being married. He's a family man at heart, but his children are grown." She chucked Tawny under the chin. "Like mine. He's about to retire and he doesn't want to live out his retirement alone."

"That's a lot of information for one night," Stack commented with a grin. "Men usually hold some of that stuff back." He sipped his coffee and looked at Tawny with a dark focus that made her wonder what thoughts were rolling around in his head.

But this conversation was about her mother and the colonel. "You like him. A lot." The signs were clear as glass, Pansy was deeply interested.

Pansy nodded. "He's funny and smart, and he's here to look at some boats. He wants to sail to Mexico and Alaska, and I didn't sleep with him." The last part came out all in a rush.

"TMI, Pansy," Stack commented. "Tawny, I'll wait for you downstairs, but we've got to go. We're behind schedule."

"And whose fault is that?" she said tartly.

Pansy looked wide-eyed.

Stack hummed in his throat. "We'll continue this discussion later." He looked at Pansy. "Would you like to come with us to get the package from the post office?"

"Absolutely. And Jeff will be there incognito for backup."

Tawny rolled her eyes. "Stack's arranged for his own backup. Right?"

"I told him last night a military man could come in handy." So that's what they'd been talking quietly about. Protecting the women. Tawny rolled her eyes but felt the warmth of their concern.

Stack opened his cell phone, hit a button, and headed out the door. From the sound of his fading conversation, he was being filled in on some background information.

Pansy collected their mugs and put them in the sink. "I want you to get to know Jeff, Tawny. I like him so much. I haven't laughed as much with a man in my whole life."

"Laughing's good," she said on the way out the door, thinking of Stack.

Pansy caught up on the landing. "What will you do with the diamonds, honey bun?" she asked on the way down the stairs.

Tawny nearly stumbled. "I'm not sure. I haven't thought that far ahead."

Her mother tapped her shoulder. "Well, it's time."

9

On the way to the post office, Stack recited what he'd heard on the phone. He'd set an operative to work on Lenny's disappearance. This time, Pansy had insisted Tawny take the front seat.

"The last known sighting of Lenny Tucco seems to be an interview he had with the Las Vegas police. He was questioned with regards to their investigation of a theft of jewelry from a private home. It was a very successful break and enter. The thieves got away with the wife's jewelry case that contained over twenty thousand dollars' worth of necklaces, bracelets, and earrings. All diamonds. Her husband was a jeweler, so she had the best."

"So it wasn't armed robbery?" Pansy asked.

"No, in fact, no one was home at the time. The wife had apparently picked up her collection from her husband's store vault to wear for a family wedding. They were out at the rehearsal dinner the night before."

"Someone knew the jewelry would be there that night," Tawny suggested.

"Absolutely," Stack said. "The wedding was a somewhat connected event."

"Connected?"

"A mobster acquaintance or business partner of the jeweler was invited to the wedding. So it's possible he sent Lenny to the jeweler's house."

Pansy nodded. "If Lenny worked for this mobster, it could be that Lenny broke into the house and took the case and never handed it over to his boss?"

"Possible. Not likely to ever get the real truth now."

"If he did, he was pretty ballsy."

"Or stupid," Tawny said.

"Agreed on both counts," Stack said with a chuckle. "But remember, he was in love with a pregnant Loretta. Maybe he wanted a fresh start with her. Could be he wanted out of the life."

"For love," Tawny said. Stack reached over and clasped Tawny's hand in his.

"Love can make men do stupid things to get what they want."

He pulled into the parking lot of the post office and found a spot near the door. It was a tight squeeze because he was next to a huge black car. Large and boxy, the car was clearly a collector's favorite.

"Look," Pansy said from the back seat. "It's a sixty-four Chevy. Frank had one just like it."

"I saw a picture of it. You were at a picnic with Loretta. That car stood in the background." Tawny jumped down from the passenger seat and walked toward the post office door. They'd missed the opening by five minutes, but to her mind, those five minutes had been well spent back on Stack's bed.

She turned to see what was taking Stack so long to catch up with her.

He was staring into the Chevy, like a love-struck fool. Men, they couldn't resist gawking at their dream cars. She liked old cars as much as the next person, but she had business inside.

She opened the door and walked in. There were a couple of other people ahead of her, though the doors had only just opened. There was an old lady who needed to mail a package. A birthday gift, she explained to the clerk.

The other clerk was reading a pile of identification cards that a man had handed over. "I swear!" he was saying. "This is my sister. She's sick and can't come in."

The conversation reminded her that she would need to produce photo identification. She dug through her bag for her wallet.

Pansy stepped up beside her and gasped.

"What?" Tawny looked at her.

Her mother stared hard at the guy harassing the clerk. "It—he—looks like Frank! Just like Frank." Pansy grabbed her arm. "Tawny, that car!" she whispered tensely. "It doesn't just look like Frank's, it *is* Frank's."

"But Stack said he saw a rental car at my place."

"I guess he wanted to switch cars to confuse you if you noticed him." Pansy shrugged. "I'm sure it's Frank's car. When he died it went to a stranger. The guy went to the law firm, proved he was the one named in the will. Loretta woke up one morning and the car was gone. She was so happy to have it out of the driveway, she laughed like a loon."

The man turned, caught sight of Tawny and Pansy, and went red in the face. He stalked toward them, slamming his shoulder into Pansy's on the way by. She had to take a step back to keep from falling. He slammed out the door and stepped straight into Stack and Jeff.

Both men slipped their arms under the stranger's armpits and lifted him off the ground. His feet dangled three inches above the concrete.

They sidestepped until they were out of view of the gawking onlookers and postal clerks.

Pansy's eyes went wide as she stared into Tawny's. "We have to get my package. Now," Tawny said.

She stepped up to the counter, produced her identification, and received the package her mother had sent. The clerk gave her license photo a good check, then allowed her to sign for receipt of the package.

"Guess you saw that guy trying to steal it out from under you, huh?" the clerk said with a nod toward the door.

"Yes, and my friend noticed too. We'll go see what the police have to say about it." She pulled out her phone and pretended to place a call as she and Pansy dashed back outside.

The package weighed little compared with the heavy silence that waited for them. Three men glared at each other, each one ready to spring if one wrong move was made. "Meet Frank LaMotta Junior," Stack said with a sneer.

Jeff had the man's wallet open and shoved it back at him. Frank Junior grabbed it and jammed it into his jacket pocket.

"You're Frank's son!" Pansy demanded, her voice fierce and protective. Tawny gaped at her. Her mother was never fierce; she usually kept her cool. "And what do you mean going through my daughter's belongings?"

The man with his back to the wall swiveled his head and leveled a malevolent gaze at her. Mockery filled his expression. "That's right! I'm your brother."

He flicked his eyes down Pansy and Tawny's bodies in a dismissive glance. They stalled when he reached the package Tawny had tucked under her arm. "That's mine!" he said, and tried to snatch it.

Stack moved fast as a snake and had Frank's arm in a viselike grip before he could move a fraction.

Jeff was a second behind Stack and Pansy gasped. She went

to stand beside her new man, obviously grateful for his presence.

Stack nodded to the right toward a quiet area of the parking lot. "Let's move this to the end of the building."

"That's Frank LaMotta's car," Pansy said.

"My father left it to me."

Pansy grinned. "Good for you because he wasn't my father. And that's a huge relief."

"What?" The man stuttered. "What do you mean he wasn't your old man?" He clenched his fists, but Stack slapped a hand on his shoulder, gave him a squeeze, and kept him walking.

"Loretta was already pregnant when they hooked up."

"That bitch passed you off?" His eyes burned with rage.

Angry heat filled Pansy's eyes, and Tawny read the signs the way any daughter would. "You want to be careful how you malign my grandmother," she said. "Loretta had her faults, but she did what she had to. She was a strong woman married to a difficult man."

The sneer on Frank's son's face made a mockery of Tawny's words.

"My mother should have been his wife." He slapped his chest. "I'm Frank Junior!" He turned red in the face and Tawny had a glimpse of Frank. Her belly clenched in fear.

But he wasn't finished yet. "My mother loved that son of a bitch until he treated us like garbage. And for what? She got tired of waiting for him to leave Loretta. When she tried to leave him, he went crazy, slammed her around something awful. After that, he didn't give a shit. Passed her around like a whore." The bitterness, the images broke Tawny's ice-hard barriers.

"Frank LaMotta was an evil, evil man," Pansy muttered, deep in her own memories. She shivered and Jeff put his arm around her.

"I was his son and all I got was his lousy, stinkin' car."

Jeff cleared his throat. "Hey, it's a beauty. If you hate it so much, why is it so cherry?"

"Investment," Frank Junior muttered, putting the lie to his earlier statement. He was glad and proud to have Frank LaMotta's Chevy. Maybe it was the only thing Frank ever gave him. "I gotta boy I want to hand it down to. He's sixteen next year."

Pansy said, "You're welcome to it, Frank. My mother hated that car. Said it gave her a bad vibe whenever she climbed into it. She refused to drive the thing."

All five of them turned and stared at the heavy black Chevrolet. An Impala SS, the long square box of a car, was a 1964 version of a Super Sport. But the shine gleamed sultry black from the loving attention Frank and then his son had given it.

"Frank loved that car," Pansy muttered. "I remember stretching out in the back seat. It was so long I couldn't reach from side to side until I was about ten." Her voice sounded far away while she stared.

"I remember him taking us for ice cream in it," Frank broke in. "Once I let the cone drip on the back of the front seat and he cuffed me a good one." His hand stole up to cup his ear in memory. "Last time he ever took me with them."

Pansy eyed him with sympathy. "I don't think he liked kids, period. I thought he hated me because I was a girl."

"He hated me because I was his bastard. But maybe he was pissed because I looked like him but never wanted to act like him. Never wanted to be anything like him." He hung his head and studied his shoes. "I never would have hurt anyone to get those diamonds. I just want my son and daughter to have a chance at college, you know? When I found out about the diamond heist, I kind of lost it. One more secret. One more thing he wouldn't give me."

"If it means anything to you, he didn't die easy," Pansy offered. "It was painful and he was alone. Loretta didn't care enough to go."

Frank nodded. "My mother wouldn't go either. If there's any justice, he's burning in hell."

Tawny's eyes met Stack's and flashed him a message. Stack nodded and relaxed his guard. Frank was no threat, not anymore.

"Your father never knew about the diamonds." Tawny explained that Loretta and Lenny planned to run away together, that Lenny and Frank had gone for a drive and only Frank returned.

Frank Junior spun, slammed his hands to his head, agonized. "Maybe we should take that car out to the desert and burn her to the ground. I knew my old man was a bastard, but a murderer?" He looked at the car again and horror filled his features. "Burning it sounds about right."

Pansy put her arms around him in communion. She whispered words no one else heard, but eventually Frank nodded in agreement.

Whatever passed between them, Frank calmed. His rigid stance eased. Tawny ended their painful private conversation with a buss on his cheek.

They were done.

10

Back at Stack's apartment, Tawny and Pansy sat on his bed, with Loretta's showgirl costume laid out between them. "Here goes," Tawny said, and stripped out of her bra.

Pansy lifted the white cotton contraption. "Aren't you taking this a bit far? This looks more like a straitjacket than a desire for support."

Heat rose in Tawny's cheeks. "Stack doesn't seem to mind it."

Pansy snorted. "You can find a bra that's pretty and supportive. We'll go shopping."

Tawny felt an eye roll coming on but stopped the childish gesture. "The last time we went bra shopping together I was eleven." And in full eye-roll mode.

"I remember, now try this on." And she handed Tawny Loretta's diamond-studded costume. The heavy top glittered in the light.

She stood in front of Stack's dresser mirror and gasped. It fit perfectly. Pansy's eyes glittered as she held Tawny's hair up in a mimic of Loretta's upswept beehive. It seemed as if the three of them were together, all young, lovely, and connected in a way they'd never been before.

"She loved you more than her own life," Tawny said.

"I know that now." Pansy smiled and gazed into the mirror at their reflection. "I told Frank Junior that by the time that car goes to his son, all the evil would be cleansed. Now that we all know the truth, there's no reason to hold on to the old feelings."

"He wants to give his son and daughter an education," Tawny said. She leaned in to inspect the bodice properly. She counted at least six good-sized diamonds. "I'm going to sell these and split the money with him. How would you feel about that?"

"I'd feel that you were a kind and generous woman, and a gesture like that would wipe out a lot of the past ugliness. Giving two innocent children an education could never be wrong."

"Something good will come out of that long drive into the desert."

Stack shut off the ignition and removed the key. He and Tawny were back from dropping Pansy to spend the day with Jeff, ostensibly to look at boats. Stack had his doubts they'd ever get out of Jeff's hotel room.

"I want to know this and I'll ask it only once." Tawny's hand sat on his thigh, burning a hole through to his flesh. "If this is not what you want," he ground out, "I mean, longer term, I need to know now."

His gut contracted as she slid her hand to his bulging cock. "Long term?"

Without meaning to, his thighs spread so she could stroke and cup him more fully. His jeans nearly cut off the circulation to his legs. "Right now, long term apparently means holding on long enough to get my fly open."

Something about her using a question to answer a question

drilled a hole into his head. His bloodless brain still had enough function left to know this was a loaded moment. He lifted her hand from his bulging, straining cock.

It nearly killed him. "Tawny, we need to get out of this truck. Now." He opened the door and the cab light illuminated her flushed, beautiful, distressed face. He lifted his hand to her face and let his fingertips trail from her temple to her chin. He tilted her head gently.

Her lips parted, her breath slowed, her eyelids drooped.

If he kissed her, he'd be gone. He'd fall into the essence of Tawny. An essence that would grab on and not let go. He'd be lost to himself and given to her.

He kissed her anyway.

By the time they got inside the lower door, he had her against the wall, tight. Her mouth tasted better than ever before, her hands moved faster, her thighs opened at the first brush of his hips. No one could imagine that the woman in sack dresses was a wild cat.

He pulled back, stared into her glassy, come-fuck-me gaze, and said, "Why did you run off like that? You quit me, you moved. You fucking disappeared!" He wanted to pull back completely, get his cock out of touching range, but his hips wouldn't obey.

So he pressed hard instead.

She squirmed against him, sending his arousal through the roof. "I saw the way you looked at me and figured I'd killed our friendship. My stupid jealousy about that woman in your office ruined everything!"

It was more than that, he figured. It had to be. Whatever had driven Tawny away had been deep. Rooted down where her reactions were fight or flight. She'd chosen to fight by showing him her body, got scared, and her flight response kicked in. Women didn't usually light out that way when they wanted a guy.

He should know. He'd been aimed at by some of the best heat-seeking missiles ever created by woman.

Tawny was different. Always had been. Always would be.

And with any luck at all, he'd be there to live with it.

His next thought threw him against the other wall. He pressed his shoulder blades hard into the drywall. Crap, he loved her!

Wanted her.

Goddamn it. He even figured he needed her.

"Stack? What's going on?"

"Nothing. We've got to get to a bed. Right now."

She sucked her lower lip into her mouth, then headed up the stairs at a dead run.

He had to move slower because his cock was throbbing to the point of pain.

Each step was agony, but he went as fast as the heavy throb allowed. She waited at the top, doing some kind of little bouncy thing. Her ankles and knees were bobbing.

"I hope that bounce means you're as excited as I am."

She grabbed his ears and slammed her mouth against his.

He fumbled in his pocket for his keys, managed to get them inside, and kicked the door shut.

His jeans were undone and her dress was up to her waist before he knew what was happening. Once this woman got going, she was fast as a train.

His kind of woman.

Thank God he liked her so much, he planned to have her in his life a long time.

"Forever," he said against her lips.

"What?"

"Condoms. Bedroom. Now." He broke free, stepped out of his jeans, and lifted her into his arms. She gave a girly whoop, grabbed on to his neck, and let him carry her through the living room and down onto the bed.

He moved all over her, sliding and lifting and moving until they were both naked and needy. She helped as much as he'd let her and then settled back on the bed so he could look his fill.

She didn't plan to take the money from the diamonds and run. She planned to stay here, near him. That had to mean something. "I love you, Tawny."

The words hung between them, bald, flat. But he felt free, complete, now that he'd said them.

He waited, expecting some reaction other than the one he was getting. Tawny chewed her lip, her eyes wide. "Why?" she asked, her voice quiet, hesitant.

Suddenly, everything fell into place. Everything. "I love you not because you're the most spectacular woman I've ever seen. Not because you have long, shapely legs, perfect calves, and long, lean thighs." He slipped his hands to the flare of her hips. "Not because your waist is small, your belly's flat and soft. Not because you have the barest shadow of ribs and full, round breasts with dark strawberry nipples. Do you have any idea how much you make my mouth water?" But he didn't give her time to answer. "You're full, luscious, long, and all woman. I want all of that, Tawny. In my bed, in my life. I want you to bear my children, to live with me when we're old and getting a little off the wall." He grinned and tapped his temple the way Pansy had.

She went to speak, her eyes full of fear and some kind of excitement he was too wound up to read. He held up his hand to forestall any questions.

"I'm not done. I love your body, Tawny. Don't ever doubt that. But I've missed you so much. You. The woman inside." He shrugged. "It's simple, I guess. I love you. Just you."

He finally stopped, afraid that he'd missed something she needed to hear. But he tracked back and couldn't see anything he might have said differently.

If she took off now, she'd be lost to him for good.

"You're scaring me here, Tawny. You could say something now."

She stopped his mouth with a fingertip against his lips.

"You want children?"

He nodded.

She bit her lip. "So do I. More than one, please."

He was on her then, fully, deeply engaged in every slick, sliding part of her. He scooped her hips up to meet his, held her close, and let the naked tip of his cock slide in. "Let's start now."

The slick, wet feel of her sheathing him made him shudder. "Tell me, Tawny. I need to know."

"I love you, Stack. I always have."

Body By Gibson

1

Mariel Gibson sat in her usual seat in the corner of the teacher's lounge. She flipped to the arts and culture section of the football coach's copy of the newspaper. An announcement caught her attention, and as she leaned in closer to read it, her shoulders pulled tight and a light sweat broke out on her forehead. A competition for artists. One of the judges was Nigel Withers. *Rat bastard.*

She took a surreptitious glance around the lounge. No one watched her, they never did. In a sports-mad high school full of jocks, mousy Mariel never attracted attention.

Without so much as a niggle of guilt, she tore the page out of the super jock's paper and folded it neatly into quarters, then eighths. She doubted the strutting jockstrap would ever notice the arts and culture page missing. Slipping the square of paper into the front pocket of her denim jumper, she stood and headed into the ladies' room. A splash of cool water on her neck and wrists calmed her. A competition! Dare she enter?

Nigel Withers. The idea of facing him in such a public forum made her belly roll in dread. She lowered her head to watch the faucet drip into the sink and remembered how he'd sliced her to ribbons. Cut out her heart. Stole the love of her life!

Rat bastard.

She'd suffered for three years because of him. She turned on the cold water again and shoved her wrists under the stream in a bid to regain her sanity. If not her sanity, then at least her good sense.

But still, the chance to prove that she was better than mediocre didn't come along every day. *Mediocre.* Was there an uglier word? She doubted it. A do nothing, says nothing word that killed her artistic soul. After all, there was only so much *bland* to go around, and she'd had more than her share.

It would have been better if he'd *hated* her work. Then she would have known she'd created some kind of emotional response. But mediocre? Arrgh!

Just to add salt to the wound, the pompous ass had leered at her breasts. "I often tell artists they have a good hand, but you, my dear, could do better with your mouth."

The pig.

He'd pinched her cheeks to make an O of her lips. Nothing hurt but her pride. She'd slapped his hand away in a reflexive motion and shoved her canvases back into her portfolio.

He wore an expression that said being serviced was his due. After all, he owned one of the city's most prestigious art galleries. He said, calmly and cooly, that his word could make her career, bring her art the attention she hoped for. And for one brief second she wanted, really wanted to prove to her family that she could make a living with her talent.

Hearing him, wanting what he offered, she had the sickening sense that if she refused him, she would never muster enough courage to show her work to anyone again. Nigel Withers hadn't hurt her physically, but her creative spirit shriveled.

"You want me to—you hate my paintings and you want me

to—" She was near breathless with shock, needing to understand.

"Hate your paintings?" He looked at his well-buffed nails. "No, you misunderstand, your canvases are too mediocre to hate. They're beige, lifeless." And then he dived in for the kill. "There isn't enough talent on those canvases to cause a reaction."

She ran out, devastated, her movements stiff and awkward.

Three years later, she still suspected he was right. She lifted her head and stared into the mirror. She'd let that rat bastard ruin the last three years of her life. But she refused to let him ruin the rest of it.

The fire of determination filled her eyes and she straightened. She would enter this competition for better or worse, and would learn the truth.

Could she live with a confirmation that she would never be more, be better, than a wannabe? Yes, because at least she could move on with the other areas of her life. She could say she'd given it one more shot and done her best.

She gathered the tattered remnants of her pride and turned the dripping water faucet off tight.

She had to face Nigel Withers again, or she'd be stuck in this stasis forever. The thought was not to be borne.

Two hours later, she sat in her car inside her garage with one foot on the floor and the other still inside the car. Her car keys filled one hand and her briefcase sat on her lap. She'd been sitting there for three full minutes, frozen in excited fear.

She was too rattled to think clearly. Rattled. Exhilarated! Terrified!

A glance in the rearview mirror told her she looked a mess. Her eyes were bright, her cheeks pink, she had a fine sheen across her forehead. If she didn't know better, she'd think she'd just been having sex. Great sex. Hot sex.

Hah! Like she even remembered the last time she'd had sex

when she wasn't alone. She let her head fall back on the head-rest, closed her eyes, and allowed her mind to wander to Danny.

Danny Glenn. Her carpenter.

He would finish building the deck soon; then he'd move on to a new job somewhere else. For six months, he had been coming to her house, working on various renovations. For six months, she had been running out of batteries once a week. Nice, but not enough to keep the man off her mind.

It was one thing to try to show Nigel Withers that she was an artist with merit, it was quite another to tempt Danny into seeing her as desirable.

Maybe the two were connected. The stereotype of an artistic woman was a free spirit, flamboyant and confident. A sexual being, ready to explore her boundaries.

Mariel the mousy high-school art teacher exploring her sexuality? Oh, please. The jocks at the school would have a field day with that idea.

Still, if she managed to seduce Danny, then she'd feel much more confident about this competition. She could face Nigel Withers without blinking. She'd know that even if she wasn't the artist she hoped to be, that at least she'd discovered herself as a woman. Maybe she could become a free spirit. Maybe she could be flamboyant and paint her nails black and dye her hair green.

So, she now had two ways to seize control of her life. The first plan was to get with Danny Glenn, to gain the confidence to face the rat bastard, Nigel Withers. Her belly clenched. And if Danny didn't take the bait? If he laughed at her awkward moves?

In her dreams, she was never awkward. What she needed to do was simple. She needed to think like Jayne. Jayne never shied away from hot, sexy men or hot, sexy behavior.

She closed her eyes and brought an image of Danny into her

mind. The man was a perfect specimen. Sun-bleached brown hair, wide shoulders, long, lean legs, and forearms that made her drool.

Some men knew they were gorgeous and played it up, but other men just *were*. He didn't have a clue how he affected her; he never would unless she showed him. Talk about terror, her heart palpitated to think about showing Danny her wild side when she wasn't even sure she had one.

The first thing to do was to break with her after-school routine. In her mind, she walked into her bedroom for a change of clothes. But what to wear for a seduction when her closet was full of coverup clothes.

Dig deeper, Mariel. There must be something that screams sex.

Anything?

Full cotton panties. Heavy-duty bras. The mental list continued with long skirts and wait, in the back of her closet, a short, tight skirt that Jayne had bought her. A gift for when they went out clubbing. But Mariel had always had a reason not to go.

The cool air of the garage chilled her as she still sat like a dead stump. Could she do this? She had to. Daydreaming in the garage would get her nowhere. And she wanted Danny. If she didn't have the nerve to go after him, how could she ever enter this competition and show Withers how wrong he'd been?

If that smarmy blowhard Nigel Withers could make her feel inferior, a rejection from Danny would flat out kill her. The last smidgeon of self-esteem she had would disintegrate.

She'd be a dried up, lonely woman trapped teaching art class in a football-crazed high school forever. In a sea of testosterone-laden jocks, she was an island. A completely deserted island, artistically and sexually.

A silent scream filled her head at the idea.

She forced herself to climb out of the car and walk through

the entrance door to the mud room. For a panicked moment, she yearned for her comfortable routine. But no!

She turned into her bedroom, then immediately stripped off her clothes. Step one: In her bra and panties, Mariel dug into her closet. In the back, exactly where she remembered, was the skirt.

She tugged it on. Black, tight, it showed off her butt to perfection. It also showed her panty lines. Off they came, with a shock of cool air against her pussy. She had a pair of slim heeled pumps in her shoe tray. Not stilettoes, but they were pretty just the same. And they were purple! Not mauve or lilac. Purple.

She bent over at the waist to find them. More air hit her slit, reminding her that if this didn't work, she'd be mortified. But she couldn't think of failure. She slipped on the pumps and examined the effect in the mirror. They thinned out her ankles and made her legs look long and shapely.

So, halfway there.

Her bra looked dingy in this light, so she slipped it off. Her breasts were full enough to bob lightly when she walked. Her hair was just long enough to brush her nipples, and they rose in response to the light, swishy feel.

She turned to view her backside. Not bad. Her ass was high and full, her waist narrow. Trailing her hand up the back of her thigh, she exposed the plump, round flesh of her right butt cheek.

Still holding her skirt high on her hip, she turned to face front again. Her dark red curls peeped out and she combed her fingers through the hair with light, sensuous tugs. Blood rushed to respond and her belly felt heavy with need.

Her pussy moistened, ready for the vibrations that would give her relief. But not today. She refused to use any more batteries in the pursuit of pleasure. Not until she'd at least taken a shot at Danny Glenn.

Now, what top to wear?

If only she had the nerve to walk out to her kitchen like this. She cupped her breasts, tightening the fall of hair across her nipples. She opened her stance, the skirt still hitched up to expose her pubic hair, while she cupped and squeezed her breasts.

No bra, she decided. She slicked her fingers over her slit, gathered some of the moisture there, then swiped it across her neck. She was brave, she was bold. She was determined.

The skirt was black, the shoes purple. She'd bought them to match a silk camisole she'd worn once. Digging it out of the back of her lingerie drawer, she kept up a steady stream of affirmations. You can do this, you can, you can!

You will!

Dressed and primed, she took a calming breath and left the safety of her room. She crept along the hall toward the kitchen. Her appearance dressed like this would shock Danny, she was sure. But shock and excite him enough to respond?

But how to act? She couldn't just walk out on the deck and lift her skirt. No. Not even Jayne would behave that blatantly.

No, she'd act the way she did every day. The idea of using her routine while staying bold and brave eased her way along the hall.

Tea, she'd make her usual cup, call Jayne the way she always did. Tell her friend about the competition and about her decision to be bold. Bold and brave.

It was a whole new Mariel who walked toward her kitchen. She only hoped she wasn't cut off at the knees once she stepped out onto the deck to see Danny.

Just like usual. Just like never before.

2

———————

Danny Glenn had wanted Mariel Gibson for months. Not at first glance, but she'd grown on him slowly. First, she'd laid a foundation built on intelligence. Next, she'd framed herself in humor and wit. After that, she'd been sheathed by shy glances and pink blushes that turned him into a house of lust and need.

At least, he figured it was lust. After his divorce, any time he'd wanted a woman this much, he'd burned up and burned out pretty quick. But those women had been different. He'd started out wanting their bodies first. He hadn't taken time to get to know them the way he'd taken note of Mariel's personality.

Immediately after his marriage ended, he'd been pretty busy fucking every woman he got his hands on. He'd explored every option available to a fully heterosexual male. It had been fun and easy, but eventually, empty.

And then he'd walked into Mariel Gibson's house. She'd smiled and drawn him in with the light of achievement in her eyes. Not many single women bought houses on their own. She explained her dreams of renovating the house to suit herself.

Her excitement had been contagious, and her desire to include him in her vision had been infectious.

They'd argued over points of design, over structure and form, but in the end, they'd compromised. Or he damn well figured out a way to incorporate what she wanted.

She was challenging and bright and decisive, and he liked her. Every day since then, he looked forward to these next golden moments when she checked on his progress for the day. After the kitchen job, he'd been relieved when she'd called him back for the built-in shelves. Now, it was the deck. But he was more than half done and the end loomed like an ax over his neck.

He'd heard her drive into the garage. But she seemed to be taking an extra long time to show up in the kitchen. She was a creature of habit, so any moment she'd walk into her kitchen and put the kettle on to boil. That done, she would call her friend Jayne. While chatting, she'd flip through her mail.

All the while, she'd be framed by the kitchen window as she glanced outside at him. Sometimes he would catch her eye and hold it, wishing like hell that she'd break with routine and step outside without her mug of tea clasped like a shield in front of her chest.

But she never changed a step. Never. If he was lucky and the sun was shining and she wasn't too cold or too warm or too shy, she would hang out for a couple of minutes and talk about her day. Small talk, mostly, but he loved that she shared the time with him. He'd hoped for a while that she wanted him to make a move, but she was quick to back away. He'd decided to wait for a time when there could be no mistake.

If he didn't see a chance soon, he'd call her in a week or two. He doubted she was dating, because she cooked dinner for one every night. No men ever stopped by, and he'd never heard her talk to anyone but Jayne on the phone.

He checked the time. Mariel was fifteen minutes behind

schedule today. Something was up. He heard the clatter of the kettle before he saw her, but when he looked up to catch her eye, he dropped his hammer.

His throat went dry when he saw the skimpy top she wore. Her lustrous hair covered her nipples. Her breasts moved fluidly under the deep purple silk. No bra. His time had run out. She was dressed for a date. With another guy.

He couldn't drag his eyes from her. Some other man would run his hands across her chest tonight. Some other man would kiss her neck, her lips, and maybe more.

Right on cue, she picked up her phone and dialed her friend Jayne. But Mariel's movements were jerky, her voice excited as she began her conversation. He picked up his hammer and gave her a wave through the kitchen window.

She waved back. A brief flash of her hand while her eyes caught on his and held.

Not for long, though, and never for long enough.

Today, something had her so excited she was bouncing on her toes. Which was great, because the movement made her breasts jiggle. She couldn't be aware of that, though. Couldn't be aware that every smooth undulation of her heavy flesh was a stroke on his burgeoning cock.

He had it bad for her. So bad.

He moved closer to the window in a shameless need to catch some idea of what had happened to make her look this wired.

"I would need to find a man, Jayne," she was saying. "A hot body. He's got to be firm, muscular, but not steroid huge."

Dressed like that, she'd have a man in record time. Danny had no compunction about eavesdropping. Any red-blooded male would sit up and take notice if a woman like Mariel needed a guy with a hot body. His prick sang hallelujah.

Every day, Mariel and her friend Jayne talked about a lot of stuff. Mostly their conversations revolved around Mariel explaining why she couldn't, wouldn't, shouldn't do something.

The majority of her excuses were lame. The woman needed to shake things up.

Clearly, today was the day she'd chosen to shake. One look at her flushed cheeks, her bright eyes, and Danny wanted to be the man she needed, for whatever reason.

He would do whatever she needed him to do. He would be whatever she needed him to be. Mariel was hot as a rocket, compact and tight, ready to launch. And God he wanted to catch her!

Today's talk about needing a body was definitely not the girlfriends' usual conversation. This was crazy different. Her voice was wired with excitement, her tone vibrant and husky. If he didn't know better, he'd think she was on the brink of doing something wild.

He was more than happy to provide the body she wanted, but he needed more details. So, he held the nail in place and froze with his hammer raised. If she looked outside, she'd think he was lining up the nail head.

While what he wanted was to drop his hammer, walk into the kitchen, and nail *her*, on the counter. Hard. Deep between her thighs. His cock rose to attention, with a gimme, gimme, gimme wail that made his teeth clench.

These last few weeks, he'd learned to work around an erection. But lately, it was next to impossible. His balls were blue by the end of the day, and his hips ached for want of her.

Mariel's voice went silent while she listened to her friend. Jayne was a hot blonde Danny had seen a couple times. More blatantly sexual than Mariel, but much happier too. Jayne had the look of a woman getting laid and loving it.

He hammered a couple more nails while Mariel moved away from the window. Her kettle whistled. The signal that any minute now she would step outside and hold on to her mug of tea with both hands. Her wide eyes would flick down his body while her sexy hands with the long, slim fingers and the clear polish on her nails held her mug close to her chest. He loved the way Mariel's breath caught when she talked to him. Her beautiful blue eyes went foggy when she looked at him.

But just as he would gather his wits long enough to think about making a move, she'd skitter away, back into the house, and the chance was lost.

He couldn't get enough of watching her, wondering about the slope of her breasts, the scent of her skin, the way she'd pant in orgasm. Oh, yeah, he had it bad for her.

If only she would step outside without that mug in her hands. He could brush her fingers when she pointed to something. He was tired of standing close to catch her scent. He wanted to touch the small of her back, lean in close when he pointed out the work he'd done. He wanted to know that if he kissed her, she'd kiss him back. He wanted to feel the sunshine of promise in her eyes when he needed to gather her close and hold on.

When he'd first come to work for her, he hadn't seen what he saw in her now. She was quiet, cool, aloof. She wore a lot of beige and other bland colors. She spoke softly and listened attentively. But today, with her chest covered in purple silk, her skin glowed. Her shoulders were lovely. He was tired of knobby bones sticking out. A woman's skeleton belonged under the skin, not poking up through it.

She turned away and continued to chat with Jayne while she made her tea and gathered the makings for salad. He couldn't hear her now. She'd lowered her voice.

Mariel gave the impression of being a pushover or too gentle for her own good. But six months into the client-contractor relationship, he knew she was no pushover. When they discussed the plans for a renovation, she stated her desire clearly, even if it clashed with his suggestions. She never hesitated to praise him when the plan came together the way she'd envisioned.

She admitted when she was wrong too.

She was bright, assertive when she needed to be, and fascinated him because she hid more than she revealed the longer he knew her.

He'd built the shelves that now housed her flat-screen television, some books, and a shitload of family photos. Every person in the pictures looked uptight and prim. Any shots that included Mariel showed her standing off to the side with her arms crossed.

He figured she held herself in a lot. Like if she ever let loose, she'd go so crazy she'd never come back.

And now, she needed a man with a hard body. If he had anything to say about it, she wouldn't look any farther than right here.

If he didn't make his move soon, his chances to engage the serious Mariel Gibson in anything more than a conversation about his invoice would slip away.

He could show up at her door next week with a bunch of flowers, but with her dressed for a date tonight, next week would be too late.

She was still on the phone, her voice soft and urgent. In his peripheral vision, he saw her snug the phone tight between her shoulder and ear. When she moved to stand in front of the open window again, he leaned in to hear.

"No, not a body builder," she said. "Someone with a more natural-looking body." Her head lifted as if she knew he was standing five feet away, outside the window listening.

He turned to stare back at her, caught her look, and grinned when her eyes widened. Hot damn. Mariel was like a tentative deer, delicate in feature, graceful in her movement, but strong and lithe. She could bound away at a moment's notice, never to be seen again.

She spoke into the phone. "With Nigel Withers judging I won't have a prayer of winning, but I need to do this. I need to try. I can't believe he would deign to show up at a competition like this. I wonder what he hopes to accomplish?"

Danny had no idea what she was talking about, but her eyes never left him. He'd slipped off his T-shirt an hour ago. With her eyes on him, he ran his hand down his chest and stared right back. A crude impulse caught his mind, but he let it go. If Mariel was the kind of woman to respond to crudity, he'd know it by now. Hell, he'd have been in her bed already.

She was far too skittish and would run like hell if he was blatant about what he wanted. She was cautious. He had to follow her lead.

His chest was slick with fresh perspiration. This was the worst thing about working as a carpenter and the main reason he'd been frustrated all this time. She was a lady, and he didn't think she'd want down and dirty with a guy who smelled like he'd been hammering nails all day. Tomorrow, he'd watch the clock better and freshen up before she got home.

He grabbed his T-shirt from on top of his lunch cooler and swiped slowly at the damp on his chest hair, never taking his eyes from the woman in the kitchen window. She bit her lip but didn't look away. Today, she played at being bold, and he wondered, no, hoped, it would last long enough for him to make a move.

He slid his balled-up T-shirt down to his belly.

Mariel dropped the phone.

Danny felt the joy of quiet victory while she cursed softly and grabbed the phone again. "Jayne, are you there? Sorry, I got distracted and dropped the phone." Silence while she listened. "Yes, he's here."

Hell, yes! Jayne had asked about him. Mariel turned her back to the window. He couldn't hear what she said next. *Game over.*

He lined up the nail head one more time. Damn deck would never be built if he kept this up. His cock throbbed when he landed two perfect blows and the nail disappeared into the cedar.

He'd need shock absorbers on his balls if she kept staring at him while he worked. He set another nail, hammered it home, while the pounding made his mind go to sex all over again.

"Danny?" her soft voice came at him through the open window. The sound slicked around his ears, dipped into his chest, plucked at the top tab of his jeans. The woman could get him off with her voice!

3

Danny's belly clenched with need and he turned away from the kitchen window so she wouldn't see how hard he was. She might have been staring at him, but he'd been here long enough to know that, if she knew what he wanted, here, now, she'd kick him off the job and call in the competition.

After calling 911. And rightly so.

Not to mention that she was dressed for a date with someone else. Rather than her usual light browns and greens, today she wore a purple top without a bra. She looked spectacular.

For some other guy.

Unless she came outside and he made his move.

He cleared his throat, not sure he'd be able to speak, let alone be coherent. "You want to check out the deck? Step carefully. I spilled some nails earlier." Come out here and leave the mug behind. Come out here and let me touch you. Come out here with your excited eyes and edgy energy.

Thank God he'd worn his roomiest khaki shorts and boxers. He'd given up on his jeans and tighties a few days ago. He dropped to a crouch to give his heavy balls some room and groped behind him for his water bottle. He sluiced some down his chest to wash the salt off, then tipped the bottle to drain it. Maybe the cool water would wash away his urgent need to touch her. The urgent need that might frighten her.

"Good heavens," she muttered. He barely heard her through the window.

"Yes?" He rose and faced her, holding the liter bottle in front of his crotch for camouflage. With some luck, she'd mistake his woody for a shadow.

He moved closer to the window. He wanted his voice low when he coaxed her to come out and join him.

At the sight of Danny splashing water down his chest, Mariel's voice deserted her. Danny Glenn *was* perfect and exactly the body type she needed. Jayne had known it all along, which ticked her off. Jayne had a lover, she shouldn't have noticed Danny.

Mariel pressed her mons to the counter and enjoyed the delicious pressure, the secret thrill while she allowed the sight of water sluicing down Danny's chest to mesmerize her. Her nipples hardened, but she doubted Danny could see through the curtain of her hair. She pulled it back to fall down her back, exposing her hard tips to his gaze. She moved her hips from side to side, increasing the friction near her clit.

Who knew a countertop could prove this exhilarating.

Sculpted to perfection, Danny's working man's body was hard all over. His shoulders, tanned and powerful, gleamed in the sun. He had a six-pack, but only when he moved and stretched. His forearms were strong and muscular, and his hands were to die for. Long, strong fingers that ended in square tips with clean nails held the bottle he'd emptied across his chest.

Which was why her voice had disappeared into the lowest reaches of her belly, never to be resurrected. She swallowed as she became aware that she hadn't yet been able to tear her gaze from that empty bottle, where something else grabbed her attention.

The shadow from the bottle seemed remarkably phallic.

She tried to swallow, but her throat was dry. Evidently, all the moisture her body produced had moved south of her waist and pooled between her legs. She bit her lip as sexual need suffused her.

"Dear heavens," she said again. Her voice! She'd found it!

She'd promised Jayne she'd ask Danny about modeling for her, but she hadn't mentioned the first part of her plan. Her plan to seduce Danny.

The plan she needed to put into motion now. She braced both arms on the counter and leaned forward an inch or two. The action pressed the sides of her breasts in and caused the lace of the camisole top to droop. Danny had a full view of her cleavage if he cared to look.

He flushed a deep blood red and she watched as he, too, swallowed. Heat filled her cheeks, but still, she had to get through this conversation.

She had to ask.

She had to.

And not just because she'd promised Jayne. Because if she was going to enter this competition, she needed a body.

A man's sculpted-to-perfection body.

And Danny Glenn's body was exactly what she needed.

Gathering her nerve, she left the kitchen window and stepped outside onto the deck. Her empty hands filled with the itch to touch him. She turned back to get her mug of tea but remembered that she'd stepped out here to be bold and brave.

"Going on a date?" he asked, with a flick of his eyes down her body.

She shook her head, unable to speak as she let his gaze move more slowly up and down.

If only he'd stop looking at her with such intense focus, she'd remember what she needed to ask him. She wanted to turn and run, but if she did, she would never screw up this amount of courage again.

So, instead of skittering back into the kitchen, she ran her hands down her thighs. The impulse to lift her skirt to show him her curls flitted unanswered through her mind. His eyes flared into twin flames as he watched her hands move. The side of his hard, sexy mouth lifted. "You look different today. All dressed up and pretty." He dropped his gaze to the hem of her short skirt. Her other skirts were longer and never hugged her legs and butt.

"I, uh, made some tea," she blurted. "Would you like some?" Her hands fluttered in front of her. Stupid, she'd left her mug on the counter and he stared at the movement she couldn't seem to control. "It's supposed to be good to drink hot drinks in the heat." She was flustered and babbling, and her hands kept moving and—"Something about making you sweat more so your body cools." Asking him if he wanted hot tea was not the question she needed to ask. She darted a glance at his eyes, but nerves attacked, and she looked away again just as quickly.

He flashed a grin that sucked the air out of her lungs. She gasped as he chortled. "I think I'm sweaty enough." He ducked his head as if the natural bodily reaction to too much heat, sun, and work embarrassed him.

She suddenly remembered why she was out here. What she wanted. And more to the point, what she wanted to do.

Seduce Danny. She fingered the hem of her skirt with a nervous twitching motion. "I don't mind if you want to use my shower before you leave. In case you have a date or something."

She twisted her fingers around each other as she clasped and unclasped her hands. *A date or something?* How lame. But there it was: a blatant invitation to get naked in her house. She cast him another glance and he looked thunderstruck. Any moment now he would realize what she'd said and laugh at her.

Shy, docile Mariel Gibson, the high-school art teacher, brazen enough to ask if he had a woman. Not only that, but she was dressed like a woman who knew what she was after. Some bold, brave woman when she was nothing of the sort. Pathetic.

"No date, Mariel. I'm not seeing anyone. Except you every day." He lifted one side of his sexy mouth again. He had a dimple just east of that corner. He used it like a flag to draw attention to his mouth, his grin, his sexy as sin perfect jaw. "Is that what you wanted to ask?" He shifted the water bottle.

The phallus she imagined was no shadow.

Danny Glenn was rock hard. And smelled delicious. And he'd called her Mariel in a warm, intimate tone that rocked her back a step.

She blinked and felt a hot chasm of need open to swallow her whole. She half turned to run into the house, but his hand on her arm stopped her.

"Mariel, stay. Please."

She wanted to run inside, but she'd grown roots that held her to the new deck. She looked at him, and his yellow hazel eyes glowed with humor and dark need.

His voice went throaty and dark, a muscle jumped in his jaw and the backyard narrowed down to these few feet between where Danny stood, poised and ready, and Mariel, frozen and rooted to the spot. "You looked at me, Mariel. You looked and you saw."

She swallowed again but still couldn't speak.

"Surprised I'm hard for you?" Danny put his empty water bottle on the deck railing behind him with a precise, even movement.

He faced the railing, giving her his profile. Then he settled the bottle on the top rail with great calm, slowly. His fingers slid down the bottle to the bottom, just so.

"Because I'm not surprised I'm hard," he said clearly. "I'm hard for you morning, noon, and night. Have been for months."

She swallowed quickly. This couldn't be happening. She was still in her car with her eyes closed, deep in a fantasy.

"Dear heavens," she muttered for the third time. The air was gone, the glaring of the afternoon sun faded to something rosy. No, that was the blood rushing into her head, making her eyes swim with lust.

She blinked. Danny was haloed with an aura of sexual need and desire that coaxed and tantalized. "What was the question?" she asked.

He turned to face her again. Stood still, but for his hands. They flexed at his sides as if he wanted to grab her and drag her off somewhere. She took no time to warm to the wildy erotic idea.

"No more questions. Time for answers." He stepped toward her until his chest butted up to hers. Touching this way, Danny was hot, hard, immobile in his stance. His scent made every feminine instinct she possessed respond. She closed her eyes, drank him in.

"Answers," she repeated. She needed an answer to a question, but she could no more remember what she wanted from him than—no!—that was wrong, she knew exactly what she wanted. The seduction of Danny Glenn had been her intention, but somehow that intention had become his.

She felt a bull's-eye on her chest, knew the pressure that built there would take her to exciting heights.

She wanted the heights. So, instead of saying the wrong thing, the thing that might change the mood or ruin the vibes, she kept silent and waited.

"I'll give you answers," he murmured, as his hand came up

to wrap a piece of her hair around his finger. "I want to kiss you." His voice, a low croon, took her to bed.

"You what? Where?"

He chuckled, low, seductive. "I want to kiss you all over, Mariel. I want to kiss your lips, your neck. I want to kiss your ear, your breasts. Your belly."

"Oh, I'd like that." She nodded, far too many times. They wanted the same things. She wanted him in her room, in her bed, where she saw him kiss her from head to toe. She blinked in shock, needing to pull back from the erotic image. But there he was, incongruous in her frilly, girly room. She blinked away the images. Had to.

He stood so close! His chest brushed against hers with each breath. He tugged on the hair he held, swept the ends across her cheeks like a fan. He moved in close while her belly swooped and dived.

His face came near enough to kiss, then diverted to her ear. His tongue touched her lobe. He drew in a deep breath and went still. Very, very still, as the scent of her juices caught him. He sniffed and she felt moisture pool again. If he touched her there, he'd come away with wet fingers. She pressed herself to his crotch, urging his exploration. His hands roved across her back, down to her ass and kneaded her.

"Then I want to fuck you, long and slow," he explained, so softly she barely heard him.

The feel of his breath tickled her ear and neck, fanning the hair with each exhalation. "Does that shock you, Mariel? Because I don't want to shock you. I don't want to see you run back into the kitchen the way you always do."

She swallowed hard. "I do?"

"You do."

"Oh, I won't run. Not today." Not while she was being brave and bold. "Um, what else do you want to do?" Her hips moved forward and back and she set her feet apart. Cool afternoon air brushed at her curls.

"Then I want to fuck you hard and fast. Fuck, fuck, fuck you," he said as if she might not have heard him clearly the first time. The softness of his tone seduced her as much as the raw images he put in her head. He was clever, her carpenter, talented at seduction.

She turned her head just enough to see his eyes. They were too close to focus on, but she felt their heat. "Then touch me," she whispered. "Fuck me."

She lost all purpose, all thought as weeks, months, *years*, of self-denial fell away. This was no small rebellion. This was no easy seduction. This was life altering. If she took this step, she would never be the same again.

She lifted her lips and brushed them against his ear, his neck, and at long last, his jaw. Her hand moved to his fingers, twined with them. Time hung for a long moment while she drank in the scent of his skin, the heat of his flesh, the roaring in her ears of her own blood, pulsing and rushing.

Then suddenly, Danny was on her like water on a river bank. He flooded her, washing away the bits of debris from her uptight, sheltered life.

He wrapped his arms around her, took her right hand up to his mouth and kissed her palm. She melted at the drawn-out sensation of firm tongue against warm flesh. When he spread her fingers and licked her in each V, she closed her eyes and drank in the eroticism he brought to her mind. "May I?" he asked.

"May you what?" She could hardly think.

"May I kiss you now?"

"Oh, yes. Yes, please."

4

Danny cupped the back of her head and tilted her to meet his lips. Hard, firm, his lips enticed and coaxed, carried her to some high place where she hovered over the deck more aware than ever before that she was a woman and Danny Glenn was a hard, hard man. Her soft parts opened and gave way; her soft lips, the flesh of her mouth, her breasts and nipples plumped and flattened against all his hardness.

She heard him sigh once. Then a shudder ran through him. Relief? Then he kissed her forehead with quiet reverence, as if he were afraid she might change her mind. "Don't deny me, Mariel. Please."

"Anything. Anything you want." This was happening. Really happening.

He kissed her again, more times than she could count. Exploring kisses, tender kisses, hard kisses and soft.

The flavor of Danny aroused and tantalized. His hands spread across her ass, cupped and molded her to him, tugging her hard against his erection. Swept up into him, she lost track of where and who she was.

She wasn't Mariel any longer. No, she was a nymph—voluptuous, young, sexual, wet, open, moist.

Danny dropped to his knees and wrapped his arms around her thighs, burying his face in her soft belly. She cupped his head, held him to her and waited, breath held, for what he'd do next.

Whatever he wanted, she would give him. He ran his calloused hands up the outside of her calves, lifting the hem of her skirt to find her naked and open.

She braced her feet wider apart so he would know she was his for the taking. He brushed at the curls with his fingers, then asked her to lean back against the deck railing, while he undid his tool belt and set it down.

His fingers skimmed and tingles raced, while she raised her face to the sky.

Mariel melted in the sun with a man on his knees before her. He combed through her curls, tugging in much the same way she had earlier in her bedroom. The gentle tugging created answering need deep in her womb.

Next, he leaned in to nuzzle her pussy with his nose and chin.

She couldn't possibly be fantasizing to this degree. Danny's hard hands slid to the inside of her knees, where they pushed her open wider. She could stop him now, but the feel of his head in her hands, cupped like a bowl against her belly, opened her up, let her sinews and muscles go liquid where she stood.

Her knees loosened and suddenly her ankles were three feet apart; his finger parted her outer folds. She bit back a moan and shivered at the trickles of awareness that sparked out from everywhere he touched. She felt wild and rebellious.

"You're so wet, you're glistening."

"Yes." She waited, breath held for his next move. But he waited for a long moment until she asked, "What are you doing?"

"Touching you. Learning the feel of your skin, getting the scent of you in my nose, down my throat, filling my head with you." He burrowed his face into the apex of her thighs and rubbed his nose across the hair that covered her. She held his head and let him move, his chest rising and falling heavily as he scented her. She wanted to melt onto the deck, splay her legs open, and let him pleasure her. She trembled while the moment hung like a gossamer thread of anticipation overhead. "I love the scent of you, Mariel. Your hair, your body. I want the scent of your cunt on my skin, the feel of your juice on my chin, the taste of you in my mouth."

The words were too much and not enough. Moisture pooled, and her lowest belly warmed to melted honey. "My head's been full of you for weeks," she confessed. His fingertips, parting her folds, inspecting her inner flesh, undid her.

He looked up her body and into her soul. Her soul looked back.

"You're sure you want this?" His voice moved to husky. The sound of sexual desire hummed through the words, while one wicked hand slid up the back of her leg to cup the split in her ass. He spread her pussy with the other hand, holding her open, his mouth a breath away.

She rolled her hips toward him, felt the welcome heat of his breath on her clit. "Lick me, Danny. Please."

He did and she moaned and writhed as he suckled on her tender flesh.

"You taste so good." His tongue delved deeper while she heard the sounds of his mouth working and laving and driving her wild.

"But I've never done anything like this before," she said, as she braced more solidly against the rail at her back. "You should know that." Oh, hell, she sounded like an untried virgin. Or the next best thing. She gulped.

His dimple flashed before he pressed his face against her pussy again. His chin pressed against her mound while he rolled his head there, enticing her with the erotic image while his hands squeezed her ass. He pulled her cheeks open while she tilted toward him. "You can tell me to stop at any time. I'll stop, Mariel. I promise."

She nodded because she had no breath with which to speak.

His gaze clouded. "You live a quiet life. You're, ah . . . not a virgin, are you?"

Her cheeks heated. "Technically, no. I've had experiences." She raced to grasp the memories. "Not bad, but not good either." A boyfriend in college who'd known less than she did. They'd figured three times would be the charm, but when things had gone from bad to worse, they drifted apart. The most they'd shared was relief it was over. "But I've never had this before."

He grinned and a chuckle rose from his chest, throaty and sexy.

"Then you need gentle and soft this time. But I'm still gonna fuck, fuck, fuck you."

Those words made her belly clench in anticipation. Wild. Hot. Yearning anticipation. "Yes, please," she sighed. "Gentle and soft would be perfect." She considered fast and hard. "Hard might be okay too."

He grinned and she felt his fingers slide along her ass toward her cleft. "That'll come later. When you're ready."

"Ready? How will you know?" But she already was. Her hips were easing toward him, her channel felt more open, wet, soft.

"Trust me." He slid a fingertip into her and she moaned with the exquisite sensation. "You'll be aroused to a fever. You'll shimmy and shake and groan. And nothing but fast and hard will do." He pulled his fingertip out, then pushed in again, deeper. Again, deeper, until he was all the way inside. He plunged in and out, while she felt her muscles relax and moisten even more.

"So pink and responsive. You're beautiful. A ripe, perfect plum with a pretty little hole made just for me."

She bore down, needing more than a finger. She groaned.

"I'm going to eat that plum until you come like a queen. Would you like that, Mariel?"

Danny saw Mariel's slit flood cream. She clenched her muscles in an effort to stem the flow. Her breath caught and he imagined the feel of her muscles working. She sighed and her breath hitched when he slid his finger in deep, so he did it again and again.

Like a fluttering of butterfly wings he felt her clench around his finger. "I can feel you working it," he murmured as he tipped his tongue out to catch some of her tasty juices. The flavor burst, ripe and hot on his tongue. He swirled and lapped for a moment, but he couldn't let her come out here. She might scream and thrash, and draw unwanted attention.

With one last flourish, he whispered his intention to stop so they could go inside. When she nodded in agreement, he rose to his feet and took her hand in his.

"About that shower? Might be a good idea." He ducked his head again. "We need to go inside anyway."

She pursed her lips. If she had to wait while he took a shower, she might chicken out. He led her through the slider into the great room. They'd been in her back garden all the time! Exposed to the neighbors' yards and windows.

Her pussy throbbed in need, while her belly felt hot and heavy. Her knees were stiff while she walked. "I'm glad everyone around my house works later than I do." It was an area filled with first-time owners and young couples. The houses were old, compact, and most, like hers, needed renovations.

When they'd cleared the door and stood in the quiet of the

interior, he turned her into his arms and held her easily. Then he snugged her hips against his and she felt his hard cock press against her, but his smile was easy. The smile of a man who knew he'd get what he wanted when he wanted it.

"No one's ever around in the daytime but me. I wouldn't have touched you if I thought you'd be on public display."

She felt surprisingly safe with him. "Thank you." She raised up for a kiss, and it was her turn to press and retreat and skim and delve and . . . want.

She kissed him freely, cupped his tight butt and squeezed. Then she moved to his cock and squeezed again, surprised at his size and breadth. "Oh, I hope you get me good and ready for this. You're huge."

And hot, and hard. She bloomed completely, open and eager for him now. She took his hand and led him to the island he'd built for her.

There, she pressed her mons to the edge and lifted her skirt to show him her ass. Then she leaned over and offered herself.

5

Danny knelt behind her and parted her ass cheeks for a better view. The rosebud she presented could wait until another day, he decided. Right now, he needed to claim her cream-filled slit. He tongued her there, lapping and swallowing her moist offering.

She rolled her plump ass higher so he could see her clitoris peeping out at him. He stretched the tip of his tongue to lick her. The soft bud hardened under his tongue.

He pressed two fingers into her wetness, amazed when she opened wider and her clit grew long and firm. He flicked the dark bud with his tongue while she moaned and rocked back toward his plunging fingers. He slid his hand to his cock and rubbed the pulsing flesh against her calf.

She stiffened and came, sending a stream of fresh cream over his fingers and down her slit to his waiting tongue. She was wide open now, so he plunged a third finger into her hole and let her ride out her orgasm while he pumped in and out.

When she was done, he rose to his feet, turned her to face

him, and pressed his forehead to hers. He dropped a kiss to the tip of her nose, bringing a sliver of sanity to the moment. "I need to shower."

"You smell rugged and manly." Her eyes were glazed with sated afterglow. "But I appreciate the sentiment."

He chuckled. "You can call it what you want, but I've been working all day. We don't know each well enough for me to take that kind of chance."

"Okay. If you can wait, I can."

He wanted this to be right, perfect.

"I'll wait in the bedroom," she said, after a long kiss. "You know where the bathroom is."

Danny had wanted her for so long, it would be hard to hold back, but he had to give her what she needed. Gentle lovemaking now would prime Mariel properly for everything he wanted later.

And he wanted it all. He wanted her mouth on him, her pussy on his face, her slick moisture on his tongue.

Because he planned to fuck, fuck, fuck her.

And then he wanted to do it again.

"Five minutes, tops," he said as he stepped away and moved down the short hall to her bathroom. She followed him, stopping at a narrow door. She opened it and handed him a fresh towel. Her eyes were wide and eager.

"I've waited a long time for this," he said.

She grinned and set her hands on his arm and shoulder, giving him an ineffectual shove. "Go, don't waste a minute."

He soaped in the warm sluice of water, spending extra time on his cock and balls, thinking of Mariel's wet mouth and wetter cunt sheathing him, pumping him. His balls tightened and he had to squeeze the head of his cock to prevent ejaculating. After that he showered quickly, slipped back into his boxers, and grabbed a couple of condoms from his pocket. He squirted some of Mariel's toothpaste onto his fingertip and did the best he could to freshen his mouth for her. He finger-combed his hair and sucked in his gut.

He hadn't felt this way in years. Nervous, anxious to impress, and out of his depth. Mariel wasn't herself today. Whatever had happened to bring on this change, he was afraid that one wrong move would ruin things. In spite of her lascivious behavior on the deck and in the kitchen, she was usually sensitive and shy, and that had him in knots.

Most of his women were confident and definite in what they wanted. Mariel was only like that when they discussed the work she wanted done on the house. She was decisive, a rare client in the renovation business. If he held an opposing opinion, he had to prove why her idea wouldn't work. She knew her own mind, stated her desires, and it was up to him to find a way to give her what she wanted. But that was their customer-contractor relationship.

This side of things would be different.

He opened the door and stepped into the hall, wearing only his boxers. His cock was so hard it stood straight up his belly, so he pulled his waistband higher to cover it. No point scaring her.

Light glowed softly, spilling yellow onto the hall carpet from a room across the hall. He peered through the doorway and found her.

Mariel was apparently naked under the covers. Her blankets pulled tight across her breasts, tucked demurely under her arms. But the sight of her purple silky top and hot short skirt on a chair in the corner added to the excitement. Her shoes rested by the closet door.

Mariel, naked and waiting in bed—life didn't get any better. "Is this okay?" she asked.

"This is fantastic." A lit candle sent a light vanilla fragrance through the room. The flame showed a tentative expression on her face. "You've been fretting."

"How do you know?"

"I've seen the look before. I know you better than you think. We've worked together. Made decisions together." He strode into the room, cock fully loaded and aimed straight for her. "And I've watched you." It was good to know a woman well in one area of her life, then add this dimension to their relationship. "And you look perfect." He stood over the bed to let her absorb the fact that he stood in her room, seconds from climbing into her bed with her.

A moment of hesitation warred with desire in her eyes.

To tilt the outcome toward the desired result, he held up the condom packets. "I worried you might have changed your mind. I'm glad I was right to bring these with me."

Desire won out over hesitation. "Oh, thank God you brought some! Mine are too old to be safe."

He chuckled. "You'll always be safe with me, Mariel." To that end, he picked up the candle and moved it to the dresser, to reflect in the mirror. "The flame will be safer here."

She blinked and blushed and looked away all at the same time. "I thought we'd be covered up."

"I want to do a thorough inspection." He dropped his boxers and slipped into bed beside her, but she'd planted herself dead center and he had to stay on his side.

Propping his head on his hand, he leaned over and kissed her mouth with a soft brush of his lips, when he wanted to dive in and take. She kissed him back and reached to hold his head.

Mariel may have looked nervous for a moment, but her kiss told him she was his for the taking. Whatever doubts she'd had while he'd left her to take a shower were gone. With a sigh that invited more, she shifted over and gave him room. The sheet loosened with her movement.

He wasn't about to refuse the invitation. Scooping her into his arms, he ran his hand across her chest, enjoying the feel of her plump breasts. Mariel was well-formed and full, and he loved that her nipples were hard as pebbles. Her breath caught when he focused on one and rolled it between his thumb and forefinger.

She arched and caught her breath when he tugged the sheet lower so he could see her. Her breasts lay rosy and round against her chest. Perfect spheres topped by luscious red berries ripe for sucking. He bent his head, took one delicately between his lips, and licked. She moved her legs.

He sucked. More movement.

He opened his mouth wider, took more of her flesh, and sucked deeply, strongly.

She opened her legs and he took quick advantage. He moved his hand down over her pliant belly, her lush hair, and deep between her legs.

"You're hot and wet, Mariel."

She nodded. A whimper escaped and her eyes flew wide as he plunged a finger into her. He pressed higher and used his thumb to burrow for her clit. He found it hardened into a firm nub. "You wanted this for a while? You thought about it?" So much wasted time.

"Yes. Oh! Do that again." She rolled her hips and bit her lip.

He rocked his hand as he pumped in and out, keeping his thumb planted firmly on her clit. She liked that he stepped up the pace.

"Soft and gentle could be way behind us already." He'd never seen a woman so ready, so ripe for sex so fast. He slid a second finger into her slickness and felt her open like a Morning Glory in the sun. Pop!

"Faster!" she pleaded. "Harder! I need more." Her hips pumped and rocked as her need to come built.

His balls tightened just watching her. "Want me to take you

there? Should I let you come on my hand?" She moaned and thrashed, her legs wide open, her pussy weeping.

His cock flexed at the sight of her, at the scent of her creaming mound. "Open your eyes, Mariel."

She did. They were wild and damp with need.

He pulled his fingers out of her soaking cunt and licked them while she watched. Then he placed her hand on his cock so she could feel his pre-cum. She swirled her thumb across the moist droplet and wrapped her hand around his shaft. "Squeeze," he said.

She did, making arousal and the urge to shoot spike through him. He arched into her hand while she played him.

He plunged three fingers into her and pressed her clit with each slide in and out.

Her hand on his cock went slack as her own need took over. She arched and groaned, legs wide while he pumped into her slickness. He slid down her glorious open body to settle his mouth on her mons, feeling her curls tickle while his hand worked her into an orgasm.

The feel of Danny's head on her lowest belly, the weight of it, undid her. Pulsing sensations rocketed up from her pussy and clit as he rubbed and plunged and took her over the edge into full orgasm. The inner clenching went on and on while she felt the release through her hips, chest, legs and arms.

She felt wetter than she'd ever been as the feeling of completion settled. He still kept his head down at the apex of her thighs, but now it felt quietly gentle to have him there.

Threading her fingers through his hair she quieted, spent and replete.

His cock nudged her leg while his fingers stilled inside her. The echo of her pulsing contractions faded gently. She may be spent and wrung out, but he felt hot and ready.

"I love the scent of your juice," he said. "You're fresh and creamy." He removed his fingers and slid his face to her open pussy in a sly move that surprised her. Gentle strokes of his tongue and his moans of appreciation broke the last of her shyness, and she opened wide again.

With a move that surprised her, he rose up to straddle her upper body. His knees pressed into the mattress. The position made it easy to guide his cock to her mouth for a taste of that slick pearl she'd found earlier. His whole body stiffened as she took the tip of his cock between her lips. Tension coiled through his body.

She swirled her tongue in imitation of what he was doing and he grunted his approval. Carefully, she rimmed his ridge with her tongue and delighted when he flexed forward for more. She slid her mouth higher on his shaft and worked at suckling him strongly.

"Keep that up and you'll get a mouthful."

The words thrilled her. Danny sounded throaty and needy. She'd never caused such a reaction before. She settled her ass on the bed and lifted her legs to wrap around the back of his head. She couldn't be more open as he speared his tongue deep into her.

He worked her with tongue and fingers. On her clit, then her pussy. He jiggled her swollen, sensitive labia, fluttered his tongue across her clit, and plunged in and out of her channel. Deep and hard, gentle and soft he took her to new heights of sensation.

His cocked flexed deep in her throat and she wondered how he tasted. It wasn't fair that he'd tasted her come while she hadn't tasted his.

There was only one thing to do.

She reached for his tightened balls and squeezed gently. Playfully, she tapped them with her fingertips while she rolled her tongue around the ridge of his cock. His body flexed and tensed, her cue to squeeze his balls lightly. With Danny's harsh cry, a warm gush filled her mouth. His fingers stilled inside her while she milked him.

She lunged her hips upward and pressed her clit to his chin and mouth. She swallowed and took what he gave her while rubbing herself to full orgasm again.

He trembled over her as they cried out their release, and when it was over, he tumbled to the bed beside her. Head to toe, they lay quietly while their hearts' thunderous beats eased to normal.

The seduction of Danny Glenn had been a roaring success. She hoped with all her heart this wasn't the only time.

That idea flitted away as he combed through her pubic curls with languid fingers. Her heartbeat slowed to normal while her breathing slowed.

She raised her head and looked at him. "This was spectacular. You're spectacular."

He grinned. "Right back at you. If we're this good together now, imagine how great it'll be when we're used to each other's bodies."

Her mind boggled. "You won't get bored?"

He raised her foot nearest to him and kissed her arch as he draped it over his shoulder. He gazed at her between her legs in a blatant show of curiosity. "You're beautiful. Plump and pink and wet. Perfect just like the rest of you. I can't imagine ever getting tired of this."

Before she could comment, he slipped one finger into her to the hilt.

6

"Let me play a moment," Danny said. Her belly dropped with the invasive rub against her vaginal walls, but it felt too good to stop him. Deep inside, he bent his first knuckle and found a spot she didn't know she had. Circles of sensation built while he played. More moisture filled her and she felt it run down her slit to her bed.

Oh, to hell with it. She was decadence personified, womanly and fulfilled. She gave up to him and stretched back. Flinging her arms and legs wide, she let Danny look his fill. He played and experimented with her tender flesh. He opened her outer lips and speared his tongue into her. Then he lapped like a cat with cream. "See? You bloom open like a flower."

"I feel it." Her belly clenched and she gushed against his mouth. She would come again if he continued. The feelings were building, the urge to arch into his mouth got stronger. He went back to finger play to tease and tantalize some more.

Her pussy melted around him as he played. He built her up to gasping, then retreated again several times.

She didn't care. Trusting that he'd take her to the peak again and again, she settled back and let her lover play as he wished. All the weeks she'd wasted being shy washed away. She would make up for lost time while she could.

Eventually, after long moments of quiet exploration, she couldn't take his retreating teases anymore. She rolled her hips in need. He chuckled when she slid her fingers to the back of his head to hold him in place. "Your clit gets long and firm, like a tiny cock."

"It's sensitive."

"And delicious." Cool air drifted across the area. He opened her and blew seductive puffs of air across her hidden flesh. "Want me to kiss it?"

"Yes."

"Suck it?"

Yes, yes yes! "Yes." The circling continued, faster. She rocked toward him in offering. Why didn't he do what he promised?

"Want me to suck it hard?" His breath curled around her exposed clit, tantalizing and warm.

"Oh!" She came in a wild gush. In an act of sympathy she'd never forget, he set the pad of his tongue to her clit and pressed and held and licked and sucked until she couldn't come another second.

Wrung out, she opened to whatever he wanted, however he wanted it.

"I want to fuck you now, Mariel. Gentle and slow."

Oh, God. This was murder, she realized. Murder by orgasm.

The condom slipped over the head of his cock swiftly, surely, bringing Mariel's restful abandon to an end. She raised up on her elbows to watch Danny settle in the V of her body. "You're still hard, even though you've already come. Are you always like this?"

He slipped his hands under her butt and pulled her close to his full cock. "You don't want me to apologize, do you?" He spread her inner lips and pressed the tip of his cock against her opening.

"No, ah," she sighed. He raised her ass higher, his muscles bulging in his powerful forearms as he held her up. He pressed ever so slowly into her, his face intent on watching as his cock slid deep. She gasped and felt the width as her vaginal walls grasped him. He pulled back out a little, then in a fast, hard lunge buried himself to the hilt. The exquisite push-pull of his every inch made her gasp.

She moaned and bucked with him. As much as she loved the orgasms Danny had given her, this deep fullness completed the act. Completed her.

She wanted the feel of his chest on hers, needed the weight of him. Gathering him to her chest, she hugged him to her and twined his legs with hers. He felt right and close and heavy and warm, while she marveled at the smooth rocking that took her closer and closer to the edge.

He whispered words. Sexy, dark, hot words that put images in her head of heavy need and deeply delicious desires. Anything he wanted was his. Anything.

She would gladly give Danny any part of herself, including her heart. "Fuck with me," he whispered. "Let me slide into you, take your cunt." He slid to draw her nipple into his mouth and suckled her. Her womb tightened as he plunged harder, faster, deeper. She answered each lunge with a buck of her own and spoke to him in dark whispers of yearning and passion.

"I want you inside me, I want your cock, hard and full. I want your mouth, your wonderful fingers, fucking me, taking me past anywhere I've been." The whispers moved them faster toward the brilliant ending that took them with surprising speed, tumbling over and around each other.

Danny shuddered and shook inside her melting channel while she felt the wracking spasms that signaled her release.

."Fuck! I'm so deep! You're hot—so wet—tight." He groaned and burrowed deeper still as the last surges rolled through him.

He sagged into her, letting her rock him gently while he gathered enough strength to roll to the middle of the bed. He scooped her close to rest on his chest. She finger-combed his chest hair while he smoothed her soft shoulder.

"Mm, that was the best time I've ever had."

"It's nice of you to say so," she murmured, content and sated.

He slid his fingertip to her chin and tilted her face up to look deeply into her eyes. "There's nothing nice about this. Nice is a boring word, said about boring people. What we've got here is exciting, flat out roller coaster exciting. And, no, I won't get bored."

For a moment, she believed him, and that was all right with her. "Me neither."

They rested for a few moments, too spent to say more. Mariel refused to consider what would happen when he finished the deck. And she'd completely forgotten about the competition, *and* about asking Danny to pose for her. She raised her head to ask, but he spoke first.

"I know you often make salad for your dinner, but I know a burger joint that serves the best steak burgers in town. Come with me tonight. They've got picnic benches. We could eat under the stars." His stomach growled and he grinned. "I need to eat."

"After all this, I need protein, not just a green salad." So this wasn't just a convenient way to get laid. He'd been serious when he said he'd watched her, wanted her. "I'd love a burger." And she loved that he'd invited her.

For Danny, her response was perfect. He hadn't demanded too much and he hadn't frightened her. A tight coil of dread sprung free. "I was afraid to scare you off," he admitted. "I wanted you for so long, I worried that I'd tear into you if I wasn't careful."

She wiggled her hips. "Not torn, but definitely stretched and deeply satisfied. When you bent your finger inside me I thought I'd go through the roof, because it felt incredible."

"I'll do it again, then."

"Please. Did I do everything right?"

Relief made him playful and he teased, "You mean sucking my cock?"

She flushed a delicious shade of pink. "You're so free and open."

"No point pretending we didn't do what we did. I ate your pussy, sucked your clit, finger-fucked you, and fucked you with my cock."

Her eyes went wide, then filled with an easy humor. "Okay, since you want a list." She counted off on her fingers. "I kissed you, shoved my pussy in your face, came all over your hands and face, and took your cock deep into my throat." She went redder. "And I swallowed your semen. Which tasted deliciously salty and hot by the way."

He laughed. "And here I decided you were demure and shy."

"I am. But like you said, there's no point pretending we didn't do what we did. I liked it. Very much. All of it." She hesitated, then added, "I like you, Danny. I like doing this. With you."

"Good, because I'm not done with you yet." He rolled to the far side of the bed and sat up. "We'll shower and go get those burgers."

The juice from the minced steak oozed out of her bun and ran down her hand. Mariel sat snuggled up close to Danny on the top of a picnic bench beside the diner. They faced the back fence that ringed the parking lot. She licked the juice from the inside of her wrist.

Beside her, Danny froze. "You have a way with your tongue that makes me crazy. Did you know that when you drink your tea you put the tip of your tongue on the rim of the mug just before you take a sip? Makes me hard as nails to see that."

"Believe me, I had no idea." But it pleased her that he'd seen past her nerves and shyness. She reached for his forearm and pulled his hand close enough to lick. Turning her head, she licked the stream of burger juice from the thick muscle at the base of his thumb. "God, do that again, but lower. Much lower."

She gave him a throaty chuckle and couldn't believe this was her. "You make me feel free, so unlike myself. I want to enjoy these moments to the fullest." She would remember them later when she was alone again.

"I'm enjoying you to the fullest. You're the hottest woman I've ever met. I knew it before, with your pretty blushes. But now? You're flat out killing me."

"Funny, that's what I thought earlier. Death by orgasm. Is there any chance we could achieve that together?"

He leaned his shoulder against hers. "Absolutely. When can we try again?"

"When we get home." She still hadn't asked the question she'd wanted to ask. This was a night for brave, bold Mariel and she had to continue. "You know I teach high-school art, right?"

"I've seen your easel in the back bedroom." He sipped at his soft drink.

"That's right, you stored tools and wood back there when you built my shelving unit."

"You haven't used that easel in a long time. All your art supplies were covered by sheets." He chewed the last bite of his burger. "I confess, though, I looked at some of your paintings."

She probably should have thrown them out, but she hadn't. "They're not very good."

His brows knit and he shook his head in disagreement. "I thought they were nice."

That was the problem! Art wasn't supposed to be nice. It had to be *more*. Like the sex they'd shared. If she told him that it had been nice, he would be offended. Nice was almost as horrible a word as mediocre.

But she didn't want to bring her private pain into the bold, brave night. "Thank you," she said, but the words were flat, like her paintings. She gathered her nerve. If she didn't ask him now, the chance might not come again. She either wouldn't have the guts to ask, or he'd have had his fill of her and moved on to his next woman. If she asked then, he'd see her as desperate and clingy, and he wouldn't be inclined to do her the favor she needed. "I need a favor, Danny, a big one."

"A body? I gave you that not an hour ago." The twinkle in his eye made her grin and gave her the courage to ask.

"You heard me talking to Jayne?"

"I love the sound of your voice. It's got a husky undertone that's sexy as hell. Makes me want to kiss you." He kissed her mouth, long and slow, tongue deep and stroking. "And kissing you makes me think of sex with you."

He cupped her breast, molded the fullness until her nipple hardened and shot an arrow to her womb. "I love your nipples, they stand up proud."

She melted and let him play and pluck. The sun had gone down, and because the parking lot was behind them, no one could see where his hand had wandered. The public sexual exploration excited her.

"I'll do whatever you need," he offered.

"I want to paint you."

He pulled his head back and stared at her. "You want to do a nude? The paintings I saw were landscapes."

"No, I want to paint your body." Her landscapes were too safe, too controlled. Too ordinary. They were, indeed, nice. Mediocre. "I want to enter a body painting competition."

"Like naked?"

"Mostly."

"All right."

"That was easy."

"I figure it'll give me more time with you, right?"

"Yes."

"And that's what I want. More time with you."

Her belly dropped at the easy way he spoke. "I'm glad." Happiness bubbled up and out from her mouth in a light giggle. She clapped her hand over her mouth. "Sorry, I never do that. Makes me sound like a fool."

"Stop doing that."

She sobered immediately.

"No, not the laughing, not the being happy. I love that you're happy." The arm he'd draped over her shoulder felt warm and comforting. He squeezed her close to his side.

"Then what? What should I stop?"

"Don't apologize for being lighthearted. Happiness isn't something to be hidden away, Mariel."

"It is in my family!" she blurted. "Along with creativity, artistic expression, a love of books, whatever." She waved her hand in dismissal. "I never fit in with my family." Talking about this made her anxious, especially with a stranger. For all intents and purposes, Danny was a stranger. "Sorry, you don't know them and I shouldn't say any more."

"If it makes you feel better, I never fit in with mine, either. My sister's an architect, my brother's a surgeon." He released her to put his hands out in front of him, flexing his fingers wide. "They're brainiacs, both of them. Me? I'm happy working with these."

"Do you feel like you've disappointed your folks?" She couldn't see how he would, he was a fabulous carpenter, with an eye for detail she envied.

"Not anymore. They've accepted my decisions now that I'm making a good living." He drew her close to his side again. "Besides, I have my ambitions."

"So do I. That's why I want to enter this competition. You remember that saying: *Those who can, do, those who can't, teach?* It makes me crazy that I've never gone forward with my own art." She refused to tell him about her deeply humiliating experience three years ago. She couldn't. That time with Withers was still painful and too raw to share.

"So, I take it this competition is important to you as an artist."

"In a way, it's vital."

"Then I'm honored you wanted me."

He had no idea exactly how much she'd wanted him. She'd wanted him day and night, in daydreams and nighttime fantasies, which he'd more than fulfilled.

"There's one more thing. Paint doesn't stick to body hair." She gave him a quirked-up smile and a beseeching look.

He went still. "I'm not very hairy."

"I love your body hair. It's perfect." Just enough to look like a real man. Sadly, it would all have to go. "But—"

"I'll shave my chest. No problem."

"Waxing's probably better. It takes longer to grow back. Bodybuilders do it all the time," she said, trying to reassure him. "If a bodybuilder can take it, you can."

He squinted and looked squeamish. She couldn't blame him, her eyebrow job hurt like hell every month. He cleared his throat and visibly manned up. "How far south? Are the boys involved? Because I hate to admit it, but they're shriveling at the thought."

"We can't have that," she said with a sympathetic buss on his cheek. "The boys will be left alone. We'll just do the front of the groin. And your butt."

He looked horrified. "My ass is hairy?"

"No!" The look on his face made her want to collapse into fits of laughter, but she tried to hide the fact. "Really, it's not. Honest."

He hung his head. Shook it. "You're asking a lot, but for you, I'll do it."

"Thank you." She kissed him and slung her arm across his shoulders in fake sympathy. "It won't hurt a bit."

"To top it all off, the woman lies to me."

She giggled against his ear and nipped the lobe with a low growl. Not only was he sexy as hell, he was funny and good-hearted. If she wasn't careful, she could fall into serious like with this carpenter of hers.

He slipped a hand under her sweatshirt and fondled her breasts again. Soon she warmed all over and leaned back to give him room to work his magic. Devil that he was, he slipped from her breasts, down her belly, and into her jeans before she knew what he was about.

With unerring accuracy, he found her clit and pressed his full palm over her mound. He rubbed and fondled her until her breathing changed to light gasps. The wild, crazy, freshly bold side of Mariel sat up and took notice. She opened her legs and moaned, bracing her hands behind her.

"Easy, Mariel," he murmured in her ear. "Let yourself go. No one can see." He shifted closer to make certain.

Let yourself go. The words wound through her mind, into her heart, and she wanted more than anything to follow his advice.

She undid the top tab and zipper on her jeans, then dropped her head back to look up at the star-filled sky. Glorious! He adjusted to slide under her panties, and her clit perked up and firmed, reaching for more attention.

And then Mariel let Danny take her into a free fall of need.

7

Once Mariel opened her jeans he had more room to work on her and he took full advantage. She was wet, open, and her little clit grew and plumped under his finger. She bit her lip with every stroke and groaned when he slid two fingers deep inside her. "You're so hot and wet. You're ready to come." He loved this side of uptight little Mariel. If it was later, quieter, he might kneel and peel her out of her jeans to bury his face in her pussy. Some night, he'd find an out-of-the-way spot in a park and do just that. "Let go, baby, that's it," he said when she tried to bury a moan in his neck.

She sucked hard on his flesh, her even, white teeth nipping. "You're hanging, babe, let it go. Come for me." He swirled his fingers inside her, pressed her mons to let her feel the weight of him on her. "You're so hot."

She moaned again. Sighed and gasped when he slid another finger into her hot wet cunt.

A car's lights swept over them, and the sound of teenagers climbing out and heading into the burger joint distracted her. She started and opened her eyes. "No, don't let anything take you from me. Feel what I'm doing to you and fly." He moved his hand faster, harder, plunging his fingers in and out. He set his mouth to her neck and ear, nuzzling and crooning dark heated words.

"Fly, yes." She moaned and rolled her hips, dropped her head back while she raised her pussy for more. Her body stiffened under his hand, her mouth closed on his neck while her inner muscles clenched with orgasm. He held her tenderly, allowing her to shatter and regroup, his hand full of soft, hot cunt. He couldn't think of anything that smelled or felt or tasted sweeter.

His cock blasted to attention as she quieted, screaming that it was his turn.

Bleary with satisfaction, her eyes, softly out of focus, found his. "I came. On a picnic bench in a restaurant parking lot." She shook her head in disbelief. "I've never, ever done anything like this in my whole life."

"But it was good, right?" He pressed against her wetness one more time to be sure the tumult of release was over. He didn't want her to miss a second of pleasure.

She sighed and opened her legs to let him release her. "This was so good, I can't wait to get home and take care of you." She smoothed her hand over his erection. The intense feeling made him want to put her on her knees in front of him. Before he could put thought into action, the teens burst out of the restaurant door, laughing and insulting each other.

Their moment of privacy disappeared.

She put her clothes back together, just in time.

"Hey, man, you gonna use that bench?"

In answer, Danny stood, held out his hand for Mariel, and waved the boys toward the table. "It's all yours."

Beside him, Mariel chuckled, low and husky. "They have no idea how hot and wild you make me," she whispered.

Pleased, Danny heard the simmer of more heat under the

surface of her words. But he had to cool off his thoughts or he wouldn't be able to drive. "This competition. Tell me what it entails."

"Practice! I've never actually done any body painting." He handed her up into the passenger seat of his work van.

"Then why do it?" he asked, although he had a fair idea why. His own furniture designs challenged him all the time.

He let her ponder her response while he walked around the front of the van and climbed in. She looked pensive as he started the ignition.

"I want to sell my art. I want respect. I want to prove a couple of things to myself and my family, before I get any older. I'll be thirty in a couple of years, and I'm not ready to settle for teaching." Her voice took on a firmness by the end. "I guess I want to know that I can rise to a new challenge. To test my limits."

He nodded as he pulled out of the parking lot. A comfortable silence filled the van as the darkness held them in an intimate cocoon. He tried not to think of sex, but with his cock on a low throb, he struggled to return to the conversation. "Some artists are happy to take joy from the act, but you're ambitious. How is that a bad thing? Why wouldn't you want recognition and to be paid?"

"Spoken like a craftsman who does get paid. You're such a guy. But, yes, I want to be paid, and I do have ambition. I forgot that a while back."

"When?"

"About three years ago. I got some bad criticism and have just recently gotten over it." She sounded doubtful, but he let it rest. If she was still struggling, no patronizing words from him would make her feel better.

"How much time do we have to prepare for this competition?"

"A month." She stared out the passenger window. "If, um, this sex thing. I mean . . ."

He tugged her hand to rest on his thigh. Under his palm, her fine bones and long fingers reminded him of how her hand had looked wrapped around his cock. "As far as I'm concerned, Mariel, this sex thing's great, and I don't see it as casual. I'm not a player, and I've never been interested in bar flies and easy fucks." His sister would kill him if he behaved like a dog.

"Oh, and here I thought I was easy."

"You?" He chuckled. "No, you're anything but! I've tried and tried to get you to talk to me, but you kept your distance." He lifted her hand to his mouth and kissed the palm. "I'm relieved you've stopped running away. So, yes, this sex thing is going to last. At least as far as I'm concerned. I want to spend time with you, lots of time."

He'd probably said too much, but she needed to know she was safe with him.

She turned to face him more fully. "I'd like that too. And we'll have lots of time to get to know each other while I'm painting you."

"Do you paint my whole body?" His cock stirred at the idea of Mariel using light strokes to paint him. All over.

She chuckled. "You'll be in a thong. Nothing will be, uh, out there for all the world to see."

"My head may not be in charge all the time. Sometimes my cock has a mind of its own."

"Then we'll just have to make certain he's too tired to rise to the occasion."

He laughed and kissed her palm again. "I'm going to love these practice sessions."

"Me too! I'll register online as soon as we get inside," she said as he parked in front of her house.

* * *

Now that Danny had agreed to model for her, Mariel went into a tailspin of doubt. She stared at the filled-out online form and let her finger hang over the Enter key. Once she committed to this, there would be no going back.

She settled her hand beside the keyboard, then turned on her chair to face Danny. "Do you think I should enter? I don't have a chance of winning. Some of the best body painters in the world will be there."

"Are you entering to win? Or for the challenge?"

"Some of both, but winning is a pipe dream. I have a much less noble reason for being there." She might as well show him now, he'd see it all soon enough.

She led him down the hall to the back bedroom she used as a studio. In the corner, stacked against the wall, were her paintings. Her failures. "I want to prove to one of the judges that he's an ass."

"Okay." But his tone said: Explain.

She tugged away the sheet she used to cover her stacked paintings. Turning the paintings face out so Danny could see them, she held her breath while he looked his fill. "These paintings you think are nice?"

He nodded, looking wary.

"I took them to a gallery owner. He laughed at me. Called me no better than mediocre. Told me I should consider teaching high-school art class."

"Well, that's what you do, isn't it?"

She threw her arms up. "That's right! But how did he know that? Am I so bland? So predictable? So fucking mundane that teaching art to kids who want an easy pass is all I'm good for?"

He stepped up close to her and his deep, hard hug flowed through her aching heart. Eased it, warmed it, maybe even saved it from breaking. "Oh, Danny, I'm afraid I'm not an artist at all."

The fear that she'd never break free of her family's expectations was worse. She couldn't share that with him. No one except Jayne knew how her family looked at her art. She sank into Danny's embrace, allowed his crooning to soothe her into mindless dreams of deeper intimacy.

She moistened and raised on her toes to kiss him. He took her mouth, her breasts, her heart, and then her body on the floor of her studio. In front of her mediocre paintings, her blank easel, her empty sketch books, Danny filled her with glory and took her to places she only dreamed about.

His mouth found her wet and open, his lips worked her into a frenzy while he fumbled to get his jeans off. She helped and dug into his pocket for a condom.

If this was what lay in store for them while she practiced painting him, she'd have to buy a carton.

He protected them and positioned himself at her opening. Braced over her, Danny grinned, his smile a brilliant, joyful contrast to the failures that loomed in the studio. "You are wicked, Danny Glenn, and I love it. Now, slide in and take it all home."

He stretched her with his pulsing cock as he seated himself deep inside. The rocking started slowly with each of them keeping a fresh rhythm. A renewed energy rolled through with every thrust and retreat.

Danny groaned, signaling his loss of control and rush to the end. His deep thrust and flex triggered her newly responsive body to flush with orgasm as he came with her.

After a pulse-pounding moment, she heard his urgent whisper, his breath hot next to her ear. "Now that was a hard, fast fuck." His chuckle sounded sexy and deep. "Go send in your entry, Mariel. I'll be with you every step of the way."

8

"He's late," Mariel told Jayne on Monday, three days into their practice sessions. "He left here before I got home from school and promised to be back by seven."

"It's seven fifteen, hardly late enough to panic about," Jayne responded. Easy for her, she never worried about anything. And she was chronically late herself. "Has he done this before?"

"No." The admission made her sound petulant and demanding. Character traits she abhorred. Traits she recognized from her family. "I'm stressed about this competition." Deeply stressed. Strung-out stressed.

"It means the world to you. I understand. I'm glad you entered, but I'm even happier you've hooked up with Danny. In spite of him running behind today, you've been much happier since last week." They'd gone shopping together on Saturday afternoon and Jayne had insisted on buying Mariel some sexy, flirty lingerie in celebration.

"I know, and I am happier. The sex is great; he's fun and sweet and brilliant when it comes to his work. This is an old house, and every job I've given him has presented unique challenges. He's patient when he explains things, and he never makes me feel stupid about what he's doing."

"A man who doesn't talk down to you about construction? Wow. You sure he's not an alien?"

She laughed, as Jayne knew she would. "Okay, point taken, I need to calm down and go with the flow. But with Nigel Withers judging, I want to shine in this competition. I don't have a chance of winning, but I need to show him I'm not a mediocre nothing."

"He ruined your confidence. It's up to you to get it back, no one can give it to you." She clucked her tongue in pique. "I wish you'd never taken your portfolio into his gallery. The man's a total ass!"

"But he sells well. He has connections I can only dream about." Her doorbell rang, and through the door window she saw Danny waiting on her front step. "Danny's here."

"Do not rag on him about being late. He probably just got caught in traffic."

"You're right. Talk to you tomorrow," she said as she opened the door for Danny. She put the receiver back in its cradle. "Hi, that was Jayne," she said, and bit her tongue about the time.

"Sorry I'm late. I guess you couldn't start without me," he said as he gathered her into his arms for a deep kiss.

She could get used to kisses like these. Maybe that wasn't smart. Maybe she shouldn't depend on them, on him. His not showing up on time had rattled her. "Very nice," she said by way of a compliment, "but we need to get started."

"Great, I'll go get naked," he said, and sauntered down the hall to her studio.

She followed and turned her back while he piled his clothes on a chair. She'd learned quickly that if she watched him, he got turned on and no work got done. Unless it was on her.

The memory of how good he was while he worked on her made her moisten. Depend on him? Addicted felt more like it.

"The theme of this competition is The Garden of Eden, right?" He stepped on the stool while she settled in a kitchen chair to work. She was painting his lower half today and needed the extra height.

"Yes, I like landscapes," she said, and started on his right buttock. "Hey, you got waxed!" His skin was pink and hairless but still pink as a baby's. "Is that why you were late? Did it hurt?"

"I don't want to discuss it. But the boys are fine, if you're wondering." He did a theatrical shiver that made her chuckle. "The woman who waxed told me to have a cold shower to close the follicles."

She looked closer. "Maybe we shouldn't work today. The paint may bother your skin." She kept the disappointment out of her voice. "I wish you'd told me you were planning this today." She set her palm to his buttock and patted him gently.

"I didn't want you to come along and hear me scream like a girl."

She tried to dispel the mental image of Danny having his body hair ripped off. She turned off her sprayer. "I planned on doing the tree trunk up your spine today." She needed to get it right, the details exact, the bark itself could take an hour. But that would take too long. The artists only had two and a half hours to do the actual painting.

She didn't have to just be good, she had to be fast. She broke out into a fine sweat just thinking about it.

Danny's voice broke into her thoughts. "I'm not an artist, not by a long shot, but didn't that gallery owner dislike your landscapes?"

"What? Yes, he, um, hated them."

Danny looked over his shoulder at her. His eyebrow quirked up into an arch. "So why try to impress him with the work he's already decided to hate?"

"That's not it at all," she cried. "You don't get it. Don't bother trying." The sting from his comment hurt, but he looked contrite at her reaction. She forced herself to calm. "You're right, you're not an artist," her tone softened. "I need to prove to Nigel Withers that he made a mistake." If she didn't make him see her art in a different light, she feared she might give up altogether.

"And rubbing his nose in it will make you feel better?" He turned and faced her fully, bringing his erect penis directly in front of her face. He put his hands by his thighs and stared down at her, his eyes burning with need.

He slipped his hands to the back of her head and held her gaze. She melted the way she always did when confronted with Danny's blatant sexuality. She leaned in, released him from the confines of his thong, and kissed the tip of his penis, tasting the lovely bead of moisture she found. Then she rolled her tongue around the rim.

He sighed and strained toward her, silently asking for more.

She slid her palms up the back of his smooth thighs to hold him still and took him into her mouth. He jerked and groaned, trembling as she mouthed him. "Oh, yes, this is good. Just what I need. Your mouth, your kisses."

She let his words soothe her sorry soul, taking comfort from the knowledge that at least she was good at *this*. It was childish to harbor feelings of resentment over what Withers had said, but still, it rankled. And frightened her into fretting day and night that this competition was a mistake for her.

She lost herself in Danny, let his words of praise cover her artistic insecurities. She gave him everything he craved, and as his arousal built, her own followed.

Soon, she let go of all her thoughts, her dreams, her ambitions for her art. All she wanted was Danny, inside her.

She nibbled her way down his shaft to his sac and with delicate precision rolled one of his balls with her tongue. He shifted and his foot slipped off the stool.

"I need to be inside you now," he murmured. Stark need laced through his words. "Right now!" He stepped down, tugged her to the floor with him, and slipped his hand up her skirt. He tugged her panties down her legs and tossed them to land on the corner of her easel.

She decided to leave them there. Maybe forever. "Oh yes!" she cried as he roughly entered her with two fingers. The claiming was quick, firm, and she arched into his hand, responding to his need. She melted and widened her legs so he could go deeper, harder, faster.

"Fuck me, Danny!" *Make me forget!*

He reached into her bra for the condom packet she'd taken to storing in there and used it.

She still harbored leftover anger at Withers, at Danny for being late, at herself for feeling this way. Her anger-tinged desire drove her higher and higher. She had to let go of her nerves, her raw emotions. She wanted to be in the moment with Danny.

He lifted her ass in the air, held her high and open before he speared his tongue into her. She came in a wild gush while Danny lapped at her open pussy.

She expected the orgasm to wash away the anger that still burned, but the urge to fuck hard only intensified the feeling.

"Fuck me, Danny! Now!"

Danny's grin fired through her as he entered her fast.

He rocked and thrust, his hard body pressing hers into the floor. His cock slid deep, his pubis pressed and retreated against hers while her clit responded with fresh bursts of sensation.

Still, she glowed with rough anger, at Danny, at herself for entering the competition, at the judges, even at her family. With a terrific lunge, she pushed at him to roll over.

He followed her lead and she straddled him, taking control. She swore and strained, opening wider, taking more, pressing harder as she slammed down on his cock. Her clit protruded, sticky and rubbery as she slid figure eights around his groin.

"Fuck! Fuck!" she screamed as her orgasm exploded. Moisture flowed with her coming, and she screamed again as wave on wave rolled through her, washing her free of all that had driven her to take him. She'd lost him. She had ignored her lover while she'd pummeled her body into roaring ecstasy.

She opened her eyes when she could, gasping with triumphant release. Bones and muscles melted, no longer able to hold her. She eased down to his chest and lay with her head on his shoulder, completely spent.

A flex in her channel reminded her that she hadn't been alone in the throes of sexual abandon. Danny was still with her, still needy.

"You didn't come?" She couldn't believe he could hold on while her world had shattered more completely than ever before. She'd been a greedy bitch, taking and not giving. Driving hard and harder still while she crowned at the pinnacle.

"I got caught watching you. Are you all right?" he asked, but she could see the price he'd paid for his control. He was about to snap, and she loved that he'd held on to allow her to ride out her anger.

"Sorry, I got carried away."

"No problem. You can use me that way any time you'd like." He arched up into her in a plea. She leaned back and gave his sac a gentle squeeze. He groaned and flexed inside her.

"Do you like that?" she asked, with a teasing lilt in her voice.

"I love it, but—" He grabbed her ass cheeks and rolled her to the floor. "I need to be in charge now." He sat on his heels and grabbed her hips. She straddled him while he pushed her down on his bulging, purple cock. He was stiff as iron and ready to pop. She'd never seen such control, but still he pressed his thumb to the rose bud of her ass and wedged his heavy cock into her pussy.

He let her feel the press of his thumb without pushing inside. Then he raised her ass until just his tip was inside. Slamming her down onto his cock, he strained up, buried himself deep and hard. Then he braced her high again, taking over completely. His muscles strained, his arms bulged, and still he dropped and raised her for his own pleasure.

He took her completely, stole her breath, reached so deep inside her she stretched and gave. "Touch my clit," she begged. "Fuck me and rub my clit."

"You're so wet, you're glistening." The new angle took him deeper as he increased his pace, but he was too far gone to touch her where her need felt greatest.

She pumped up and down. Rode him again while his focus went to the exquisite sensation of sliding deep and pulling out to the tip.

He grabbed her hips to make her move faster, deeper with every stroke. His cock roared into orgasm as he pulsed and shot into her. He held her hips in place as he spurted and spewed deep. His orgasm triggered another for her and her pussy clenched around him, milking the last drops of semen from his balls.

When it was over, Danny didn't speak. Instead, he lifted her into his arms and took her to the shower, where he gently soaped and rinsed them both. He kept the water cool and soothing for his skin.

They stumbled into her bed, still damp, and crashed into dreamless sleep together, sated.

The next day at school, Mariel felt uneasy about her behavior the previous evening. She'd had angry sex! She'd never expected to feel anger and desire at the same time before. But when she examined her anger more closely, she saw that it hadn't been directed at Danny. If she'd been truly angry with him, she could not be aroused.

No, she'd been angry with herself. This competition had opened too many wounds, too much fear within her to be comfortable. Every day, she worked on her design during her lunch hour. She'd even made minor changes when she should have been cruising the room giving advice and encouragement to her students. She no longer cared about what the students were doing, her teaching went by rote and she was angry about that too.

She was a mess! An emotional wreck. The only good thing in her life at the moment was Danny. Her carpenter had so many wonderful attributes, she glowed whenever she thought of him. The sex was unbelievably good. She'd never been more satisfied in her life.

She'd wanted to discuss the whole anger thing but didn't want to come off as whiny. It seemed insane to be ticked off about entering a competition that she'd *wanted* to enter. Maybe it was fear masquerading as anger.

After all, if she didn't enter the competition, she couldn't lose, could she? She would never learn or suffer over what a panel of judges thought about her art.

She stood and set aside her worries as she walked through her class and checked on the students' work. Again, she couldn't bring herself to care, and ended up distracted and disconnected from even her most promising students. One of her students had a real flair, but even Rajid's work looked flat and uninteresting today.

She saw no point talking to Danny about any of this. He was a carpenter, not artistic, not creative. He used angles and form and structure, but it was more mathematical than truly creative. He would never understand her fear.

What Danny understood was sex. He was completely physical, sensual. He fed her body, not her soul. He understood how to make her wild, how to make her body sing with desire, hum with urgency and flood with release.

He'd never understand the unique delicacy of her creative soul.

That evening, Danny was late again. It was only ten minutes this time, but his breezy apology grated across her nerves.

She couldn't work, couldn't decide on a color for his spine. She wanted a tree trunk, but got a snake. She wanted controlled lines, not a froth of streaks that led nowhere. Frustrated, she set down her airbrush and shut off her compressor.

"I'm done for the night."

"That was quick. Not going well?"

"I don't know what's wrong." She shrugged and cleaned the nozzle. "You can shower now." She kept her back to him, unwilling to let him read her disappointment.

He stepped close, crowding her. His heat and energy pushed through her frustration. "I'll need you to scrub my back."

She straightened, nipples already peaking. "Great idea." She could wash away her fear, be in the moment with Danny again. By using sex, she could hide. "Be right there."

But by the time she'd cleaned her equipment, the shower had stopped running. Great, now he was early!

"We're due for a night out," Danny said from the doorway. He wore her best indigo bath sheet low on his hips. His arms were crossed, making his forearms bulge and his pecs stand out. Her mouth watered. "We've stayed in most of the time we're together and you need a break. Think of it as creative therapy." He reached for her hand and linked their fingers. "Besides, I have something I want to show you."

She tugged at the towel hard enough to draw him two steps closer. "I've seen it before, but I'd love to see it again."

He covered her hand with his. "No, Mariel. We need to take a break." He retreated to the bathroom and closed the door.

On numb legs, she walked into her bedroom and removed her painting smock. A break. He was done. It was over. Her heart stumbled in her chest, and all she could think was that she would soon be coming home to an empty house. No more banging, or sawing, or the sound of power tools. No more Danny.

For months she'd climbed out of her car in the garage after school, thinking of Danny. And now the house would be empty. He had finished the deck today and she loved it. He was no longer her carpenter. She'd paid him in full when he'd arrived and their professional relationship was now severed.

He was only seeing her because he'd promised to model. A thought crossed her mind, but it was so disheartening she tried to deny it immediately.

She slipped into a fresh blouse and headed into the living room, where Danny waited for her. The idea she tried to hide from sprang out of her mouth unbidden. "Do you want me to pay you?"

"For what?"

Did she really want to say this? "For modeling."

His gaze narrowed and a muscle along his jaw jumped like a nervous tic. "I'm modeling for you because you asked me to, because I want to spend time with you."

"Oh." Her mind stopped spinning while she took in what he said. But his face said way more than she wanted to know.

"That better be all you think I want money for." He stalked out the front door, anger clearly set in his straight back and shoulders.

"Way to keep a man interested, Mariel," she muttered as she followed him out to his truck.

Obviously, Mariel was tied in knots about this competition and Danny needed to cut her some slack, but her comment about paying him to model was over the top. He wasn't sure what he'd done to make her think he wanted to be paid to model. He'd do anything to help her, but if she didn't see that by now, he didn't know what else to do to prove it.

He'd had most of his body hair torn out by the roots. He stood like a statue for hours after long work days, when what he wanted was to kick back with her.

Telling her that he liked her, wanted to be with her hadn't worked, because she didn't seem to hear him. Apparently showing her how he felt about her in bed wasn't enough, either.

They were involved in such an artificial way that he had to take a step in a new direction. As much as this competition meant to her, Mariel meant more to him.

There was only one thing left to try. If she didn't see who he was after tonight, he doubted she ever would.

And that would be a shame, because he cared for her.

His wife had expected him to read her mind. If he didn't guess what the problem was and do handsprings to correct his many failings, he suffered the silent treatment for days.

He'd been frustrated as hell to go along day after day walking on eggshells and not knowing what Serena expected or wanted from him. He was tired of the guessing games he'd had to play with his ex.

He would not go down that road again. He wanted Mariel, but not at the cost of his good sense.

Mariel had been clear in her wants and desires when it came to the renovations. They'd worked well together. He'd listened to her ideas, tried his best to incorporate her design suggestions and needs into all the work he'd done for her.

That experience told him she liked to communicate, to state what she wanted, but maybe that was only because she'd been paying him.

This modeling thing was different. She was afraid of the artist inside her, afraid of cutting loose, afraid of her inner passion, so she took it out on him. By refusing to tell him what was pissing her off, she shut him out, trying to place the blame elsewhere. And that blame seemed headed straight for his shoulders.

He wouldn't let her get away with this. He couldn't. If he allowed her to continue to be angry and resentful and just plain scared, then their relationship would be over.

He cared too much for her to lose her without one more attempt to let her know that he understood. But she had to start talking too.

She sat tightlipped in his truck, the blue dashboard glow making her ghostly. From the looks of things, getting her to open up wouldn't be easy.

"How was your day at school?"

"Fine. It's always fine." She bit her lip but didn't say more.

"Listen," he began, "I don't want you to keep tearing yourself up about this competition."

"You don't understand," she muttered.

He stopped at a red light. "Why wouldn't I understand? I'm not a caveman." He tried to keep a lid on his temper, but she was doing it again. "Don't shut me out, Mariel. I don't like it. I won't accept it."

Eventually, with his wife, he'd stopped trying to figure out what he'd done wrong. He'd handled things badly by going cold and silent too. He and Serena had been two stubborn people who cared about each other but were torn apart by their refusal to communicate. He owned up to his part in the divorce and had vowed not to let the same thing happen again.

He shook his head, brought himself out of his memories and back to Mariel. "What's going on with you," he asked. "Explain."

"You're a carpenter! How can you possibly understand what I'm going through?" Her voice got high, then broke over the last word.

"You do think I'm a caveman. You assume because I work with my hands, I can't see the artist in you. Worse, that I won't understand your creativity. Maybe even that I don't *want* to understand you."

Now he was angry. And what was worse, he was now convinced she saw him as a good lay and nothing more.

She didn't respond, just sat there, dark and stiff, her face mutinous.

"You sit tight, I'm taking you to my place."

"Sex won't help this, Danny. We're good at coming together. What we're not good at is being together, being partners."

"Whose fault is that? You're the one who refuses to share your frustration."

"If you cared, you'd show up on time!"

So that was it. He'd been late a couple times. It was on the tip of his tongue to explain the reason, but his being late was just the surface. She'd been miffed with him but wouldn't ask why he was late. Then, she'd stewed about it without clearing the air.

She was capable of being straight with him, she'd proved it time and again in the past few months. Her decisiveness and flair for design had intrigued him from the first time they'd talked about her plans for her renovations. They'd butted heads a couple of times; but with compromise and communication, they'd come to agreement with every project.

"I'll do my best to get to your place on time," he promised, "but I start a new contract tomorrow and the building's across town. Traffic's a bitch."

She nodded, her face a pretty pink. "Not everyone works as close to home as I do."

"Glad you conceded the point. And I'm not taking you to my place for sex. I want you to see something."

"What?"

"You'll see when you get there." He turned onto his block and headed toward his place, hoping things would turn out right for them. Telling her that he understood her frustration and fear regarding the competition hadn't worked for them. Now, he had to show her.

9

Danny lived in a house surrounded by wholesale and retail businesses. This was no family neighborhood. Next door to Danny's place sat a plumbing supply shop, while on the other side stood a rental business. Wheelbarrows and various other landscaping tools and equipment lined up along the fence that bordered his property. He parked in front of a huge workshop at the back of his wide yard.

He jumped out of the truck and jogged to open her door for her. She let him take her hand to help her down. He ducked his head when she landed on the ground beside him, reminding her of their first time and how he'd been aware of needing a shower.

"Why are you suddenly shy?" she asked.

"I'm not. It's just, I want you to like what you see."

"I do." She ran her hand up his chest to his neck.

"You need to see that I understand your frustration with the art."

"I'm sorry I was churlish about you being a few minutes behind schedule. It was selfish and silly. I'm letting the pressure get to me." He couldn't possibly know how she worked herself into a frenzy of doubt and fear every day after school. From the time she climbed into her car and headed for home until he walked in her door, she agonized over every inch of paint. No, he could never understand, so there was no point telling him that a coil spring of tension built every day.

Sex was her only relief. She'd become a sex maniac just to avoid her artistic frustration. Even now, she wanted to climb all over Danny and take the oblivion she craved. Take it, not give it. Despair threatened her mood.

He unlocked a door and ushered her inside what looked like a workshop. Inside, she gasped and covered her mouth in shock. "Furniture!"

Beautiful chairs, tables, chests, and desks with elegant, flowing lines and rich hues of oak, maple, and pine filled the room. The floor was clear of shavings. They filled barrels. The scent of clean wood filled the air.

She took two steps farther into the room and reached out toward a chair with arms designed for comfort. "For an office?" she guessed.

He nodded. "You can tilt back and put your feet up and work with your laptop here." He pulled up a tabletop from the side. It swivelled and tilted every which way. "I still need to decide on the stain and finish. Every piece needs the right color, the right patina. I like my pieces to glow, even under low light."

Her eyes followed the lines of chairs to the wall and up. He'd made so many he'd had to place them on racks that lined the walls.

She gaped at him. "I had no idea!"

"I never told you. This is something I do for the joy of it."

"You're an artist. A true craftsman." In every sense of the word. "Creative and free." His designs were individual, unlike anything she'd seen before, although they reminded her of the best she'd seen of the most famous eras in furniture. He had buffets that reminded her of the Shaker style. Chairs that looked like something from a French palace. Cocktail tables that could grace a mansion's library.

"This is magnificent work, Danny. Incredible!" She walked toward his work bench. "May I touch this?" *This* was a free-form piece of wood that smelled heavenly. "Cedar?"

At his nod, she leaned in and sniffed deeply while she ran her hand along the sweeping curves. "It looks as if you followed the flow of the wood. Does that make sense?"

"I hoped you'd recognize what I was trying for." He shook his head and stared at the floor. "Sometimes I doubt I can pull it off. You know, what's in here." He tapped his temple to indicate his vision of his creations.

She wanted to cry. To hide her weakness, she walked to him and stepped into his arms.

Danny held her for a long moment, his hands smoothing her spine and shoulders. She shuddered and let relief fill her. "You understand me better than anyone I've ever met."

"This competition would scare me too. Putting my designs out there, only to have snooty judges walk by and sniff at what I think is good. It'd be tough to see what other designers are doing better." He rocked her gently from side to side. "I'm impressed as hell that you're willing to enter. You're working with new equipment, a body instead of a canvas. It's all new and you just keep forging ahead."

"I've let it get personal, which is a mistake. I'm determined to impress Nigel Withers, and it's foolish and wrong. Creatively, I should let my art fly and not worry about one particular person's opinion, but he was cruel when I took my portfolio to him."

"And now you can't get his comments out of your head?"

She sighed and rubbed her achy forehead on his shirt. He smelled great, like fresh air and sunshine. "No, as hard as I try, whenever I choose a color, I wonder what he'd say. Every line and stroke is under his watchful eye. I hate it! I've lost all the joy, but if I *don't* paint, that pompous ass has won. I don't know how else to get over this mountain of doubt."

She loved that he'd shown her his designs. "You're so strong in your work. I envy your confidence."

He tilted his head back to look into her eyes. He held her there, locked on like a missile. "You'll notice I'm not the one taking my work to design shows." The raw honesty impressed her.

"Are you selling privately?"

He gave a dismissive shrug. "I've sold a few. My sister's an architect and she's working on getting some pieces into a couple homes she's working on."

"That's great! What awesome support. My family insisted I get a degree so I could teach. They always told me I would never make a living with my art."

"So, you never talked much about it?"

"Never. Talking about it was an open invitation for ridicule." It has closed her up, shut her down. She bowed her head. "I had to work up my courage for months to take my work to Withers's gallery."

"And he took up where you family left off?"

She nodded. "Pretty much."

He crooned in sympathy and she soaked it up.

"I don't mean to whine. Whining is unattractive. I should just paint my landscapes on weekends and try to find the joy in teaching." She sniffed, horrified that she was close to tears. "I should just be satisfied nurturing the one in a thousand students who has real interest and talent."

"You were one of those students once."

She grinned into his great-smelling shirt. "You're right. As a child, I was convinced the world was wide open. But once I got old enough to talk about my dreams, my parents hammered home their points until I cracked under the pressure. I never gave myself time to develop as an artist." The results of which were mediocre but nice landscapes. She went straight into teaching afraid. Intimidated. "But when I was a child, I had all the confidence in the world."

"You need to get your confidence back. You can do that by going into this competition. You don't have to win, or even do better than anyone else, you just have to be free and let your talent shine." Danny stepped backward until he sat in one of his unfinished chairs. With a rounded bottom and no arms, it reminded her of an S with the top curve missing. He sat and pulled her into his lap. "You can do it, Mariel, I'm sure of it."

She wanted to believe him. "Are you sure we won't break this chair?"

"I'm sure. There's a titanium rod embedded."

She gingerly straddled his lap. The chair gave a couple of inches, then moved back to proper position. "This is fabulous. Where would you use a chair like this?"

"At a computer desk, although arms would probably be a necessity. But I prefer this look." He shrugged and the chair moved fluidly.

She kicked off from the floor and the resulting movement intrigued her. "What if I did this?" She pressed down on his lap and grinned. "This could be fun," she said, and gave a bounce.

He slipped his hands to her belly and slid them up to cup her breasts. "Naked, just the way I like them." He undid her buttons and fanned out the sides of her blouse to expose her chest. "Perfect nipples," he said just before he suckled her left breast. A direct line to her womb went taut as he worked her nipple with his tongue.

He rolled the other nipple between his thumb and forefinger. The chair moved as she braced her feet on the floor. A hard ridge of muscle grew under her as she slowly rose and fell, teasing him with kisses while he licked and suckled her.

"Take off your clothes," he whispered before he took her mouth in a kiss designed to pull them off of their own accord. She worked her fly zipper down, then stood and shucked off her jeans as fast as she could. Danny did the same, then settled back on the low-slung chair, his cock a raised flagpole and his eyes on fire for her.

She was slick for him, open and ready, and his eyes flared as she raised one foot to rest on his knee. He used both hands to trail the inside of her thighs and open her outer lips. A finger traced along her rim delicately, and she had to close her eyes as anticipation built. Her belly clenched as she allowed the finger play. "So wet," he said softly, with a reverence that pulled her into his desire.

She dropped her head back and thrust her hips toward him in invitation. Moisture slid down her channel to her inner thigh while his finger continued its wide circles around her. Would he never touch her clit, or plunge his fingers into her to ease her ache?

Apparently not.

"What do you want, Mariel?"

"You have to touch me deeper. You have to." She pushed with her foot to make the chair move.

He chuckled. "You're delicious. Your scent changes with your desire, calls to me." He tapped his thumb against her full clit and she groaned.

"Yes, do that."

He did. "More?"

"Yes, put your fingers inside."

He did. Heaven. Then another slipped in and he found the spot that drove her over the edge into an orgasm that fired through her. Her legs gave way, but he held her while her muscles contracted around his fingers.

She opened her eyes, found herself on his lap again with his cock edging into her open pussy. She deepened the connection and felt him, full and hard, go deeper than he'd ever gone. "I love this chair!"

Then he moved and the chair moved with him, sending her into paroxysms of pleasure. He grabbed her shoulders and looked down to watch as he plunged in and out. She rocked, he rolled, and when he came in a wash of urgency, he took her with him.

"Thank God you keep condoms in your pocket. I didn't see you slip it on," she said as she climbed off his lap.

"I'm pretty fast. And getting faster. There are times I want inside you so much, I can't think straight."

She paused and considered the possibility of doing away with the condoms altogether. "If we promised exclusivity, we could get tested. Start fresh."

"Promises? From the first time I saw you, I wanted you. Since we've been together, I haven't wanted anyone else."

"I assumed you'd have lots of women."

"I admit that immediately after my divorce I ran wild, but that got old fast. I like my women smart and talented. It's a waste of time otherwise."

"A waste of time?"

Danny shrugged, then set his features to bland. "I want a wife and family one day, and I'm not about to screw that up with playing games."

The idea of a family with Danny, a future with him both frightened and thrilled her. But she had to be careful. She had to keep her heart safe. To be anything less than cautious would be reckless. Reckless wasn't something Mariel Gibson did well.

10

Mariel had to call Jayne. *Jayne* was no stranger to wild impulsive living, and she'd encouraged Mariel many times to break free. If she dug deep, she would admit to a nugget of jealousy over Jayne's ability to take what life had to offer.

Danny was exactly one of those things life offered. A couple of weeks earlier, they'd agreed to be exclusive, which was no strain for Mariel. Danny was her perfect lover and a perfect model. Her work on his body improved daily. The theme for the event fit her penchant for landscapes, and even if she said so herself, the Garden of Eden she conjured on Danny's gorgeous body got better and better.

If only he could arrive on time for their sessions. The competition was three days away and she still wasn't satisfied with the lines of the river she wanted to flow down his chest. At his thigh, she tried time and again to create a plume of water cascading over rocks into a pool that was actually Danny's right foot. She'd tried for an entire session last night, but it just wouldn't match her vision. She remembered Danny tapping his forehead in his workshop. He understood her frustration with vision versus the end result.

They'd come to a perfect understanding, in bed and out.

For the first time in her life, she was in a fulfilling relationship.

If only he could arrive on time for their sessions. Maybe he'd be punctual tonight.

She entered her house through her laundry room at the end of her kitchen. Her renovated kitchen, thanks to Danny. Cherry cabinets, granite countertops, deep drawers, and under cabinet lighting combined to make her cooking area a dream.

If she managed to get through this competition, she might succeed in breaking the bonds of fear that ruled her life. She called Jayne. "I think I'm in love," she said, when her friend answered.

"Are you crazy?"

"Probably. But Danny's—"

"A carpenter you *employ.*"

"—so supportive. And creative. I'm very happy with him."

"Then why are you upset when he doesn't get there on time?"

"I don't know. My head says traffic's murderous at that part of the day. My head says there are times he needs to do estimates for jobs. He has to be available when potential clients want to meet. I'm being unreasonable. I know that. But still, I can't get it out of my heart that maybe his being late is a kind of sabotage."

"You mean the way your family sabotaged you?"

She closed her eyes, held the phone tight, and nodded. "Yes, sort of."

"Have you explained this to Danny?"

"Not exactly. I told him how they browbeat me into teaching and never believed in my art. He knows my parents refused to buy me art supplies."

"Does he apologize for being late?"

"Yes, he says he understands that I let my confidence waver when I'm away from the work."

"This being aggravated with Danny is a symptom of your own reaction to stress."

"You're right. And teaching's getting to me. I hate being there, and my students have noticed. I'm turning into one of those bitter teachers who wants to be anywhere else but in the classroom."

"Ugh. I hated those teachers."

"And I hate that I've become one!"

"Why not withdraw from the competition? Would the world come to an end? Would you stop painting?"

She'd wondered the same thing all day. "Quitting now is not the answer." She couldn't imagine never painting again. "I would still be a frustrated, bitter teacher, and that's not helpful to any-one, least of all my students." Not to mention her self-esteem.

Danny walked in. She waved to him while she gave Jayne a quick good-bye and hung up. "You're here and on time! Thank you." She walked into his arms for a deep kiss. As always, his cock rose between them. She laughed and cupped him. "Way to say hello, big man."

He slid his hands to cup her breasts and fondled her in ap-preciation. "After holding a hammer all day, these feel soft as pillows."

She laughed and danced out of reach. "Not tonight. I'm still fretting over that waterfall."

The night before, Danny had stayed still as stone while Mariel worked on the rocks by his thigh. The brush strokes had felt intoxicating, and seeing her lively lovely focus, he'd been almost ashamed to have his cock rise and break her concentra-tion.

She'd ignored the tip of his cock peeking up out of the thong for a good fifteen minutes while her breath fanned out across his upper thigh. She took her interest in detail to the extreme, and he'd been suggesting for over a week that she lighten up. To his mind, a body art competition was about the overall effect, not the minutiae she seemed to get caught up in.

She never listened, though. In fact, Mariel seemed tighter and tighter every day.

His cock had stayed hard for her. How could it not? Her wet lips were mere inches away, and every few moments, the pink tip of her tongue would come out and lick her lips. His balls contracted every time he saw her tongue, until finally, he couldn't help shifting an inch just as she tried for a shadow by the waterfall.

She looked up, her eyes filled with pique. "You made me mess up. Can't you wait?"

"I am waiting. Don't you think longer, less detailed lines would work? How about some mist as the water sprays over the rocks?"

"No, that won't look right. That's not what I see."

"I've never seen a waterfall without mist."

She settled on her haunches and glared up at him. "Fine!" Then she pulled his thong down and attacked his cock like a starving woman. He loved the deep, rhythmic strokes, the way the fine edge of her teeth scraped the underside of his shaft. She gave his balls a firm squeezing and pumped her head up and down while she fluttered her tongue around his ridge.

He groaned when he saw her fingers slide under her smock. Her knees spread wide so she could work herself. He imagined her firm clit standing on end, her fingers trailing juice from her slit to her clit.

Her mouth worked him faster, harder, and he pumped gently, fucking her mouth and throat with delicate precision. He knew her so much better now, that he could feel when he was deep as she could take.

She was angry again. The tension in her strokes, in the way

her hand worked under her smock. She groaned, but the quality of the sound was all wrong.

He heard frustration and heartbreak in the sounds she made. Her frantic movements were beyond sexual need.

Danny stepped off the stool, pulling his cock free of her mouth. She cried out and kept working her pussy. "I need— Help me!" She fell back on the floor and he covered her with his body, oblivious to the paint smearing across her smock.

He gathered her close and crooned in her ear, while she sobbed in wretched gasps. "Baby, baby, it's all right. You're fine, you'll do fine. You'll be great. Slow down, now. Just slow . . ." She sniffed and her stiff body responded to his comforting croons. "Let me love you. Let me be gentle and take you there."

She sniffed and nodded, while he settled his head between her thighs. When he looked at her beautiful pussy, the full, plump labia, the darker slit that opened at first touch of his tongue, his heart melted in sympathy. She used sex to work through her anxiety, but even that failed her this time. He'd do anything, be anything she needed, but he wasn't sure she understood how much he cared.

He wanted to tell her where his heart was headed, but she was in no kind of head space to hear it. No one under this kind of pressure needed more.

He kissed her folds softly, let her feel his delicate touch, his gentle, swirling tongue. She sniffled, tense and too upset to respond. He slowed to calm and ease her with his lips and tongue. He pressed on her low belly gently to steady her, letting his touch warm her through. She quieted after a moment.

Her clit receded, her thighs relaxed while he took her down from the angry place she'd been. Once she eased back to pliable and soft again, he crawled up her body for slow, deep kisses. She sighed into his mouth and accepted his comfort.

He had his lover back, the wonderfully giving woman he loved. This was his Mariel.

Slowly, carefully, he used what he'd learned about her to build her need to a peak before he settled his mouth on her again. This time, when his tongue delved into her, she creamed for him. When he suckled ever so gently on her clit she moaned for him. When he pumped his fingers in and out of her, she bucked and wept as she came.

He kept his raging hard-on away from her, determined to keep this about Mariel's needs, not his own.

For the first time, he held her instead of taking his own relief. He carried her to her bed, then showered. She'd had all the comfort he could give her, and when he checked on her after his shower, he found her asleep.

They hadn't spoken of those moments afterward. But today, he read anxiety in her jerky movements again.

"I'll take a shower first, Mariel. Take the edge off, so to speak. I want to get through this session without a hard-on, if you can get through tonight without getting angry."

She flushed. "I'm sorry, I just get so damn wired." She kissed his chin, his nose, then his lips, lightly. "Thank you for last night."

"No thanks needed. I live to serve."

The night before the competition, Danny loved her to the point of exhaustion for both of them, but it hadn't done any good. She'd dreamed over and over again about that day in Nigel Withers's gallery.

She walked in with her portfolio under her arm, murmuring a thank you to the man who was leaving when he held the door open for her. The man who walked away without a backward glance. The man who looked like Danny.

She turned and watched as he strode away, his burnished brown hair and broad shoulders receding into the distance while her heart turned to shards of pain. She loved Danny and he had left her here alone. Once Danny disappeared, she saw Withers inside the door, his expression impatient. His sparse mustache twitched.

He was busy, he said without speaking. Too busy to see yet another artist without an appointment. The words echoed in her head while her heart pounded. She had tried over and over to book a time, she explained, but he'd refused her calls.

If she didn't already have a name in the art world, he was unavailable. Until he looked at her. She wore the clothes she'd worn to tempt Danny.

Her blood heated when she looked down and saw the tight black skirt and purple camisole. Withers's white, narrow hand tugged her skirt up to expose her pubic hair. Then he turned her so he could see the cheeks of her ass, which he palmed and squeezed. When a finger extended into her pussy and shoved in hard, she opened her legs and took it. He slid his finger in and out until her body betrayed her and moistened as his finger pumped faster.

Withers expressed no sound, made no comment while he showed passersby on the street how easily he manipulated her. She held her portfolio open, but he refused to look at her work while his finger pumped roughly, his thick knuckle swirling and plunging to make her wetter and wetter.

He stepped away and, still without speaking, swept his hand to point the way through a doorway that opened into a pitch-black space.

When she walked through the door a light overhead came on to reveal a table with a pillow at one end. The table was spotlighted by a yellow glow.

Withers never spoke, not a word, but she understood she had to lie on the table. Her landscapes littered the floor now and Withers walked across them, unseeing and uncaring. Her life's work lay under his feet and he refused to look.

No, look! Please.

His hand entered the glow of light and motioned her to take her place on the table.

She did, but she kept her head turned toward her scattered landscapes abandoned on the floor.

Leather-clad hands opened her legs. Her wet pussy twitched with the cool air. Strangers' hands hiked her hem to her waist, while others pulled her top up to expose her breasts.

The table was surrounded by men. Men wearing tight black leather gloves. Men whose faces she couldn't see, but whose hands stroked and plucked at her nipples and the soft flesh of her inner thighs. She wanted to rise, but the sensations were crowding her, the hands touching her in too many places, swamping her.

She wasn't bound by anything but her fear and sexual need. She felt more moisture gather in her pussy and behind her eyes. Her belly felt the feather light wisps of breath as the men leaned over her to scent her entire body. They murmured approval, but the words were lost in the cavernous dark.

Fingers skimmed her pubis, lightly, lightly, until she was driven to the point of madness for a real touch, a real caress. Even Withers's rough finger work would help, but she couldn't see him now.

All she had in her world were silent men with gloved fingers in the dark. She arched toward the brushing fingers and the men clapped, slowly, in ponderous time to see her arch and moan. They enjoyed seeing her arousal, and their enjoyment tormented and teased.

Withers appeared at the end of the table, by her feet. His face was the only one that showed in the glowing yellow light. His tongue flicked out to wet his lips and his trim black mustache. He flicked the tip of his tongue toward her pussy in time to the rise and fall of her chest. His tongue was not lewdly fast, but slow, like a lover's laving.

She thrashed on the table when she saw him nod his approval at the sight of her wet, creamy slit. The leather gloves were gone now, and she could feel soft palms and naked fingers. The men who surrounded the table pulled on her thighs to open her legs wide. Other hands wedged under her ass to hold her crease open to their view. She felt exposed, vulnerable, but needy and sexually open to all of them. Her belly clenched in need, and one of them saw and rubbed her there in a deep massage that reached her womb. She gasped at the heavy hand and needed more, lower.

Instead, he kept the pressure on her low belly and refused to cover her distended clit. A man on each side clasped her legs and bent them to split her wider. Nothing was hidden. Her stiff clit was exposed and her folds opened to their view. Moisture slid from her pussy to the table, wetting her completely.

More ponderous applause. She'd pleased them with her response. Her need built higher as fingers on her nipples plucked and pinched. Her womb pulled taut, and she felt her inner lips open. The hand on her belly continued to massage but never moved to where she needed it most.

One by one, the faceless, nameless men moved along the table. In turn, they studied her streaming slit, her vulnerability, her deepest secrets. Stretched out for their enjoyment, her pussy wept, while tears streamed from her eyes. But they wouldn't touch her there, wouldn't ease her need. And she was needy. So needy, she felt shamed.

She arched in a wordless plea for release until Nigel Withers leaned in close, his tongue extended toward her swollen clitoris. One swipe and she'd come, one touch, one lick was all she needed.

One finger plunging would take her over the edge, but he did nothing but gaze at her with an arrogance that aroused and humiliated her.

She held her breath and waited interminable moments while

her nipples tightened against the pinching, grasping hands. They wanted her to plead for release, but she wouldn't. She held her lips shut tight against her own desire.

Male voices rose around her as Withers's mouth brushed across her pubic hair. She gushed cream in response to the light arousing sensation. She bit back the moan they wanted to hear. She would deny them their satisfaction as they denied hers.

The men at her sides released her breasts, her thighs, and her ankles, and began to rub their thick, impossibly long cocks. The heads were dark purple, like her camisole and her shoes. The slits in the heads dewed with drop after drop of pre-come, and their long fingers could barely encompass their thick shafts. These were no ordinary men, and she cringed to think of them entering her with their massive organs.

Suddenly, Withers leaned toward her pussy, eyes lit with delight and lust as he studied her, undulating his tongue ever closer without touching. Never touching.

Suddenly freed from the cloying hands, she was more trapped by her sexual craving than before. Withers's mouth opened, blew air across her wet cunt, and brushed tenderly across her curls, damp now with his moist breath.

One by one, the men tapped the bulbous heads of their cocks on her closed lips. Tap. Tap. Tap, in time to their jerking, manipulating hands.

Their pre-come made her lips sticky, until she licked them. When she loosened her pursed lips, fingers set into the corners of her mouth held her open.

Man after man slid his cock across her wet, open mouth, never entering, but sliding, seeking the moistness. She felt their massive balls press the side of her head as their cocks slid across her mouth. Man after man jerked in spasms as they spewed streams of come across her face and neck. Ropes of semen lashed her thighs, her belly, her breasts, while Nigel Withers's mouth retreated into the gloom without touching her clit. Without settling that greedy, avid mouth on her needy cunt.

Without giving her the release she desperately cried out for.

She woke with a strangled cry. Danny kissed her as she cried in his arms, worn down by fear and loathing.

For Nigel Withers and herself.

"What have I become, Danny?" she whispered in the warm dark of night.

But Danny had no answers.

11

Mariel never explained her nightmare, but whatever had happened in her dream had shaken what little composure she had left. He tried to get her to talk about it during the two-hour drive to the competition, but she refused. He'd expected her to be tense and quiet, of course, but when he looked at her, she seemed buried in black thoughts. She kept her arms folded over her chest and her gaze fixed out the side window of his van.

An hour into the drive, he flashed on a memory of his ex doing the same thing time and time again. "Mariel, I'm pulling over and we'll work out whatever it is that's eating you up." He pointed out a rest area.

Her shoulders sagged. "Oh, Danny, I'm sorry." She sniffed and tried not to cry, but one tear slid down her cheek. She swiped at it, and when she looked at the moisture on her fingers, sobbed like a little girl lost.

He took the exit for the rest area and parked. When he reached to pull her close, she shook him off. "No, I have to apologize for using you. I'm sorry. You've been nothing but kind and loving, and I've been awful to you."

"In what way?" he wondered how far down this road she wanted to go, but he wouldn't stop her.

"I've turned into some kind of needy, whiny sex maniac. I use sex to hide from my fear. I use sex to cover up my insecurities. I use sex to hide my anxiety." She looked at him, her face all blotchy and wet from crying. It was the dearest, most vulnerable expression he'd ever seen on Mariel's face.

"Danny, I've been using *you*, when you've been so giving and loving and sweet."

He bit back a grin. "It never occurred to you that I was fully engaged during all this sex you've been using, and that I got my rocks off too?"

"Yes, but—"

"And that I told you when we started that I'd do anything for you?"

She swiped at her nose. "Yes, but—"

"Would you like to forget this competition? Want me to punch this Nigel Withers in the nose for making you doubt yourself for all this time?"

She smiled at that, her eyes filling with humor. "You would, wouldn't you?"

"Damn straight."

"I had a nightmare about him last night. He refused to give me something I wanted really really bad." She ducked her head and her face flushed in the way he remembered when she used to be skittish around him.

"And? You want me to punch his lights out for that? Make him give it to you today?"

"Oh! God no!" She looked so horrified he wanted to laugh.

She twisted her fingers in her lap, the way she used to twist them when they talked about whatever project he was working on. Mariel had regressed to her previous, shy, frightened, uptight self.

"I think . . ." She hesitated. But then he saw her settle, her spine straighten in the seat. "I think the nightmare represented me needing his approval desperately. For three years I've let his nonreaction to my work dictate how I felt about my paintings." She thumped her chest with the flat of her palm. "*My* work! Mine! No one should make me feel this way. No one."

"That's right. If you let someone else belittle you and make you feel unworthy, you're the one who suffers."

"I let him get to me. I let him steal three years. Worse, I let him darken the light of my creative soul." She blinked and sniffed. "Does that sound melodramatic?"

"Not if that's how you feel." He thought it might be over the top, but he wasn't about to stifle her revelations at this point. "What happened in your nightmare to bring you to tears?"

She raised one eyebrow. "I'd just like to forget it. Can we please go now? We still have twenty miles to go before we get there."

The community center's main room stood wide open, and each artist and model had their own numbered ten-foot square. Mariel lined up to check in with the registration desk, while Danny humped her equipment in from his van.

Excitement thrummed through the crowd and Mariel soon felt the refreshing change to her toes. After her nightmare and her confession to Danny, her anxiety had drained away. She felt loose all over. Her shoulders relaxed, she could even turn her head without hearing her neck grind.

She rolled her head and shoulders, pleased with the physical release of tension.

A man's voice caught her ear and she turned to see if she recognized the man who belonged to it. A former student? An instructor of her own?

No, not five feet away stood the rat bastard himself.

Nigel Withers, black mustache and overbite just as she remembered them. He seemed shorter and less reptilian than he'd been in her nightmare.

Coming so soon after a twisted, sexual dream about the man, she blanched where she stood. Every drop of blood drained from her face, and she prayed for the floor to open and suck her down into a vortex.

She shuffled her feet on the tiled floor. No vortex opened. Damn.

In her time with Danny, Mariel had changed her look considerably. No more ponytail. Her heavy auburn waves were free to float across her back and chest. She wore a soft green shade of eye shadow to brighten the look of her eyes.

Her clothes reflected her more sexual outlook. As Jayne said, she now looked like a woman who was gettin' some and lovin' it.

From across the room, she caught Withers's eye. He ran his gaze down her body, allowing it to linger at her breasts, the way he'd done that day in his gallery. The day he'd intimated that a blow job might change his mind about her landscapes.

The pig.

She shuddered. She hated that she'd dreamed of him leaning over her vulnerable body. That in her nightmare, she'd let him look his fill, breathe on her, and make her weak with need.

The faceless, nameless men that stared at her on the table were just part of a weird sex dream that happened of its own accord. She could deal with that, maybe even share it with Danny some day. They might share a laugh about it. But the idea of Withers leering at her most vulnerable parts sickened her.

The rat bastard in question angled his way over to her, exposing his overbite in a smarmy smile, his pathetically thin mustache stretched across his lip. The sparse hair looked dyed.

She remembered a decision she'd made weeks ago, to be bold and brave, and that had worked out better than she'd hoped.

Bold and brave was worth another shot. She pulled it together again and faced the rat bastard head-on. He was only slightly taller than her. She looked him in the eye and lifted the corners of her mouth in a tepid smile.

"You could be one of the models, my dear. So lovely." He lifted too-white fingers toward her cheek, but she dodged him.

"I'm an artist."

"A fine one, I'm sure." But his eyes skimmed down her body again. Her skin crawled.

He didn't recognize her and didn't recall their meeting.

She'd beaten herself up for three long years over this rat bastard's response to her work and he couldn't even recall the meeting.

"Yes," she agreed boldly, "I am a fine artist. You told me once that I have a remarkable talent."

He licked his lips and frowned, clearly trying to remember her. "Then I look forward to seeing your work again," he said.

"You may recognize it," she said with a nod and a sliver of a smile. "You asked me for a blow job, and when I refused, you trashed my paintings for spite." Take that, you rat bastard.

Then she turned on her heel and strode to Danny's side.

"I just bumped into Nigel Withers," she said, her voice stiff.

Concern filled his gaze. "How'd that go?" He put his hand on her elbow, but she shook free.

She closed her eyes, took a deep breath, and held it. "He didn't remember me." After that, she said no more about it but kept her anger to a simmer as she hurried through setting up the gear. She told Danny to get ready because the timed competition would begin in moments.

The scene eluded her. Try as she might, she couldn't get the lines right. At last, she rode out her anger, and with the release a new idea came to mind. She laughed out loud, startling Danny, and set to work.

Danny's body inspired her. Her passion for painting returned. Her joy rose. She no longer wanted to transform him into a garden landscape. He needed to be Adam. He needed to be Eve.

He needed to be the beginning of life.

From the front, Danny Glenn's perfect working man's body became bigger, bolder, stronger. His jaw was sharp, his brow high with intelligence, and his eyes glowed with healthy vitality. Over his skintight thong, Danny's groin looked heavily powerful and fecund with the seed of all humankind.

He glanced down at himself when she told him to turn around.

"What happened when you met Withers?" he asked warily.

"Nothing much, really. I'm just bolder and braver this time."

"I'll say." But he turned and gave him her back to work on.

An hour later, from the back, Danny was Eve, with smooth shoulders and hair painted to the base of his spine. A narrow waist flared to wide hips meant to bear the children of the world yet to come. Eve's butt was high, plump, and femininely inviting.

An announcement ended the timed portion and Mariel raised her head to see the complete look.

She blinked back tears of joy. Her passion had returned in full, and Danny's Adam and Eve was the result. "I don't have a hope in hell of winning," she said, "but I feel fabulous." She laughed and people around them looked over at the tinkling sound of joy.

"I overheard you earlier with Nigel Withers," said a woman from behind her.

She turned and found a flamboyantly turbaned woman wearing a yellow smock dress and purple leggings.

"You were fabulous. That man's a pompous ass. If he didn't coerce sex from artists, he'd never get any." She waved her hand in a dismissive gesture, then held her thumb and finger about an inch apart. "He tries to tell people this is eight inches."

Mariel choked back a laugh and Danny stumbled as he

climbed off the stool. Mariel steadied him. "Let's pack up and go home."

"Aren't you going to wait for the judges?" the woman asked.

"I don't need to know what they think," Mariel responded with a light chuckle.

Danny looked thunderstruck, then happy as he understood what she said.

Mariel smiled at him and held his gaze. "I know what I think, how I feel, and that's all I need." She'd been bold and she'd been brave, and she felt free to be the artist she wanted to be. That's all she'd ever need. She felt light enough to walk on air.

The woman shrugged and slipped a card into Mariel's hand. "I love what you've done here." She eyed Danny from head to toe. "And I'd like to see more of your work. Please bring your portfolio by my gallery. I don't have the following that Withers has built, but I'm getting some attention."

"Oh! I'm not ready for something like that," Mariel demurred.

"But what about all your landscapes?" Danny interjected.

"Mundane," Mariel announced. "Boring." She grinned. "And, dare I say, they're mediocre?"

"How soon can you have something else to show me?"

She studied Danny's warm gaze and nodded. "Give her six weeks," Danny said, holding out his hand for another of the woman's business cards. He read it. "Ms. Hollings. Mariel Gibson will be in your gallery in six weeks."

"Gayle, please." She bussed Mariel's, then Danny's cheek. "Six weeks. And bring something in with this kind of passion." She waved her hand down the front of Danny's body. "And I'll guarantee you a show of your own."

Mariel's head spun with possibilities.

Six weeks later, Danny held the door for her as she left Gayle's funky art gallery in one of Seattle's up-and-coming artistic neighborhoods. Gayle had been honest to admit her place didn't have the renown of The Withers Gallery, but as far as Mariel was concerned, it was heaven.

"The meeting couldn't have gone better," Danny said. "Your work's changed in ways I never could have foreseen."

She'd left behind her landscapes forever and had kept Danny out of her studio while she'd worked on changing directions. She was freer than she'd ever been. Braver too. She'd let her passion loose on the human form, and she loved painting again.

Danny hadn't seen any of her new work until she'd pulled her newest paintings out of her portfolio inside Gayle's cramped office.

The gallery owner had kept all three paintings for immediate display. "She liked them," Mariel said.

"Loved them," Danny agreed. "But does it matter?"

She laughed, free and easy. "Not a whit. I like them, and that's everything."

He snatched her up into his arms, pressed his lips to the crook of her neck, and inhaled deeply. "I love you, Mariel. I need you. Marry me."

"Danny Glenn, I always knew you were perfect. Perfect for me."

Turn the page for an excerpt from Bonnie Edwards'
MIDNIGHT CONFESSIONS!

On sale now!

1

On a mission she'd been planning for two weeks and wanting for longer, Faye Grantham took a breath, smoothed her palm up her thigh to hike her dress and crossed the threshold into the darkly lit hotel bar.

Alone.

Desperation was a harsh mistress and demanded sacrifice, and Faye was desperate. Propelled into the bar by a heat under her skin she could no longer deny, her craving exploded outward, from her skin, her hair, the ends of her fingertips. She was on fire, and it amazed her that no one in the hotel lobby had called 911.

Sex with a stranger. An *I don't want to know your name* kind of stranger, that's what she was here for, and that's what she was determined to get.

She paused inside the entrance to glance around for a likely candidate. At first she was disappointed. A sparse crowd was sprinkled around the edges of the room. Light came from table-top candles and subdued ceiling bulbs made to look like the night sky. For a bar called the Stargazer, it made sense.

Couples shared a quiet drink, men spoke into cell phones with laptops open, a woman with shopping bags sporting expensive logos at her feet sipped a martini. Her mouth was set grimly, and she downed the drink fast, nodding for the next before the glass was set back on the table. An obviously bad day.

The only men of interest were a group of rowdy suits at a table left of the door. Four men in their early thirties, happy, celebrating.

Pay dirt.

Her inner heat cranked up to unbearable at the sight of all those delicious-looking men. She kept her gaze forward to hide her interest but had to ease out a breath. She half expected to see fire blaze from her mouth.

Need. She'd never felt such need.

Forcing her legs to take her past the men and toward the bar kept her focused.

An ego-boosting silence hit the table as she strolled by. A whiff of tantalizing male cologne swirled around her head as she moved past. It was a man-spice smell that went straight to every feminine scent receptacle in her head. Her nostrils flared to catch every molecule.

If she turned her head to look at the men, she'd stop walking, and one last shred of pride wouldn't let her. She would not stand there to be ogled openly.

Moisture pooled at the image in her mind of four men touching her with their eyes, skimming her arms, her breasts, her legs, taking inventory of all her secret places. All of them wanting to be with her, inside her hot, hot skin.

Suddenly awash in heat, she took a hard breath. *Keep moving.*

If she wasn't careful, she'd end up with all of them at once! Flat out, stripped naked on a bed, with four men making her melt, making her wet.

She felt the back of a male hand brush lovingly down the

side of her naked breast. The hair on the back of his fingers would excite and entice as he pressed against the soft flesh. Her nipple would bead; the knuckles, large and knobby, would caress and inflame her areola. Another man would kiss her mouth, sucking at her lower lip before sliding his tongue deeply into her yearning, empty mouth. *Oh, yes.*

She could have two of them suckle her breasts, and one could pleasure her toes. The fourth, oh, the fourth would slide his broad fingers into her so she could ride out an explosive orgasm before he slid his massive cock into her. She squeezed her thighs together, barely able to walk the rest of the way. Melting in the heat of her own fantasy, she finally made it to a bar stool.

She'd never, ever entertained such hot fantasies before. Maybe it was turning thirty last month, or maybe it was finally being engaged after five years. Or, maybe, it was Colin's talk of her needing a sex therapist.

Whatever was going on, she loved it. She was living a sexual implosion, and she needed to understand why. And fast.

Her bra felt like burlap and scratched against her raised nipples. Sparkles of desire raced from her breasts to her pussy, and she shivered with the yummy feel. In her mind, one of the men soothed the roughened nubs with an expert tongue. She imagined a wet mouth suckling at her as she tilted her head back to offer more. She shivered as the man's lips trailed up her neck.

Suddenly remembering she was sitting alone on a bar stool waiting to be served, she pulled herself out of her fantasy and looked down the bar for the bartender. It wouldn't do to start moaning in the throes of an imagined orgasm.

She'd be hauled out of her seat and sent to a rubber room.

Maybe that's where she belonged. But before that happened, she was going to get laid. Her nameless lover would be one of those great-smelling men at the table behind her.

One of them would surely read the signs of her arousal. One of them would tap into it, want to exploit it. One of them would want it bad.

And bad was what she needed.

This craving had built for months. At first it had manifested as an unsettled feeling when Great Auntie Mae Grantham had passed away. She'd felt guilty for not going to see her more often.

Then—oh, so slowly—the unsettled feeling grew into an itch she couldn't scratch. She'd had more sex, but she'd been even less satisfied than usual. All the while the craving grew until it tore and clawed at her, bringing sexual frustration to a pinnacle. She couldn't fight it any longer.

A sexual implosion was the only name she could give the wild craving. It filled most of her waking moments and all of her sleeping ones. Sexual need crawled under her skin, oozed out her pores, scented her breath and made her carry fresh panties everywhere she went.

Everything she'd done, everything she'd tried had brought her to this moment, to these men. These strangers.

If she didn't succeed in this mission tonight, her marriage was doomed before it began.

She kept her back to the tableful of men so they could sort it out amongst themselves. In a few minutes, when they saw she was alone, one of them would stroll over, lean against her forearm where it rested on the bar. He'd burn with the fire on her skin. He'd order a drink, see if she shifted away.

When she stayed put, he'd look at her and smile. She'd cross her arms under her breasts and, without flinching, give him an eyeful. She'd chosen this bra for maximum uplift. The top of her areolae peeked over the edges of the lace cups, the rosy flesh obvious from above.

The dress she wore had practically chosen her instead of the other way around. She'd found it in her backroom inventory in a stack of men's fedoras, folded like a scarf.

Odd that she'd even thought to look there. She shouldn't have looked for a dress in a pile of hats. When she'd pulled it out and held it against her body, it screamed *come fuck me*, and she knew it was the one to wear.

She'd checked the tag and found it had been worn by a B actress in a 1957 sex-kitten flick. Not much cachet in the vintage clothing business, but a whole lot of "hot" in the seduce-a-stranger realm.

She smiled and felt her sexual aura shimmer again as she tilted her hips just so toward the men and placed her beaded clutch on the bar top.

Beaming a smile at the bartender, she leaned toward him, her nipples grazing the round, leather, rolled edge of the bar top. Enjoying the pressure, she swished her nipples back and forth to ease herself.

Big mistake. At the faint abrasion, moisture pooled again and slid down her channel to wet her g-string. She crossed and uncrossed her legs to appease her inner ache.

Her focus turned inward at the first sensation of moisture between her legs. The bartender had been wiping up a spill a few feet over but let the cloth he used dangle from his hand as she settled herself. Idly she wondered if he could see sparks in her eyes.

She tilted her head, gave her hair a fluff, then raised her arms so her breasts jiggled just for him. He woke from wherever his thoughts had taken him and came over to her. Young, handsome, and randy, he leaned across the bar and took a good look at her cleavage.

"Aren't you breaking some bartender's code by staring at my breasts?" But she squeezed them together again to ensure his interest.

He grinned and looked into her eyes. "What can I give you tonight?"

"I don't know. What do you have that's juicy and wet? I'm a thirsty girl."

His eyes flared, and he folded his arms on the bar. Strong forearms, with a sprinkling of hair showing out of the sleeves of his brilliant white shirt.

"You must work out. Your upper arms bulge with muscles. You look very strong." She trailed a fingernail across the back of his hand, down to the tip of his middle finger.

One of the suits moved in beside her before the bartender could answer. "I'll have a whiskey and soda. And for the lady?"

He followed the script, and with a look that scorched, peered down her scoop-necked bodice. Faye gave him a slow, welcoming smile and crossed her legs again. "I like your cologne. I smelled it when I walked by."

He caught the movement of her legs and grinned. "I'm glad you like it." He reversed her seductive movement and traced a fingertip from the pink-painted nail of her index finger across her knuckle and along the vein in her hand to her wrist.

Fire raced along every nerve he danced against. *Touch me, touch me. Oh, touch me.*

When he stopped the delicate caress, she thought she'd beg for more. She bit her lower lip, wetting it, plumping it, preparing it. He watched her mouth with deep focus.

Their bodies turned toward each other; their heads dipped even closer.

A strong jaw, even teeth, and intelligent eyes made up her first impression. His control of the situation was apparent when he looked at the younger man and cocked an eyebrow. Quick as that, the bartender bowed out of the equation.

Faye had found her man.

Aside from the sexy cologne, he smelled of success and

power, and she blinked up at him as if surprised he'd be so bold. His forearm burned along the length of hers on the bar, right on cue.

She swiveled her ass toward the other three men the man had left behind. An appreciative hiss came from one of them.

She imagined the man beside her skimming his hand down her back to cup a cheek and squeeze. She had to blink to dislodge the image.

His eyes were hazel and hot, his hair neatly trimmed, his hands the hands of a businessman. Clean, neat nails. She'd already learned his gentle strength when he'd traced her finger and hand.

His lips were hard, though—exactly the way she liked them. She saw them bearing down on her own, demanding she yield her mouth to his. The strength of her fantasies unnerved her. As if they'd come from somewhere outside her own psyche.

Each fantasy was more powerful than the one before until she wondered if she was projecting them onto her forehead for all the world to see.

She'd never been so imaginative. Never so hot, never so needy, never so alive.

"I haven't decided what I want yet," she said, finally remembering to reply to the stranger's question. "I can be very picky."

She cleared her fantasies away with great effort and took stock of him. What she saw fit her requirements. Healthy looking, interested, no wedding band, and keen intelligence. Yes, he'd do.

"I'm Faye Grantham," she said, tossing away her anonymous-sex fantasy. Giving her real name came naturally, and she wasn't an easy liar.

"As in, grant 'im his wish?" One side of his hard mouth quirked up.

"If you'd like."

"I'd like."

"Miss, can I get you something?" The bartender interjected, all business now.

"Like I said, I'd like something wet, something juicy." She arched her neck, trailed her fingertips down her throat. "Maybe an icy drink; I like the way they cool me when I'm hot." Her fingers drew down farther along the line of her cleavage.

There was a long moment of silence from the two men as they watched her fingers trail between her breasts. Her nipples stood out prouder, the areolae hard.

"Do you have something that will cool me off? Something juicy and wet?" She emphasized the *t* sound, drawing it out only to clip it off at the end.

The gulp the young bartender gave was audible. "A Bellini. You'll like it, I promise."

The man at her side—older, more experienced than the bartender—narrowed his gaze. Then he slid his hand to her back to a spot above the low material of her dress. Her flesh tingled where he touched.

His fingertip drew slow, hypnotic circles on her naked flesh. Her spine straightened in response, lifting her breasts higher. If he didn't do more than skim a finger along her skin soon, she'd shimmy right out of this bodice. She looked into his eyes and saw the promise of a sure thing.

He was hers for as long as she wanted to play.

"I don't need that drink after all," she said. "I think I see what I need right here."

She slid off the stool, making certain to brush the length of his body. Her pebbled breasts skimmed his chest, her knee bent as it caressed the side of his leg. More juices flowed at the thought of sex with this man with the hot eyes and hard mouth. She licked her lower lip in anticipation.

"You have a room?" she asked him on a husky note, surprised at the deep timbre.

He nodded and turned his head to the bartender. She liked the sharp angles of his profile, took a complete inventory and burned again.

"Champagne. Suite twenty fourteen," he ordered from the gaping young man on the other side of the bar.

She slid her eyes to the younger man. "Make it the best you've got."

She turned, took her clutch from the bar top and headed toward the exit that would take them through the lobby and up to his suite. Her hips swayed seductively, her shoulders straightened and she could feel the heat of his stare through the silk of her dress.

"My card," he offered. He took her elbow in a firm grip to guide her through the tables. She took the card, glanced at his name in spite of not wanting to know it. Mark McLeod.

It was a good name. She didn't recognize the company logo, but it didn't matter; they'd never be in touch again. She slid the card into the outside pocket of her clutch next to the very convenient letter from Watson, Watson and Sloane.

She looked up at his profile once more. Strong chin, bold nose, hard lips, and great shoulders. She warmed through and through at the idea of skimming his collarbone with her mouth, allowing her teeth to leave small marks of possession along the path.

He did not look back at the table of companions he'd left behind. No, his focus was on Faye and Faye alone.

She knew he'd keep it there. How refreshing.

They strode across the lobby together, his fingers firm on her arm. Her breath quickened with each step, her breasts bounced, each movement a secret abrasion on her sensitized nipples. Her knees quaked at the knowledge of what she was about to do. Sex with a stranger in an airport hotel room.

Coolheaded logic flushed through her body, washing away the rapacious desire that had brought her here.

The inherent danger in her plan finally rattled her. Faye glanced at Mark out of the corner of her eye as they walked together. He looked like a decent man, a kind man. A normal man. A hot and ready man she'd deliberately enticed. She couldn't go back on her offer now.

Her body wouldn't let her, she realized, as the warmth in her loins spread upward again. She tried to tamp it back, but it was useless. This was a battle she'd lost many times in the last three months. Her body wanted what it wanted in spite of her attempts to hold herself in check.

She wanted to scream her need out loud, but she didn't have to. Mark had picked up on her sexual craving, had responded and answered the call of woman to man. He knew what she wanted, and he would give it to her.

Once alone in the suite with Mark, anything could happen. Any sexually deviant behavior he favored could occur, and she'd be trapped in it with him. But wasn't that part of the whole thing? The fantasy of being unable to put a stop to things, of being swept up into something forbidden, exciting, and wild. Excitement mixed with a healthy dose of fear twitched and grew and made her pant.

Mark slid a finger over the elevator keypad and grinned into her eyes. "Okay?"

"I'm fine." Fear mixed with anticipation was a heady blend—arousing and spicy.

"You're more than fine, Faye. You're a dream come true." He let go of her arm and ran his hand down her back to cup her ass the way she'd envisioned earlier. Thrill trails followed his movements. "You're perfect."

"Really?" She bit her lip. She shouldn't sound so ingenuous, so stupidly inexperienced. He'd be surprised enough by her behavior once they were alone.

The elevator doors opened, and they stepped inside the smoke-mirrored quiet. They turned as one to face the doors, bodies thrumming, heat rising, minds racing with images of what was to happen when the door closed, hiding them from public view. Mark frowned at a harried-looking bellman with a luggage cart.

The bellman nodded and stepped back. The last chance to change her mind disappeared as the doors slid shut, closing Faye in with this stranger. This Mark McLeod.